FALSE FRONT

FALSE FRONT

DEBBIE BALDWIN

Columbus, Ohio

This book is a work of fiction. The names, characters and events in this book are the products of the author's imagination or are used fictitiously. Any similarity to real persons living or dead is coincidental and not intended by the author.

False Front

Published by Gatekeeper Press
2167 Stringtown Rd, Suite 109
Columbus, OH 43123-2989
www.GatekeeperPress.com

ISBN (hardcover): 9781642379259
ISBN (paperback): 9781642379266
eISBN: 9781642379273

For my children, who define love for me

and

For Richard, who puts no limits on what's possible

PROLOGUE

Two Years Ago ...

Emma Porter looked bored. No surprise there. It was her standard expression—her failsafe. She, with some effort, avoided the imposing lighted mirror in front of her and kept her gaze on the screen of her phone. Her violet eyes, masked by colored contacts that turned them an unremarkable blue, glazed. It didn't help that the stylist was working his way around her head in a hypnotic rhythm, pulling long strands of honey-colored hair through his enormous round brush. He would have put her to sleep but for the incessant chatter. *Sister, do you model? How has no one approached you before?* Oh, they'd approached her.

She gave her standard reply.

"Nope, just in school."

She checked her phone again. A text.

We're good for Jane Hotel. I talked to my buddy. Bouncer's name is Fernand. See you at 9!

The exclamation point annoyed her. *You're a guy,* she thought. *Guys shouldn't use exclamation points when they text.* She'd probably end up dumping him over it. She'd done it for less.

"Big night tonight? It's a crazy Thursday. Are you going to that thing at Tau?"

"No. Just meeting a friend for a drink."

A friend? She guessed he was a friend. She'd met him twice—no, three times; he'd kissed her on 58th Street before she got into a cab three nights ago: hence the big date.

"A friend, huh? Sounds like a date."

"Yeah," Emma sighed, "it's kind of a date."

"So, no one special? No BF?"

"Nope. No boyfriend. Just a date."

"Well, I imagine the boys are climbing through your window, gorgeous girl."

She wanted to say *the last time a boy tried to climb in my window, security guards tackled him on the front lawn, as a leashed German shepherd bared his teeth at his neck while Teddy Prescott cried that he was in my seventh grade ceramics class, and he just wanted to ask me to a school dance.* Instead, she buttoned her lip and checked her phone. Again.

"No, not so much."

"Well, my work here is done. What do you think?"

He ran his fingers up her scalp from her nape and pushed the mass of hair forward over her shoulders, admiring his handiwork. She managed as much enthusiasm as she could muster.

"Looks great. Thanks."

She grabbed her bag, left the cash and a generous tip—partly for the blowout, mostly for enduring her mood—and headed out.

The walk home was a short-ish hike. While Broadway up ahead was always jam-packed, the little Tribeca side street was surprisingly desolate. Scaffolds stood sentry, and crumpled newspapers blew across the road like urban tumbleweeds. Emma's footsteps clacked on the pavement, and her shopping bags swished against her legs. In the waning daylight, the long shadows reached out. Emma moved with purpose but not haste, running through the plan for the evening in her head. Across the street, a pair of lurking teens stopped talking to watch her. The jarring slam of a Dumpster lid and the *beep, beep, beep* of a reversing trash truck echoed across the pavement. Near the end of the block, a homeless man in a recessed doorway muttered about a coming plague and God setting the world to rights. Emma forced herself to keep her pace even but couldn't stifle her sigh of relief as she rounded the corner and joined the hordes. A businessman let out a noise of irritation as Emma forced him to slow his pace when she merged into the foot traffic. Yes, this was better. She hurried up Broadway and headed for home.

Spring Street was insane. The stores ran the gamut from A-list designer shops to dive bars and bodegas. Beneath the display window of Alexander Woo, a ratty hipster strummed a guitar. In front of Balthazar, there was a hotdog vendor. The street was dotted with musicians and addicts and homeless and shoppers and tourists and construction crews and commuters and students. There was a French crêpe stand next to Emma's favorite Thai place that was next to an organic vegan café. It was like somebody took everything that made New York *New York*—the art, the diversity, the music, the food, the bustle, the noise— and jammed it all onto one street. The street Emma called home.

Outside her building, a group of guys from her Abnormal Psychology class was coming out of the corner bodega.

"Hey IQ, what's up tonight? Heading downtown?"

"Maybe."

"Martin's parents' brownstone is on Waverly. Party's on!"

"Okay, I'll try to stop by."

"Cool."

The guys in her class had started calling her "IQ" freshman year. She was flattered at first, thinking it bore some reference to her intellect. A few months in, she discovered it was short for "Ice Queen." That was fine with her too. Whatever.

Her elegant but inconspicuous building sat just down from Mother's Ruin, her favorite pub, and next to a heavily graffitied retail space for rent. She waved to her doorman, who rushed to help her with her bags.

"Hey, Ms. Porter. Shopping, I see."

"Hey, Jimmy. Yeah, just a few odds and ends."

He glanced at the orange Hermes shopping bag and raised an eyebrow but didn't comment.

"You want me to take these up?"

"Yes, please, Jimmy." She handed over the bags and pushed through the heavy door to the stairs, while Jimmy summoned the elevator.

As she climbed the seven flights, Emma felt pretty calm. It was just a date. People had them all the time. *Normal people* had them all the time. She was normal. Well, she was getting there, and this outing tonight was proof of that. She had met a cute guy. She liked him well enough, and he was taking her out. She was excited about it; well, the *progress* more than the date. Another box to check on the list. She could crow about it to her therapist next week. The guy, Tom, seemed excited too, based on the aforementioned errant exclamation point. That, and the fact that she had actually heard him high-five a guy over the phone when she'd said yes.

Her bags were waiting by the door when she emerged from the seventh-floor landing. She fumbled with her key and pushed the door open with her butt as she scooped her purchases from the hallway floor. As she walked into the small but tasteful apartment—well, huge and elegant by college standards but certainly low key for Emma—she was greeted by a squeal and then the vaguely familiar strains of Rod Stewart's classic, "Tonight's the Night," so off-key it was barely recognizable.

"Jeez, Caroline, could you take it down a notch?"

"Nope. Can't. Sorry."

Caroline Fitzhugh had been Emma's best friend since before they were born. That wasn't an exaggeration. Their mothers had grown up together, had married men who were themselves best friends, and were neighbors in Georgetown as newlyweds. The women were inseparable until Emma's mother crossed the line separating "life of the party" from "addict." Their pregnancies were well-timed. It gave the two women a chance to rekindle their friendship, and it gave Emma's mother a fleeting chance at sobriety. Their moms spent their pregnancies together, nearly every day for the nine months leading up to the girls' arrival. Well, seven months and three weeks—Caroline was always in a rush to get places. After that, Emma's family moved to Connecticut, Caroline's to Georgia, and the girls saw each other on holidays and trips. Caroline knew Emma *before*. Before what one of her shrinks had euphemistically referred to as "the event." Before she was Emma Porter. Before she was from a small town near Atlanta. Before. Caroline was one of a handful of people with that knowledge. She knew Emma, and she protected her with a ferocity that rivaled Emma's father. Tonight, however, was a different story. Tonight, Caroline was pushing her out of the nest. *It's time,* she had said.

Caroline popped a bottle of Veuve Clicquot way too expensive for pre-gaming, declaring a dispensation on Emma's father's strict alcohol ban, and poured them each a glass.

"One glass, Em, to loosen up."

Emma answered her with a sip.

"Go get dressed. The LBD awaits."

The "little black dress" to which she referred was the Versace black crepe safety pin dress. It was the sexiest thing either of them had ever seen. The sleeveless dress hit Emma mid-thigh and was accented with mismatched gold safety pins at the waist and hip. Caroline had bought it for Emma on her credit card to avoid any questions from her father. He was generous to a fault, but anything remotely provocative was frowned upon. Emma garnered enough attention as it was, and a sexy dress only upped the ante. Now the dress was laying on her bed next to a pair of strappy sky-high heels and a small box holding a pair of diamond hoops. *The outfit for the virgin sacrifice.* She laughed to herself, then stopped abruptly, surprised by the term her thoughts had conjured: *virgin.* It was a word she never used because it had no meaning for her. She hated the word because the status of one's virginity was inextricably linked to one's past, and she couldn't dwell on what she didn't know. Therapists encouraged her to embrace a term that expressed her "emotional virginity," but Emma never could think of one. Her shrink was not amused when she suggested "vaginal beginner" and "hymenal newbie," so they let it slide. She could be an actual virgin after all. The point was that it shouldn't matter, and if everything went according to plan, after tonight it wouldn't. She could pop her emotional and/or physical cherry and move on. At this point, she just wanted to get the damn thing over with.

They had hours before she had to meet Tom. JT, her driver and body-guard, usually accompanied her out in the evening, but Caroline told him they were heading to a study group at a friend's in the same building, so he had the night off. She was on her own, and she was thrilled.

Caroline pulled up the zipper on the dress and bounced around to Katy Perry, while Emma sipped tentatively on the same glass of bubbly.

"Oh Jeez, Em, just drink it. One glass won't have you cross-eyed. It'll calm your nerves."

She was right. Emma was nervous. For obvious reasons.

Emma left Caroline at Mother's, their local bar, with some friends and ordered an Uber to head to the Jane Hotel. As Tom had said, the bouncer, Fernand, was expecting her. Not that she would have had any trouble getting in anyway—she never did—but that dress was like a VIP pass. The group of people waiting gave a resigned sigh almost collectively as Emma deftly moved past them and entered the elegant bar. Tom had a table he was guarding with his life, and she made a beeline for him. When a guy at the bar grabbed her arm as she passed, not hard, just enough to stop her, Emma paused, stared at the hand on her bicep, and then slowly looked up at him with a perfected impassive glare. Ice Queen indeed. He released her without a word, and she dropped into the seat across from Tom.

"Hey, Gorgeous. You look amazing."

"Thanks."

"I didn't know what you like, so I ordered you a white wine."

She rarely drank. Well, that wasn't entirely true. She drank in one of her self-defense classes. Jay, her instructor, had insisted that she know how to do some of the moves "impaired," as he put it, so he'd fed her three beers and then had her train on the mat. She'd thrown up all over him.

The wine did relax her, and they chatted effortlessly. It took Emma nearly an hour to polish off the drink, and when she returned from the ladies' room with a fresh coat of lip gloss, a second glass sat waiting. What the hell. It was a big night.

It took her exactly four sips and ten minutes to realize what was happening.

Emma wasn't normal. Her father, in an extreme effort to get control of their world, made sure of that, and at this moment she was thankful for it. Most girls would think the subtle blur of vision and the slight wave of nausea were due to nerves or too many drinks. But she knew exactly what was happening. She reached into her purse and texted her panic word, "lighthouse," to JT, but he was off duty. It could take him hours. She took a calming breath, keeping her heart rate as low as she could in her panic.

"I'll be right back. I think I left my lip gloss in the bathroom."

"I'll go with you. You look pale."

"No, no, I'm fine. Just dizzy from the wine, I guess. I'm a lightweight."

She forced a giggle. That appeased him. He didn't know she knew.

"Okay, I'll be waiting."

"Be right back," she repeated.

Emma took deliberate steps. When she glanced over her shoulder, she saw Tom throw some cash on the table and pull a key card from his breast pocket. She needed to focus on making her way down the hall. She couldn't get help in the bar; a stumbling, slurring girl in a bar would only bolster Tom's ruse. There was an elevator at the end, but as she made her way toward it, she stumbled and realized that it was exactly where Tom wanted her. She needed help or a hiding place, and she needed it fast. Whatever he had slipped in her drink was strong. The symptoms were hitting her fast. She moved down to a janitor's closet. Locked. She started moving frantically hand over hand, keeping her balance on the wall, avoiding looking at the nauseating pattern of the wallpaper as it started to blur. Tom's footsteps were heavy behind her as he closed in. She got to another door, pushed it open, and stumbled into the room. A group of surprised suits looked up as she blinked at them with terrified eyes. The man at the head of the table stood.

"Jesus, are you all right?"

"No. Help."

She heard the man closest to her mutter, "she's wasted." The man at the head of the table moved like a flash. He was coming toward her, and she was losing her ability to discern whether she had put herself in more danger by stumbling into this room. He seemed to float toward her, and Emma started to shake.

"Not drunk. Drunk," she slurred. "Drugged," she amended. "Help."

"Jesus." He put his hands on her shoulders, and she instantly calmed. Emma tried to shake the fog out of her head, but it only got worse. When she looked up, she saw three of him. So, she looked straight ahead at his tie. A cornflower blue tie that hung between the open sides of his dark suit jacket. She grabbed it with both hands, crunching it in her fists. She tried to remember her training, but all that came out was a plea.

"Please."

He put his arm around her protectively and calmly spoke.

"It's okay. I've got you."

And with that soothing notion, she passed out in his arms, still clutching his cornflower blue tie.

Emma woke up nineteen hours later in a hospital room that looked like a suite at the Ritz. JT was standing at the side of the bed like a royal guard, a pissed off royal guard. He felt responsible for her indiscretion; she could feel his anger and guilt. Her father dozed, ashen, in an upholstered leather armchair. The night was a bit of a blur, and she ran through a timeline in her head to catch up. She had as much of it recalled as she probably ever would. Other than the mother of all headaches, she was otherwise uninjured. When she lifted her arm, the one without the IV, to move an itchy strand of hair from her face, the final few moments before she blacked out came flooding back. There, in her hand, was the cornflower blue tie, still knotted, with the length of it dangling down her forearm. It was wrapped around her palm and knuckles. JT informed her with a perplexed smirk that the nurses gave up trying to pry it from her, and the man, who had not given anyone his name, had ended up pulling it over his head and wrapping it around her hand as they wheeled her away on a gurney.

Completely unconscious, she had refused to let the thing go.

CHAPTER ONE

Present Day

The Harlem Sentry had begun as a conspiracy blog. A crazy bastard named Farrell Whitaker had started it to expose GMOs and lead levels in city water and Hudson River polluters and sleeper cells and anything else that occurred to him. He wasn't even taken seriously enough for anyone to refute his claims—the occasional alien abduction story that peppered the pages did nothing to help. Then one day about five years ago, he thought he saw a congressman sneaking out of a certain out-of-the-way club. A certain out-of-the-way gay club. A certain out-of-the-way S & M leather bar gay club. A certain married, staunchly conservative congressman, in town for a UN event, sneaking out of a certain out-of-the-way gay club with, *eh hem*, a companion. And just like that, Farrell Whitaker had suddenly become the highly respected journalist who headed up the most reliable online investigative news source in New York.

Emma had been working there a month, which was almost enough time to prove to her colleagues that she was an ardent, intelligent NYU grad and not some ditz Farrell wanted to fuck. Almost. So, when he called her into his office that day and gave her the good news, she knew the other writers would give her a collective WTF, and she didn't give one shit. Zero shits given.

Farrell's office looked like one of those basement rooms in a police procedural where a stalker has established his base of operation. Only, rather than one object of fixation, Farrell's obsessions ranged from political corruption to environmental toxins to animal abuse to secret government programs. A whiteboard in the corner had the ominous headline: "White Hat/Black Ops" scrawled across the top and pictures of kidnapped executives and young girls taped haphazardly beneath. Another had what looked to be a pharmaceutical pricing flowchart. Farrell could be the poster child for an ADD/OCD combo.

The charming, if neglected, arched, leaded-glass windows overlooked elevated train tracks where the subways emerged from Manhattan tunnels. His office, despite a huge cash infusion from one of the largest news media organizations in the country, had a gritty feel that Emma was sure Farrell loved. His desk was piled high with magazines, newspapers, and political pamphlets. Farrell, in his paranoia, felt that "lo-fi" was a safer way to research—Big Brother was watching online. A wall in the corner was tacked full of photos of congressmen, movie stars, news anchors, and athletes. There was a burial ground of outdated technology: fax machines, old laptops, and disk drives, some of which he still used. Farrell loved the looks on people's faces when he showed up to an interview with a handheld analog recorder and asked if he could "tape" the meeting. Amid the chaos and the junk, Farrell sat behind his desk, black Adidas propped up dangerously close to a triple espresso, with a cutting-edge tablet nestled in his lap. His frizzy dark blond hair was pulled into a ponytail. He looked like a retired BMX racer. He glanced up with a warm smile, the eye of his office hurricane, and didn't waste a second jumping in.

"Emma, take a seat. You may think you're getting canned, but you're not getting canned. No canning today. Just good news. Very, very good news." Emma glanced over at his sideboard and spotted the nearly empty pot of coffee resting on the burner.

She often wondered if Farrell had a more serious undiagnosed mental disorder beyond his fixations. He rambled like a lunatic, but he said he had good news, so she just looked at him with a raised brow.

"Nathan Hamilton Bishop. Not Nathaniel, not Nate—Nathan. Born—Greenwich, Connecticut; age—twenty-eight; height—six-two; weight—185; hair—brown…."

She listened to Farrell rattle off Nathan's stats and thought how incomplete the description sounded. He failed to mention that Nathan's eyes were a captivating emerald green or that his eyelashes were so long that as a boy he had trimmed them. Farrell omitted that Nathan's hair curled at the ends when he wore it long and that his crooked smile revealed a barely perceptible chipped incisor that he had never had repaired.

"Chestnut," she murmured.

"Pardon?"

"His hair. Never mind."

"Andover, Dartmouth, HBS. Current president, soon-to-be CEO of Knightsgrove-Bishop, arms dealer to the stars . . ."

"Defense contractor."

"Tomato, tom-ah-to," he continued as though she hadn't chimed in. "Fuck buddy to the rich and famous, charlatan, bon vivant, womanizer . . ."

"I know who he is," she snapped. Boy, did she know.

"Well then, grab a jacket because hell has frozen over."

Emma waited.

"After routinely requesting an interview every month since he took office . . ."

"He's the president of a company, not a country," she corrected.

"My sweet, naive girl." He smiled kindly and looked at her as though she had asked if Santa Claus were real. Emma mused that he would have patted her head if she hadn't been sitting across the desk.

"Where was I? Ah, the interview." Are you sitting down?"

"Sitting."

"Seatbelt buckled?"

"Farrell."

"Sorry. Nathan Bishop has agreed to not one, but a series of interviews, a six-week series on himself and the love of his life."

She thought she might throw up for a second.

"Who?" she choked meekly, not wanting to know the answer.

"Nathan Bishop. Emma, are you even listening to me?"

"No, I mean the 'love of his life' part."

"Oh, isn't it obvious? The company. Not sure Bishop is capable of meaningful human interaction."

She was too relieved to respond.

"He requested you."

"He what?"

"He requested you. You're doing the interview. I didn't even question it. When an ungettable guy agrees to something like this after nearly two years of trying, I don't care if he wants the Ghost of Christmas Past doing the interview.

No. Fucking. Way.

Her mind was going in a million different directions, so she kept it simple.

"Why?"

"I think it's obvious."

The color left her face. Normally, she was the first person to think her looks were the reason for something, but this was Nathan Bishop. The most recent photo on his image search was of him with the *Sports Illustrated Swimsuit Edition* cover model. This wasn't about Emma's looks, but it couldn't be . . . . She huffed a breath and sat back in the unsteady chair.

"Why?" she repeated, feeling ridiculous.

"Um, because he has eyes in his head. And if this were still just a nickel-and-dime blog, I would add 'and a dick in his pants.' But we aren't, so I can't."

"So, no illusions that I'm a talented upstart," she replied blandly. In a strange irony, sometimes her looks were a blow to her ego, something Caroline deftly referred to as "the problems of the pretty." She usually added a dramatic *boohoo* to emphasize her point.

"You are talented, but I doubt Nathan Bishop read your piece on arsenic levels in Sheepshead Bay."

Emma shrugged her acknowledgment.

"Look, everybody has a way of getting their foot in the door. Me? I'm willing to risk a restraining order. You? Well . . ." he trailed off.

"So, take advantage of the fact that I'm attractive and go get the story of the summer?"

"Attractive isn't even close to the word I'd use, but yes, take advantage of . . . this." He gestured to her from head-to-toe and turned to his tablet. "And if you want to sue me, I'll add your lawsuit to the pile. He wants you at," he paused as he scrolled through the email, "noon tomorrow. Lunch in his office. If tomorrow is like every Friday, he will just be back from his weekly squash game—no doubt sweating out a hangover and sabotaging some unwitting political campaign."

"I'll be there." She ignored the rest of Farrell's comments, not because they bothered her, or even because she thought they were absurd, but because the first thing he said was ringing in her ears so sweetly that she didn't want to let the sound go: *he wants you.*

CHAPTER TWO

Nathan Bishop was a scoundrel. A pig. A shark. A wolf. A fox. A dog. He was the entire zoo. And Emma had been in love with him since she was a child. They had been next-door neighbors in Connecticut, and he was her first real memory. When Emma was four, she'd gotten stuck in his treehouse. She had climbed the rickety ladder and was too afraid to come back down. She'd sat up there, balled up in a corner until she'd smelled something strange. When she looked over the edge, Nathan was sitting under the tree smoking a huge cigar and coughing. He was nine.

"Nave."

Her little voice scared the shit out of him, and he threw the cigar into the dirt and frantically looked around. Panic gave way to confusion. Then he looked up and saw her.

"Jesus, Em-em, get lost."

"Nave?" she repeated. A fat tear hit him on the shirt.

He looked up again. This time, he smiled.

"You're stuck, huh?"

She nodded. He climbed up and sat with her for a second. He pulled the sleeve of his Henley down over the heel of his hand and wiped her nose and cheeks.

"Climb aboard." He patted his shoulder, and she climbed on, her small legs dangling down his back, arms around his neck. Slowly, he took her down. "Okay, you're safe on the ground. Don't go up there again, though. It's really old. It might not even hold your ten pounds."

She nodded at him and pushed at a loose tooth with her tongue. He was just so safe. He reached two fingers out, and she took hold of them. "You going back through the hole in the fence?"

She nodded, wide-eyed. He knew all her secrets.

"Okay, get going. Mariella is probably already wondering where you are."

She released his fingers.

"Nave?"

"Yeah?"

"Don't smoke again." And with that gentle scolding and a reminder that she knew some of his secrets too, she ran across the lawn and slipped through the hole in the fence.

She saw him all the time. Their families spent holidays together and summers in Nantucket. She would wait for him to come home from school, and he would let her sit in his room sometimes while he studied. Their parents used to joke that they would get married, but a comment like that to a ten-year-old boy about a five-year-old girl was, well, ridiculous. To that five-year-old girl, though, it was heaven.

All of that changed the summer she turned nine. Emma hadn't seen him since.

Back at her desk, Emma flipped through article after article on Nathan. He had so much media exposure, it was staggering; he deliberately wanted to put himself in the spotlight, which was not like the boy she remembered. These articles painted a picture of a man she didn't know and didn't particularly care for. He was on the cover of *Rolling Stone* after Knightsgrove-Bishop funded a huge multi-use stadium in Dubai. In the photo, Selena Gomez was shining his shoes, and Ariana Grande was filing his nails as he sat reclined in a spa chair; both women wore white lab coats with neon lingerie peeking through. *New York Magazine* did a feature on his arrest record: two counts of public indecency, one count of assault, one count of public intoxication. And of course, there were the women. There were stories of kink, infidelity, broken hearts, and public catfights. Models swore they were engaged to him, a movie star left her husband for him, a royal had claimed to be pregnant by him. All the stories were sourced through the women; Nathan had never once commented. On any of them.

Coming a close second to his sexcapades were his adrenaline rushes. He rode mountain bikes in Chang Mai, parachuted in Odessa, did a survival hike in Afghanistan, climbed K2, raced camels. His extracurriculars read like a rich playboy bucket list. As she scrolled down the posts, the man painted on the page felt wrong. Was this vapid, live-for-the-moment, roué what Nathan Bishop had become? Why? The thought made her feel . . . empty.

When Emma was eight, Nathan left for his first year of boarding school. She realized now that he was young to be going, but with his British mother and his much older brothers, it was understandable. That, and his mother had left his father shortly after, so she could only assume his departure had been calculated. None of that factored into the thoughts of an eight-year-old, however.

She was playing in the backyard—dolls were lined up, and she was teaching them state capitals. Nathan walked up and gave her an exaggerated wave.

"Nave, what's the capital of California?"

He scratched his head and pretended to think.

"*Is it Disneyland?*"

She fell over laughing.

"*No, silly. It's Sacramento.*"

"*Sacramento? Okay, I will have to remember that. Em-em, I'm leaving for school.*"

A frown marred her face. Something wasn't right.

"*It's a new school.*" *He had a look on his face that spoke volumes. He should have prepared her.* "*I have to sleep there.*"

"*Oh. Okay.*"

"*Hey, no pouting.*"

"*You are supposed to take me on the boat today.*"

"*Damn, I forgot. I'm sorry, Em, I can't today.*"

Her lip began to quiver.

"*Hey, hey, hey. I'm coming back in a few weeks. We'll go then, okay?*"

"*Okay.*"

"*You sure?*"

"*Don't forget.*" *She fiddled with the doll in her hand.*

"*You bet, Em-em. I will come back, and I will teach you to sail. You'll be my first mate. Sound good?*"

"*No. You're the first mate*"

He laughed.

"Aye aye, captain. Kiss on the cheek?"

"Nope. You gotta marry me for us to kiss. Bye, Nave." She punched him in the thigh as hard as she could and ran off.

Nathan's absence hit her hard. She would stare out the window across the pristine lawn that separated their homes and quietly cry. She would sneak into his bedroom and hide in his closet. She wouldn't eat for days. Her father was about to throw in the towel and take her to a psychologist for her understandable abandonment issues when Nathan came back for a one-week fall break. After that, things had gotten easier. Nathan always prepared her before he left and made her promise to do small tasks for him while he was gone. The Bishops had a chocolate lab named Winchester that Nathan needed her to brush once a day and, hopefully, teach a trick. He wanted her to find him a really good skipping stone. He asked her to learn a greeting and three essential phrases in four different languages. He kept her busy and came home enough that she was able to adjust to his absence that year.

After that, everything changed in her world. It was like she had moved to a different planet. Now, though, she realized that she was obviously in the same solar system because Nathan Bishop was still her sun.

She was jarred from her thoughts by her phone dancing across the desk. She rarely answered unknown numbers, but her daydreaming had put her in an uncharacteristically romantic mood, and she imagined Nathan's urbane voice on the other end of the line.

"Hello?"

"Ms. Porter?"

"Yes?"

"This is Aggie, Mr. Bishop's assistant."

"Yes?"

"Mr. Bishop would like you to meet him at the back bar of the Gotham Hotel tonight at 9:30."

"I thought we were meeting at noon tomorrow?"

"Mr. Bishop felt an introductory meeting was in order. You are to meet him tonight."

No request, no option. No way.

"I'm sorry, Aggie. Tonight doesn't work."

Ha. Take that.

"Could you hold please?"

"Sure."

As Emma held the silent phone to her ear, she felt a pang of dread. What was she doing? This was the guy every journalist in the city wanted to talk to. She had him for six weeks, and she was blowing him off? Her knee-jerk reaction was going to blow the entire interview.

"Ms. Porter?"

"Yes."

"Mr. Bishop said to let you know he's disappointed you're otherwise occupied seeing as he canceled a dinner with the UN Secretary-General to free up this time."

Time to suck it up.

"I'm sorry, Aggie. I've already canceled my other plans. Of course, I'm free."

"I'll let him know."

Click.

So that's how this was going to go.

CHAPTER THREE

The Gotham Hotel was the epitome of cool. It was edgy and chic, but with an Old New York history. The lobby was an intricate mix of contemporary art, all in black and white with an occasional splash of color, and classic photos of famous occupants over the years. The suited woman with a discreet headset manning the concierge desk looked more like an event planner managing a red-carpet event than a hotel employee. She eyed Emma for a moment. Assessing. Emma was wearing a black cashmere sleeveless turtleneck, black cropped jeans, and black Chanel ballet flats. Once the woman had satisfied herself that Emma was a nobody, she gave a cold smile.

"Yes?"

Emma met her frigid greeting with some ice of her own.

"Nathan Bishop?"

"Ah."

She seemed to stop herself from adding, *of course*.

"Back bar. Down the hall."

She gestured with the back of her hand dismissively. Emma wanted to clarify that she wasn't some dessert he'd ordered, but she had no laptop or notebook to aid her in her quest to appear professional. This was just an introduction, after all, so she stuck out her chin and strode past.

As she moved cautiously down the empty hall, it suddenly hit her. She was about to have a drink with Nathan Bishop. She tried not to build him up too much, but she knew him—maybe better than anyone. The man she remembered was kind and thoughtful and caring and beautiful, and even though he didn't know Emma Porter, surely their bond was still there. Her heart was racing, but as she took hesitant strides down the empty hallway, she noticed that wasn't the only reaction she was having. There was a mist of perspiration forming at the back of her neck. Her nipples were straining against her lace bra, and between her legs, there was an unfamiliar warmth. She was *aroused*. It was a sensation she had never experienced before, but it was unmistakable. *What the hell?* It was like her body was anticipating the fairy tale that was waiting in the next room. She could picture it perfectly. *He would be sitting in a booth gazing thoughtfully into his drink. Waiting. As she walked in, he would stand, and their eyes would lock. She could practically feel the electric zing as he would slowly walk toward her and take her hand in his . . . .* She rounded the corner.

Record. Scratch.

Excitement turned to shock turned to dismay. Of course, Nathan saw none of this. He was talking on his phone in a small booth, laughing as if he'd just heard the funniest joke ever told. Crammed in across from him were two women, one of whom Emma immediately recognized as an infamous lingerie model, the other the face of a hip cosmetics brand. The lingerie model had one heeled gladiator sandal set gently on the seat of the opposite bench, between Nathan's spread thighs. Cosmetics girl was sucking provocatively on the cherry from her cocktail. Nathan ended his call and pulled on the knot of his pink tie, then spread his thighs wider with a wink. All the while Emma stood dumbstruck. *Who the fuck are you?*

As if she'd spoken the question aloud, Nathan glanced up. Their eyes met, and for just a moment she saw a sweet, sincere look of recognition. Then it was gone, and a lascivious grin split his face. He waved her over with his tumbler, scotch splashing dangerously close to the rim. He then somehow dismissed his coterie, who pouted prettily and indicated they would be at the bar. Emma took their place in the booth. Nathan didn't look up from his phone.

"Glad you were able to rearrange your plans, Ms. Porter."

"Uh, yes, about that . . . I'm sorry. Your assistant took me by surprise."

"I see."

"I want you to know I'm available for you, Nathan. Whenever you want."

He dropped his phone then quickly secured it. Was he drunk?

"Good. I've waited long enough for this."

What?

"Excuse me?"

"Ms. Porter. How in-depth are you willing to go?"

"Very. I'd like to know the real you, make the article quite revealing." She shuddered at her word choice. She didn't want to be suggestive.

"Do you have a safe word?"

"Excuse me?"

"I'm sure you heard me. I was quite clear."

The funny thing was, she did have a safe word. The word she texted JT in an emergency. *Lighthouse.* She thought about texting it now. Instead, she met the steely, drunken eyes across from her with some steel of her own.

"Yes."

"Excellent." Nathan pulled out a key card and polished off the last of his drink. "Shall we?"

"Shall we what?" She was genuinely confused.

"Take this upstairs. I keep a suite here." He eyed Emma up and down and grinned. "For revealing interviews." He tossed her word back.

"What?"

"Any questions you have can wait." He sounded almost dismissive. Like she was somehow irritating him.

"What?"

"*Tsk tsk tsk*," he scolded. "That was a question." With that, he started walking out. What the . . . .

Emma followed along to the hall. For a hot second, she imagined following him into the elevator, letting him do ... whatever he did with his conquests that left them desperate for another go. Despite the insulting arrogance, Emma could see how most of the time, when the doors on that elevator slid closed, there were two people in the car. Not this time. She withdrew her phone and texted JT to meet her at the valet stand at the front entrance. Nathan walked ahead, oblivious. He didn't even turn to check that she was trailing behind. When he did finally turn, he was a little taken aback to see her continuing down the hall, but it didn't seem to register that she was done.

"This way, Ms. Porter."

She stopped and faced him fully. Nathan grew wide-eyed at the look of wrath on her face. He looked her in the eye for, really, the first time, and he squinted slightly like he was actually seeing her. Emma fought the surge of tears that rose inside of her and stood stone still. Swamped in disappointment, she was speechless. He, too, looked at a loss for words. She scanned her brain for something to say; the only thing that came to mind was his distinguished but closely-guarded military record. So, she kept her eyes trained on him, unable to mask her sadness, and simply said, "conduct unbecoming." Then she turned and walked away.

Emma heard the elevator doors slide open and a group of bawdy men exit, calling Nathan's name and greeting him too loudly. Then she rounded the corner, hurried past the bitch at the front desk who looked surprised, and maybe pleased, to see her hustle out. Emma guessed not many women left a meeting with Nathan Bishop this early.

She rushed out the front door as a uniformed doorman held it open and disappeared into the back of the Suburban. JT looked at her from the driver's seat with concern, but she quickly dismissed him.

"It's fine. Just a misunderstanding about the time. Let's go." She ventured a glance out the window just as Nathan came rushing out. He stood on the sidewalk and looked up and down the street. She was safely hidden behind tinted windows, and he didn't give the car a second glance. Then he did something totally out of character. The calm, cool, collected Nathan Bishop shoved a rack of luggage over, sending the bags tumbling onto the sidewalk. As the car pulled away, he reached into his pocket and pulled out a wad of bills that he handed to the doorman without looking. Then, he stalked off down the street in the opposite direction.

An hour later, Emma's text alert sounded. *Meeting confirmation: Noon K-B HQ with Mr. Bishop,* then a link for directions. Okay then.

When she crawled into bed that night, she mourned the man of her imagination. The silver lining was that she still had the interview. She would still get a byline and an amazing opportunity. She half-laughed and half-cried; how ridiculous she had been to think Nathan would still be that wonderful boy she knew. That would be like thinking she was still the same little girl. Absurd.

CHAPTER FOUR

Dario Sava was eager to return to the comfort of his villa. He sat behind the utilitarian desk of the warehouse office, throwing pistachios at the chattering Capuchin monkey that caught, shelled, and ate the treat, then did a quick backflip to thank his master. Dario was still an attractive man, even in his late fifties. Known as El Callado, *the quiet one,* he had a mild disposition and a confidence that made him seem taller than his five-foot, eight-inch frame. He was calm and laconic, and a rare fit of temper was taken seriously by those around him. Few with his demeanor went into this business, which might explain his extraordinary success. Unlike the other men in his world, he had had one lover, his late wife Tala, and no children—by God's choice, not his. He was not made for such things. As he waited for an update from his man, Rigo Mendaz, Dario revisited an old wound. Rigo had promised him, *sworn to him,* years ago that the gash to his soul, like an actual, physical injury, would scab and heal and perhaps scar but cease to hurt. Unfortunately, Rigo was mistaken. It had festered.

Unbeknownst to Rigo, Dario had put out the occasional inquiry, but his half-measures had only resulted in increased frustration with the lack of resolution. Dario Sava didn't know how long he had on this earth; his business was not known for the longevity of its employees, and his health had always been poor. He did know, however, that his life felt . . . unresolved. It was an unsettling feeling for a man who dealt with incompetence and betrayal swiftly and with finality. So, on this day, the tenth anniversary of his wife's death, he came to the conclusion that it was time to excise that old wound. His sense of, not so much justice as *balance*, demanded it.

Rigo appeared at the door. He didn't spare a glance at the uniformed corpse sprawled on the floor. Apparently, the meeting with the local official had gone as expected. Rigo Mendaz looked more suited for a board meeting on Wall Street than the meeting with guerillas and mercenaries from which he had just come. He had traded in the traditional garments he had been required to wear in his previous work for Dario. He still wore the thobe when he traveled; blending in with hundreds of fungible Middle Easterners was an effective strategy for remaining anonymous. Rigo smoothed the lapels of his custom Savile Row suit, tightened his blood-red tie, and waited for Dario's nod before entering the room, stepping gingerly around the body and taking a seat in the folding chair.

"All is as it should be," Rigo spoke in gently accented English. Dario understood his colleague's native Armenian and Turkish, but both men felt they would benefit from flawless mastery of the American language.

"Very well." Dario admired Rigo's economy of words. Dario delegated, and those whom he entrusted with assignments completed them to his satisfaction or were terminated, in both senses of the word. Under normal circumstances, Rigo's response would be enough, but the importance of this particular order had Dario seeking more detailed information.

The turn of events had been quite serendipitous. A group of Chinese construction workers had been breaking ground on a housing complex in Harbin, Manchuria when they came upon a human skeleton buried in the soil. The workers concluded it was an adult male, based on the clothing. They also presumed he had been executed, based on the bullet hole in the back of his skull. More intriguing, however, was the square package, about the size of a lunch box, still intact, stuffed beneath the disintegrating coat. The Japanese writing and the date, 1945, stamped on the front made the discovery all the more puzzling. The workers left the package unopened—blissfully unaware of the danger—and followed the proper channels, but the inquiry to the local government had red flags flying. Subsequently, the item had been procured without incident by Dario's men in the convincing guise of local officials. And since the item nestled in the pelvic girdle of the remains hadn't been identified, the real local authorities had simply deleted the inquiry rather than reveal their incompetence. That wasn't to say that the item had simply been forgotten by others who had heard the rumor of the discovery. It was found twenty-four miles east of what would have been a direct route from Harbin, Manchuria to the port for Kyoto, Japan's base of operations in World War II. Most of the people in Dario's orbit, white hat or black, knew what the item potentially contained, or at least where it had originated. Months of careful analysis and testing had confirmed his suspicions. Dario Sava had stumbled upon a gold mine.

After a brief follow-up with Rigo, Dario was satisfied that the item was secure and ready for transport, a decoy put in place, the bribes paid, and the buyers apprised of the purchase protocol. That done, Dario returned to the other matter.

"I want you to locate the girl."

Rigo stared at the tiny monkey in the corner who stared back with a cocked head. Understanding dawned. Dario continued. "I suppose she is a woman now."

"Dario, this is unexpected. How long has it been?"

"Fifteen years."

Rigo shook his head as if to clear it. "So much has changed."

"And one thing has not. This eats at me like the cancer."

"El Callado . . . ." Rigo began with the term of respect before attempting to contradict his employer, but Dario preempted further comment with an uncharacteristic bang of his fist on the desk. Then, in a voice as still and calm as a quiet lake, he said, "He took my child, hermano. I will take his."

CHAPTER FIVE

Emma smoothed the periwinkle cap sleeve dress down and slipped into nude Louboutin stilettos. Her hair was flat ironed—a battle she had fought and won—but if the humidity climbed any higher, her waves would mount a counterattack. Reaching down to the bed, she scooped up the seven sets of bras and panties she had considered, ridiculous as it was, and refolded them. Anything to bolster her receding confidence was a must. As she tossed the lingerie into its drawer, her eye caught the cornflower blue tie tucked away in the corner. The reminder of the best part of one of the worst nights of her life. The tie made her feel strong, and it reminded her that there were people in the world she could trust. She pulled it out and rested the thinnest part under her nose like a silk mustache. It didn't have the soft fragrance anymore, but the action comforted her. She rerolled it and returned it with much more care than she had the underwear, threw her Mac into a leather messenger bag, and stepped into the hall, determined to put the events of last night behind her. Take two.

Caroline tumbled through the front door, looking like she'd been in a hurricane, because she had, in fact, been in a hurricane. Her stick-straight strawberry blonde hair was tumbling out of an actual rubber band hanging near her shoulder. Her startling amber eyes were ringed with makeup and fatigue. Caroline worked for CNN and took whatever crappy job they threw at her. In six months, she had been sent to landfills, contaminated lakes, disputed gang turf, and now a hurricane. She had just arrived back in town and didn't know about Emma's unfortunate run-in the night before. Emma decided to keep it that way.

"Don't you dare say it," she threatened.

"Wouldn't dream of it. It's too easy," Emma winked.

"Oh, and get this: it's Hurricane Caroline."

"No way."

"I know, right? When we left for the Outer Banks, it was a tropical storm, but when we landed it was Hurricane Caroline. It's moving up the coast. It won't seriously affect us, but we will get a shit ton of rain."

"We have to go out tonight. You're a hurricane! We have to celebrate!"

"That's not the best part."

"Oh my God, what?" Emma had a feeling she knew what Caroline was going to say.

"I'm on camera!" she squealed.

"Finally. How'd you get it?"

"Felicity refused to go." Then she leaned toward Emma conspiratorially. "The YouTube video of her hair extensions coming out in that tornado has made her a little gun shy about, um, weather."

"Should have made her gun shy about cheap extensions."

"I know, right?"

"I'm so proud of you."

"Thanks." Her fatigue seemed to resurface as she turned toward her bedroom door and pulled what looked to be a produce bag twist tie out of her hair. Emma waited for her delayed response, and just like that, Caroline turned back and gave her the once over.

"Oh, and *wow*." She ran her hand, palm up, through the air from Emma's toes to her head.

"Thank you. About time."

"Sorry, I'm going on thirty-eight hours with nothing but coffee and stale bagels." Realization hit. "Holy fuck. Nathan?"

Emma inhaled a shaky breath in answer.

"Well, keep your expectations low, Em. He's not the adorable tween you remember. The Huff Post article I skimmed last week referred to him as, 'ruthless as a landmine.' Or was it a percussion grenade? Either way."

Emma had already figured that out, but she held her tongue.

"Probably both. When you're a defense contractor, the metaphors flow."

"I'm just saying, keep the bar low."

Little did Caroline know, if the bar were any lower it would be rolling around on the floor. Emma agreed. "Just an hour of Q and A."

"And eye-fucking."

"Hell, yes. God, he's so pretty."

"I think there will be eye-fucking in everyone's field of vision. You look per . . . purdy." Caroline had quickly amended the descriptor. Emma hated the word "perfect." She had decided the reason was that it reminded her of all the ways in which she wasn't. She had an almost visceral reaction to the word. It nearly made her sick.

"Purdy?"

"You are from Georgia," she winked.

"Right. Anyway. Thanks."

"Just breathe and enjoy it. It's the first time you've been within ten feet of the man in . . ." she stared at the ceiling, doing the math, ". . . fifteen years? I'm going to pass out in my clothes. Wake me up when you get back, and we will hit the town harder than Hurricane Caroline."

Emma's phone blared her father's ringtone, "Papa's Got a Brand New Bag," in the lobby of the Manhattan behemoth that housed Knightsgrove-Bishop. She didn't want him to know she was there. Fat chance. Sometimes she thought he had been more adversely affected by what happened than she had. He was wary of anything that could topple the carefully constructed facade that was her life. She couldn't keep it from him though; besides tracking her movements with her phone, JT had, no doubt, already informed him of her whereabouts and apprised him of the short meeting last night.

"Hi, Dad."

"Hey, Beauty, what's up?"

"I'm in Fiji doing some scuba diving."

"So I hear."

"Interview. For my work."

"Nathan." It wasn't a question.

"He doesn't remember me, Dad. I haven't seen him in person since I was eight."

"All right, honey. Don't be too hard on him. I'm friends with half the board," he chuckled.

That was easy.

"Okay, Dad, gotta go. Love you." JT gave her an apologetic nod and headed to the coffee shop across the street.

She stood in front of the sleek elevator doors, her reflection staring back, and waited. Surely in a building this size, it wouldn't take long for someone to come along. Her issue with confined spaces was one of her most profound and frustrating; especially considering the source of it was lost in some mental black hole her mind apparently wasn't ready to explore. She had worked through it enough—hypnotherapy, relaxation exercises, breathing tricks—that she could handle common small spaces, like cars and elevators, as long as she wasn't alone. As counterintuitive as it was, she had realized that if someone else was there, she didn't experience that blinding terror, despite the fact that a small space would be even tighter with added bodies.

Finally, a group of men approached, laughing and ribbing each other about a baseball game the previous night. She gave a careless shrug indicating that she had forgotten to hit the button. They didn't seem to mind. A goofy blond guy in the group reached past her to summon the car with an indulgent smile. As the doors slid open, she counted down from seven, breathed in through her nose and out through her mouth, and took a confident stride in behind the men. They got off on the thirty-fifth floor, so she got off too, pretending to look confused. When a guy with a messenger bag stepped on, she joined him and sighed in relief when he hit the button for the top. The elevator climbed so high her ears popped. The security measures taken just to get this far had been staggering— her ID had been scanned, her appointment confirmed—the TSA could learn a thing or two from this place. Emma could only imagine what it would take to get to Nathan. Although why anyone would want to was beyond her. If he were as much of a libertine as the press made him out to be . . . the thought made her flop back against the wall of the elevator. What better way to make Nathan seem harmless than to paint him as a titular figurehead? That could be the reason for his well-documented indiscretions. Of course, going to Norway to BASE jump off the Troll Wall seemed a bit extreme to create that persona. She was grasping at straws—something, *anything*—to make the Nathan Bishop of her imagination mesh with whomever she was about to confront.

The elevator doors slid open, and Emma was preparing for what she imagined would be the requisite body cavity search when a striking African American woman with a nearly bald head and scarlet lips approached. Emma's four-inch heels put her well above average height, and this woman towered over her.

"Ms. Porter, I'm Iyla. If you'll follow me."

Iyla led her down the marble hall and stopped at a pair of double doors that could easily have been mistaken for a wall. She placed her thumb on an unnoticeable scanner, and the doors parted.

"It's like getting into the Bat Cave," Emma joked.

"It's mostly for show. Clients like all the bells and whistles. Honestly, it would take a SEAL team to make it this far into the building uninvited."

Emma nodded her understanding, and they continued. As they breezed into a large, open waiting area, an efficient older woman, Aggie, Emma assumed, peeked over her half-glasses and said, "He's ready for you," then returned to her phones. *I'm sorry, Senator, Mr. Bishop is in a meeting. This afternoon? Yes, sir. I'll put you on his calendar.*

Iyla gestured to the door. "Go on in."

"So, this one just opens?" Emma joked.

"When he wants it to." She turned and left.

Emma pushed the door open and saw him sitting behind his computer. He didn't look up, but he noticed her there. She mustered her easily accessible false confidence and took two strides into the room. He looked up.

Nathan pinched the bridge of his nose. He started to stand, then stopped himself. He ran a hand through his already thoroughly mussed hair.

"Ms. Porter, I . . ." She let him find the words. "I owe you an apology. I'm appalled at the way I behaved. I'm not used to. . ." He hung his head. Was he embarrassed? "I'm not used to getting a new perspective on a situation."

Emma decided to throw him a bone. "You're used to women . . . Following along." She meant it literally and figuratively. He understood.

"Can we start over?"

"I'd like that," she smiled.

He smiled too, and then he stuck out his tongue like a dog panting in relief. It was adorable.

This was the boy she remembered—tousled chestnut hair, crooked smile, the scar on his lip from when he fell down a pool slide at his summer house. And those eyes. Those grass-green eyes. Eyes that were wide and serious and always a bit sad. The last time she looked into them she was a child. But that was before. That little girl had missed him for fifteen years—that little girl who no longer existed. Still, she smiled at the thought.

"Something amusing?" He pulled her out of her trance.

"No. Sorry."

Nathan seemed momentarily thrown as well, but he quickly shifted into easy command. She wondered if his facade was as phony as hers.

"Have a seat," he looked at his computer screen, "Emily."

All the color drained from her face. Did he remember Emily? Did he remember her?

"What did you say?"

He rechecked the screen. "Emma Leigh Porter. That's what it says on your résumé. I assumed a Georgia girl would use her middle name too. Emma Leigh."

"No, sir. Just Emma."

"Okay then, Just Emma, have a seat. And call me Nathan. Officially." He winked. "We'll save the 'sir.' I'm assuming the next six weeks are going to get fairly intimate. We might as well start off on a first name basis." If his comments were laced with sexual innuendo, he didn't punctuate it with a look or gesture. He simply exited out of a document on his computer and shifted his attention to her.

The weight of his earnest stare had her shifting on her feet. When put in awkward situations, Emma had two go-to responses: aggression or flirtation. She fell into Siren-mode and twirled a pen between her lips. "Whatever you say," she cooed. What happened next never happened. What almost always happened when she used her sexy, empty come-ons was the guy would either have to shift to cover an embarrassing physical response or he would just stare at her speechless.

Nathan laughed.

He burst out laughing, and Emma found herself joining him at the absolute absurdity of her behavior. He had been hit on by movie stars and royalty. She was obviously out leagued in the sexpot department, and he had more than his fair share of experience with women using their assets to manipulate him. She tossed the pen onto his desk. "Sorry. Bad habit."

"Does that work for you? Wait, don't answer that. I already know."

"That depends on how you define 'work.'"

"Yes, I see your point. Flirtation as intimidation, yes?"

She smiled. He understood right away. It occurred to her then that that was what Nathan had done the night before in his own way, resorted to sexual tactics to avoid revealing too much of himself.

"The best defense is a good offense."

"So not a Giants fan then?" he quipped.

She laughed and gave her trained reply, "Falcons." Then she added, "But secretly the Seahawks."

Nathan had a strange look on his face, and Emma faltered. He'd had a signed Seahawks jersey on his bedroom wall when he was a kid, and she used to read the numbers on the jersey before she could read the name. *One and four!* He would high five her. Emma stiffened. She was slipping into Emily, something she never did. Ever. She needed to bring Emma Porter back, but she was having trouble containing that burning need inside of her to lead him to the truth.

"My dad spent a lot of time in Seattle when he was in the Navy. He's a big fan," Emma continued.

"Then why is it a secret?"

Nathan was suspicious, but she was sensing it wasn't personal. It was his nature. That, and he ran a business that hinged on secrets. She sighed.

"I was being cute. Again. Thanks for noticing."

He laughed. Again. Time to deflect. This was an interview, for God's sake. She had every right to be asking him questions. God, this was awkward. They kneed and jerked their way through the conversation, and Emma hadn't even started the interview.

"Could we please talk about you? I'm new at this, but I'm fairly certain you're supposed to be the one answering questions at some point during the interview."

"By all means, Ms. Porter."

"Thank you very kindly, Mr. Bishop."

For the next hour, Emma grilled him on his background: stuff she already knew, but it was important she hear it from him—in case she slipped with some tidbit she shouldn't know. He was suspicious as it was. She didn't need to add fuel to the fire. He refused the three phone calls his assistant dared to bother him with, one of which may or may not have been the Secretary of Defense. He took one call from a phone that sat behind his desk in a charger on the credenza. Her eavesdropping yielded nothing as Nathan gave a series of yes/no responses and signed off without comment. He ordered lunch—cheeseburgers and fries—and they moved from their formal position at his desk to the cozy sitting area in the corner. Nathan sprawled on the couch, jacket off, tie loose, sleeves up. Emma sat at the opposite end with her bare feet tucked under her. He was telling some story about Dartmouth lacrosse and gesturing with a fry, but Emma couldn't stop staring at his mouth. His beautiful, perfect, sexy mouth with a small but distinct scar splitting his upper lip on the right-hand side.

"What did I just say, Emma?"

"Hmm?" Her eyes shot up to his, and he looked frustrated, and maybe a tad amused.

"What did I just say?"

She hadn't paid attention to the story, so she changed tacks.

"How did you get that scar?"

"I'm sorry?"

She tapped her lip. "That scar. How did you get it?"

"I was thrown from a motorcycle."

She almost coughed up a fry. *What a liar.* When she was six, Nathan was eleven, and they were at his family's home in Nantucket for a Fourth of July cookout. She was floating in the pool on an inflatable raft, and Nathan was standing on the top of the pool slide with a spatula in his hand singing an 'NSYNC song. When he went to punctuate "Bye Bye Bye" with a hip thrust, he slipped and tumbled down, splitting open his lip at the bottom. The grown-ups all laughed until they saw Emily. She was weeping inconsolably as blood poured from Nathan's lip. She thought he was going to die. He came and got her, and when he placed her on the side of the pool, he was sucking on an ice cube. The bleeding had stopped. She touched the cold end of the cube with her small index finger. He smiled, hiding a wince, and rubbed her head. *"It'll leave a scar. It's gonna look cool, Em-em."* She remembered looking fascinated at the wound. *"Okay."*

"Really? A motorcycle?" She was clarifying, not questioning. He was unflappable.

"Yes, freshman year in college."

"Okay."

"Are you doubting the origins of my fascinating scar?"

"I wouldn't dare. And it's not fascinating. It's *cool.*" She was playing with fire, but what the hell.

"Yes. Cool." He rolled the word around. She watched him and knew she wanted him to remember her.

"Your eyes," he said.

"What about them?" She looked down reflexively.

"They're … an unusual shade."

The contact lenses hiding the distinctive violet color turned her eyes a gray blue. If he looked long enough, he would notice the colored contacts. Or maybe he already had.

"Let's talk about your personal life," Emma changed the subject quickly.

"Let's not."

"You could give the pat response and say you're married to your work."

"I could, but I'm not."

"So, no commitments?"

"No romantic commitments."

"Ever?"

"Two girlfriends in college. One in business school. I can't speak for them, but I had no . . . intentions."

"Ever been in love?"

"Nope."

"Ever given your heart?"

He ran his fingers plaintively over the chocolate brown leather of the couch, lost in thought. "I'm surprised you asked that."

"Why?"

"Most people don't see a distinction."

"Between being in love and giving your heart?"

"Yes."

He didn't elaborate. She got her answer.

"Do you think you'll ever get married?"

"Sure. If I find the right girl." She noticed he said find instead of meet, then scolded herself. She could find innuendo in anything at this point.

"Do you think that will happen?"

"Truthfully, no, but we'll have to wait and see."

His mood darkened, and the self-centered part of her wondered if he had been as profoundly affected by her circumstances as it seemed. She pushed the thought down.

"You said no 'romantic' commitments. Are there others?"

"Yes." He sounded relieved to get out of personal territory. "I have friends—brothers, really. I would lay down my life for them."

"From your military days?"

"Yes. And before you ask, I won't say more about my time in the military that isn't already public record. My field was Naval Intelligence, my rank was Lieutenant Commander. The men I served with—I work with some of them even now."

"You do? You gave them jobs?"

"More like they gave me their expertise. K-B has the most specialized, highly trained group of former military elite of any private corporation on the planet."

"Mercenaries?"

"That's a tough term. Are they soldiers for hire? In a roundabout way, yes. Am I toppling governments and installing my own puppet regimes? No."

Farrell would be so disappointed by the news.

"So, you have friends. And you have two brothers who are quite a bit older."

"Eight and ten years. Henry is a federal judge, and James is a writer. And I was a surprise."

"An unexpected pleasure," she amended.

"That's what my mother used to say."

"It sounds like you three have very different skill sets."

"Well put. And I was the only one with the *skill set* to take over."

"And the desire?"

"Sure."

His eyes told her to drop it, so she did.

"So romantically . . ."

"We've covered that."

"You vacillate between coy and evasive."

He pinched the bridge of his nose between his thumb and forefinger.

"Ask what you want to ask."

"Your 'dating' life is well-documented by gossip sites."

"Not a question. And why did you air quote dating?"

Emma shuffled through her notes.

"You were filmed having sex in a box at the Met."

"I wasn't having sex in that video. It was just a little foreplay. You try sitting through a German opera."

"You were arrested for . . ." she checked the wording, "public indecency for receiving oral sex from an unnamed actress at the Central Park reservoir."

"It was two in the morning, and the charges were dropped."

"Then there's the observation deck at Rockefeller Center. Are you an exhibitionist, Nathan?"

"Yes. Unashamedly, but the roof was closed for a private function at the time."

He made no apologies for his behavior outside of the office. That was an understatement. Last spring, he had graced the cover of *Vanity Fair* standing in the Plaza Hotel fountain fully clothed, flanked by two bikini-clad supermodels each with her hands clasped on one of his broad shoulders and a sleek knee rubbing each hip. Tie askew, big hands around their slim waists, he looked like a modern-day Errol Flynn.

"Okay, so no Mrs. Right, only Mrs. Right Now?"

"Something like that."

"You're a tease, Nathan."

"Am I?" he smirked.

She growled in frustration. She took a deep breath and danced close to the flame.

"There are times you seem serious, even passionate. Then suddenly you act like you don't give a shit about anything."

"I give a shit about a lot of things, as you so eloquently put it. I do not, however, give a shit about interviews." His face was impassive. She met his gaze.

"Then why agree?"

"I'm wondering that myself." His frustration was only apparent in the added amount of control he exhibited. He straightened a throw pillow and squared a magazine on the coffee table—one that she noticed off-handedly had him on the cover. He was keeping his external world orderly to balance an inner upheaval. She knew that because she did the same thing herself. She should have backed off, given him time to gather himself, but she didn't.

"Was there one who got away?"

His mind drifted for a moment, then he scrubbed his face with his hand. He suddenly looked exhausted.

"Not the way you mean . . . no."

"Why do I get the feeling that, like the scar on your lip, I'm not getting the complete picture?"

"It's not for public consumption," he snapped.

"Off the record?"

"Emma . . . ." He started to move to her. It was as if they were both blurring the lines of who they were, their true selves grappling with the personas they had taken on. She wanted to know if he was thinking about her. Was it her disappearance that haunted him?

"Who was she?"

That spooked him. It was the last straw. He looked angry, then distant, then he shuttered himself completely.

Emma mentally kicked herself. It was too much, too soon. Not to mention that he had served in Afghanistan and North Africa and routinely did business in Middle East hot zones. The list of things that had damaged him was not limited to Emily Webster.

He pulled out his phone and sent a text. It was strange only in that, with the exception of that one brief phone call earlier, he had been intently focused on her for nearly three hours. He had dismissed calls from high-level people and had even canceled a meeting. When he returned his gaze to hers, he was calm and remote.

"No 'she.' And like the scar, you are looking for drama that isn't there."

"So, I shouldn't put down here that you were attempting to leap the Grand Canyon on a Harley?"

He didn't even smile. "Just a standard slip on a wet road." He started scrolling through emails on his phone.

"Whatever you say." It wasn't so much the lie, but his insistence on it that irked her. She hated that he was such a smooth liar.

"What I say is the truth, Ms. Porter," he replied with icy clarity.

"What, no 'Emma' now? I thought we were going to get intimate?" She wasn't flirting, she was pissed. And now he was pissed. Why? She wasn't exactly sure, but they were both inexplicably seething.

With the effortlessness of practice, he donned his jacket, shot his cuffs, and straightened his tie, then looked at her, tense and impassive. The moment should have climaxed in a shove or a shout . . . or a sizzling kiss. They were staring at each other when his office door opened. "Ready?" They both turned to the door.

Emma Porter was a beautiful woman, stunning even. With her wavy, honey-blonde hair and striking features, she turned heads. Add to that long legs and what Caroline declared "the perfect rack," and she pretty much, again as Caroline jokingly said, "had got it goin' on." Maybe God was compensating for the mess on the inside. Who knew? But for all her hang-ups and issues and phobias and neuroses, her looks were not one of them. However, when Emma saw the woman standing in the doorway, she was swamped with a feeling of inadequacy.

Wow.

She was striking. She was easily six feet tall, wearing flared, black trousers, an ivory shell, and a simple pair of nine-hundred-dollar Jimmy Choo black peep-toe pumps. She had flawless olive skin and black hair that hung like a sheet of silk down to the small of her back. Her nails were long, but not too long, and red, but not too red. Her eyes were hazel and her lips nude. She was pin-thin but still feminine. Her face was serene, uncomplicated.

It wasn't so much the fact that she was *prettier* than Emma—that was debatable. It was the fact that she was the *opposite* of Emma: dark, exotic, composed.

Nathan shot his cuffs again, crossed to her, and gave her a chaste kiss on the cheek. They looked like a bride and groom on top of a wedding cake. Nathan was sending a message to Emma. It was more than *ours is a professional relationship.* It was more than *I'm with someone at the moment.* He was saying loud and clear: *you're not my type.*

The woman was older than Emma, closer to Nathan's age, and she hooked her hand around his bicep with an enthusiasm that didn't suit her. Nathan didn't seem to notice; he simply looked at Emma with his eyebrows raised in a smug gaze.

Nathan must have been used to a different reaction to his rejection. As the emotion drained from her face at the sight of them, Emma switched into auto-response. Her psychologist said it was an emotional safe zone that was understandable given her history. Caroline called it her "robot mode." It wasn't obvious to the casual observer, but it was there. Her face went pleasantly blank. She blinked at them calmly, then turned to gather her things. She did what Nathan had done just moments ago and organized her external world as inside she shut down.

Something about it must have alarmed Nathan because she suddenly felt his hand on her back.

"Emma?" She was uncomfortable being touched and didn't allow strangers to touch her. Ever. But this was Nathan. His hand felt so good on that innocent place between her shoulder blades, but it didn't matter.

"Yes?"

"Alex and I have plans. Are we good to wrap it up for the day?"

"Yes. This was great. Thank you." She had pushed him too far and exposed herself stupidly, and his summoning of Alex confirmed that. His force field was back in place. Emma didn't know if he regretted this extreme show of unavailability or not, but he huffed out a sigh and ran his hand down his face. Maybe he had expected a protest or nonchalance, but her subtle detachment seemed to trouble him. Alex shifted impatiently in her periphery.

"So, I'll see you Friday then?" he asked, ignoring Alex.

"Friday?" It was Wednesday. Emma thought they had weekly interviews scheduled.

"Yes, Friday. It's like my shrink says, ''I think we're going to need to see each other twice a week to get through all this crap.'" He did exactly what she had done—tried to coax her out by lightening the mood. He wanted her to laugh. She forced a smile.

"All right."

"Four o'clock." It wasn't a request. "We'll need to meet at my apartment. I'm working from home Friday." He grabbed her phone and entered his contact information, then texted himself. "I'll text you the address." Alex cleared her throat and a brief look of annoyance passed Nathan's face. Emma did nothing to indicate her inward pleasure at his response.

"All right," she replied flatly.

It wasn't an act. It was just how she was. She shut down in the face of any strong emotion. Honestly, she was lucky it hadn't happened earlier with him. Emma moved toward the door and skirted around Alex, who was standing her ground. She looked up at the other woman impassively but acknowledging her as the alpha female in the room. "Nice meeting you," she said as she passed. Alex didn't reply.

Nathan followed Emma out of the room and gently spun her to face him. "Emma?" She stared up at him. "We good?"

"Of course. I'll see you Friday," she stated without inflection.

He sighed.

"Okay, good. If I got one more 'all right' out of you I was going to stab myself in the thigh with a letter opener."

"All right." She smiled wickedly, coming back to herself. He laughed; it was relieved and genuine. His assistant, Aggie, looked up, briefly stunned. She took in the two of them and quickly returned to her work. Emma stepped toward the elevator and looked softly at him. He shook his head and headed back to his office. After his door closed, she pretended to fiddle with her phone until a harried-looking man in a rumpled suit approached, and they rode down together.

Out on the street, a black Range Rover idled at the curb. An extremely muscular, bald, black man in a suit approached her. Instinctively, Emma searched out JT, who was standing nearby and seemed at ease.

"Ms. Porter?"

"Yes."

"I'm Andrew. Mr. Bishop requested I take you home." Obviously, JT had checked out the car and figured out what Nathan was doing. Nathan would never suspect she had her own car and driver. She was making twenty-three grand a year as a reporter. He was being incredibly thoughtful. She climbed into the back of the car and thanked Andrew. He winked and Emma thought he was charming. As they pulled into traffic, her phone pinged and, when she glanced at the contact name Nathan had entered into her phone, she burst out laughing.

Mr. Wonderful: *Don't flirt with my driver.*

Emma: *No promises, Mr. Wonderful.*

Mr. Wonderful: *Well, you're crap at it anyway, so go for it.*

Emma: *There are plenty of guys who disagree.*

Mr. Wonderful: *I see through you.*

Emma: *I guess I need to work on my act.*

Mr. Wonderful: *Please don't.*

Emma: *What's my contact name on your phone btw?*

Mr. Wonderful: *Emma Porter.*

Emma: *Liar.*

Mr. Wonderful: *That information is "need to know."*

Emma: *I'll worm it out of you. I'm very persuasive.*

Mr. Wonderful: *You know I've been interrogated by the Taliban, right?*

Emma: *Seriously???*

Mr. Wonderful: *See you Friday.*

Emma: *That's just mean.*

Mr. Wonderful: *It's a teaser. I'm sure you're familiar with the concept. Gotta go.*

She tossed her phone into her bag and checked over her shoulder. JT was following in the Suburban at a good distance. Andrew was none the wiser, although surely as Nathan's driver he would have been trained to watch for a tail. If he was aware of JT, he didn't react. In fact, he didn't say another word the entire drive home. Emma rested her head on the soft black leather and closed her eyes. She briefly thought of the interview and noted with mild surprise that Nathan had not once mentioned his father. It was no secret that the late Henry Bishop was no gem, and Emma herself had witnessed his coldness toward his son, but Nathan had taken over his father's company. Surely there was some sense of, if not affection, loyalty to his father to step into his shoes.

Emma gave herself a metaphorical pat on the back for thinking like a reporter. She made a note to follow that thread. More importantly, she needed to shut down this emotional magnet drawing her to Nathan. She had charged into a situation that neither her mind nor her body was prepared for. It was all well and good to love Nathan Bishop from afar. She was good at loving him from afar. She was devoted to him. Up close? She wasn't emotionally equipped to handle "up close" with anyone. Fourteen years of therapy and countless first dates had taught her that. No. She needed to get the story, write a great piece about a fascinating man, and go on her not-so-merry way. For the next six weeks, she was going to focus on work and love Nathan Bishop from afar, up close.

That's what she kept telling herself.

CHAPTER SIX

Nathan sat at his desk finishing a conversation on the satellite phone. His best friend, Miller "Tox" Buchanan, sat sprawled on the couch. He had earned his call sign on his SEAL team, because, where most people liked to detox after a wild night, Miller liked to, as he put it, "retox." Of course, at six-feet, five-inches and 280 pounds, it took more than a couple of beers to intoxicate him in the first place, adding to his rep. Despite his size, reputation, and general demeanor, Tox was a gentle soul. The only person who ever seemed to get hurt in encounters with Tox was Tox. Andrew "Chat" Dunlap sat in the chair to his right, reading an article from a Spanish language news site on his tablet. His caramel complexion was unlined and his mocha eyes were placid. Nathan "North" Bishop ended the call and turned to the men.

Working in Naval Intelligence, Nathan considered these men his brothers. While he hadn't been a SEAL, he was integral in many of their ops, once leading them out of a labyrinth of Afghan caves better than any compass or tech, earning him his call sign "North."

"Harris and Steady handled the extraction. A certain Thai prison official can now afford a beach house in Phuket, but the boys are headed back to Duke after learning a valuable lesson about the dangers of doing drugs."

"Or at least the dangers of crossing borders with drugs in your carry-on bag. Idiots." Tox rolled his eyes. Chat chuckled.

North continued, "I'm keeping my eye on the pro-democracy protests in Hong Kong. Some Americans have been detained. Also, the British activist Toshi Peele is making noise about joining in, and the Chinese government has already promised to arrest her."

"Copy that." Tox stretched his massive frame and re-sprawled. "How's your lady friend?"

"Fine. Nothing to report there."

Chat looked up from his tablet and nailed Nathan with an assessing gaze.

"What?"

Chat quirked a brow.

Nathan sighed, "Well, I can see you're not going to let this go. I met with her last night. Cocked it up six ways to Sunday. She was here today." He swung the first ball on the Newton's Cradle on his desk. The clacking filled the silence. "She clearly wants more than the fluff piece I was expecting. She's . . . probing."

"Aww, and you wanted to be the one doing the probing," Tox smirked. Chat pointed at him with a *you-got-that-right* nod.

"Ever since she interrupted that meeting—Jesus, was it two years ago? I've just . . . I don't know, wanted to see her again."

"Get your fucking tie back. I hate it when women steal my clothes."

"You rescued her. You feel responsible for her. It's not uncommon." Chat shared his insight without looking up from his tablet.

"It feels uncommon."

"Twitch checked her out, right?" Tox asked. Their computer whiz kid could find out where someone lost their first set of keys. The youngest and most talented of the group, Twitch sported Coke bottle glasses and a long red ponytail that the guys routinely threatened to cut off. She hadn't been in the military, and her surprisingly optimistic outlook on life was a breath of fresh air.

"Of course. No red flags. A couple of speeding tickets. Arrested, but not charged, at an animal rights protest in college. Clean, but not squeaky clean." A squeaky-clean background was a red flag in itself.

Tox stood, grabbed a handful of Skittles from a bowl on the table and walked to the door. "I'm free for hair braiding and a tickle fight later, but right now I need to check in with our resident hacker—sorry—*programmer*. Little matter of national security."

"Let me know what Twitch scares up. I spoke with Cerberus. So far there's just a lot of rumor and speculation. All we know at this point is that something was recovered in China that has every terrorist with a bank balance licking their chops."

"Twitch discovered a dark auction site called River Styx. Heavily encrypted. She's trying to find an 'in' that doesn't tip them off."

Nathan gave a dark chuckle. "It's like the virtual version of the guys selling knockoffs on Canal Street. Cops come by, the vendors shut the stand down and open it back up half a block away."

"I'll keep you updated."

"All right. God, all of a sudden I hate those two words."

Chat looked up from gathering his things, then headed out without comment. Tox turned before following him out the door.

"When the dust settles on this, I want Twitch to do a deep dive on Emma Porter. Something just feels off."

"Come on, Tox. A two-year-long set up is an elaborate con, don't you think?"

"Maybe, but there's no harm in checking."

"I guess you're right."

"You good?"

"Yeah." But as Tox pulled the door closed with a quiet snick, Nathan wondered what it was about Emma Porter that was so unsettling.

CHAPTER SEVEN

Mother's was packed for a Wednesday. On the sidewalk, Caroline and Emma skirted a group of smokers and two guys having a heated argument, while the bouncer, Jorge, watched as they pushed into the bar. Caroline wore frayed white cutoffs, Chucks, and a black T-shirt that bore the caption: *it's polite to wait until you're asked.* Emma was in a flowy white camisole, torn up blue jeans and flip flops. JT was out front chatting with Jorge.

Emma ordered her usual club soda and cranberry and a light beer for Caroline. The bartender, Jake, waved off her money; he and Caroline were friends. She left a tip on the bar and returned to her bestie, who had nabbed a small table.

"Okay, talk. How was it?"

"Good. Productive."

"Em . . ."

"He's different now."

"Well, let me think." She tapped the middle of her forehead with two fingers. "He's not twelve anymore, could that be it?"

"He's a playboy," Emma despaired.

"He's hot. Of course, there are going to be women."

"You know his rep."

"I know, but the tabloids love him," Caroline soothed. "If he went for a walk in the park with a girl, it would be in *The Star*, and it would be salacious."

"True."

"What else?" Caroline probed.

"He might have a death wish."

"I've read about some of his pastimes. He missed his calling as a stuntman."

"Get this, in September he's going to free solo in the Atlas Mountains." Emma shuddered.

"Huh." Caroline paused in thought and took a swig of her beer.

"What?"

"It's just an odd location. Why there? I mean, you can rock climb anywhere."

"Maybe he's going to party in Marrakesh after." Emma rolled her eyes.

"I guess."

Something about the way Caroline said it gave Emma pause. Making a mental note to revisit Nathan's background, she returned to her train of thought.

"He's bad for me, Car."

"How so?"

"When I'm with him I'm . . ."

"You're what?"

"I'm Emily."

Caroline gasped but covered it quickly with another swig of her beer. Caroline hadn't heard Emma say her real name in fifteen years.

"What's she like?" Caroline asked with a sincerity Emma rarely saw.

"Terrifying." She shuddered and sucked on her straw. "And terrified." Before Caroline could peel the onion on Emma's response, a voice boomed from the door.

"Caroline!"

Marcus Pratt was Caroline's one friend at CNN. He was an editor and had taken to Caroline's ballsy personality right away. Perhaps because he was so shy and quiet, or maybe he could tell she was going places.

"Marcus, what's up?"

"Sorry to bust in," he panted, "your doorman said you were here."

"What's going on?"

"The hurricane is big news. I guess the damage is record-setting. Upstairs wants you to do a short piece, teasing a follow-up story. The storms are working their way up the coast and they want a story to coincide. 'Caroline talking Hurricane Caroline' has everybody totally jazzed. Felicity was there, and she was pissed. Said she would take it over, but it's your story now. Felicity said she would shoot it tonight if you weren't there, knowing full well you were gone for the day." He rested both hands on top of his head. "If we head back now, you can do the promo."

Caroline was on her feet before Marcus had finished, correctly predicting how his story ended. She gave an apologetic smile, and Emma waved without a thought.

"Go. Kick ass."

"Thanks, Em. Be home later."

Caroline and Marcus jumped into a cab as Emma waved goodnight from the sidewalk. That was going to be an interesting editing session. Emma had walked about ten steps when she felt a meaty hand on her shoulder and was hauled around to face an extremely red-faced guy with an unsteady gaze.

"Hey," he said to the side of her face.

"Hey," she replied, feeling immediately put out, "I'm just heading home."

"Here's the thing. You're hot."

"I know."

"Wow, and you're kind of a bitch."

"I know." Emma started scrolling through her phone.

"Why don't you pass me that, and I'll enter my number."

"No, thanks."

Emma wasn't handling him well, but she was out of sorts, and the guy was pissing her off. Where did he get the nerve? Although based on his breath, she knew the answer.

"Okay, how 'bout if I just feel your tits and send you on your merry way?"

The wave of laughter and fist bumps confirmed his buddies had formed an audience, and he was now showboating. JT was leaning against the storefront reading a text. He looked up when he heard 'tits' and just chuckled to himself as he backhanded Jorge on the arm with a 'get a load of this' expression. He turned to watch the exchange more closely but made no move to come to her rescue.

"Go for it." She cocked a brow at Red Face.

If he was stunned by her reply, he covered it with a forced cockiness in front of his onlookers and reached out his hand to her chest.

Thumb bent back, knee to the groin, heel of her hand to his nose. It took all of three seconds. A few of his friends rushed to help him. One yelled, "you fucking cunt!"

Yeah, I'm the bad guy here.

JT just shook his head smiling and, when Jorge waved them off, ushered her toward her building. One of Red Face's friends moved to confront Emma but thought better of it when he took in the skyscraper now flanking her. Across the street, something caught her eye. A man sat in a town car, which wasn't unusual, but the way he was holding his phone put her on edge. She had had her picture taken enough to know what it meant when someone was holding their phone like that. Maybe he had videotaped the scuffle. Although, from that angle he wouldn't have been able to capture it well. That also didn't explain why he continued to hold his phone upright. When he saw Emma looking at him with a WTF expression, he simply tossed the phone on his passenger seat and pulled out into traffic. Emma noted the license plate and that was that.

"Who was Mr. Subtle in the Lexus?"

Emma looked up, surprised to see JT watching the same thing.

"No idea."

"Nice takedown by the way. He was a big guy," JT praised.

"He was wasted."

"That doesn't make him smaller."

"True."

JT sent a text, and they walked the half-block in companionable silence, broken when JT murmured, "Huh."

"What?"

"Mr. Bishop is vetting you."

"Mr. Subtle in the town car?"

"The car is registered to his company; well, Bishop Security, it's a subsidiary."

"Why take pictures?'

"Spank bank collection." JT dodged her punch to his upper arm.

"Huh." JT continued to stare at his phone.

"What?"

"It's just . . . the car is registered to Bishop Security, but there *is* no Bishop Security. There's no website, no search engine hits . . . well, one hit. Bishop Security is mentioned in the retirement announcement of Charles Bishop in 2002. Says he started the elite subsidiary after 9/11 for specialized projects."

Emma huffed. "That tells us nothing."

JT clarified. "Means it's in-house. Explains why they don't have any Yelp reviews."

"How did he know where I was?"

JT waggled his phone in his palm. "I assume he has your contact info. With his resources, he probably knows what color toenail polish you're wearing."

Emma just rolled her eyes.

They stopped in front of her building, and JT waved goodnight. The night doorman, Ray, held the door as she slipped in and called it a night.

Upstairs, Emma changed into a pair of gray cashmere lounge pants and a worn NYU T-shirt and crawled under her duvet. She had been raised to be paranoid, suspicious of everything. A guy taking her picture rarely escaped her notice, even if it was just some creep at a bar. She was disturbed by the idea of her image being out there, in someone's phone or on their computer, but accepted it. JT was right; she probably was a welcome addition to some perv's spank bank collection. Shit happens. Emma let it go, and her thoughts once again drifted to Nathan. She didn't know this Nathan Bishop, this warlord, man-whore, tycoon. She knew a boy who pretended not to notice when she sat on his shoe, wrapped around his calf, as he walked around like nothing was amiss. Nathan Bishop, CEO scoundrel, was a stranger, but the thought that he was keeping tabs on her, for whatever reason, warmed her.

CHAPTER EIGHT

Bergdorf Goodman was a zoo on Friday. Emma wasn't a shopper and she hated crowds, but she was climbing the walls in her apartment waiting for her meeting with Nathan. She waved off an enthusiastic salesgirl and browsed halfheartedly. Across the room near the jewelry cases, a woman caught her eye. Tall, exotic, and graceful, she pointed out an item to the extremely attentive salesman helping her. Alex. As if sensing Emma's gaze, she lifted her head slightly, like a lion sniffing prey, noted Emma's presence, and moved down a case or two. Emma made her way to the exit, but before she could steer to another path to avoid Alex, she swung around.

"Emma, is it?"

"Yes, hello," she said coolly.

"Did you enjoy your little interview?"

"Yes." *What is she playing at?*

"Nathan's a master."

"At what?"

"Handling interviewers."

"Well, I wasn't *handled*, if that's what your concern is."

Her lips lifted in a calculated smile.

"Not at all. I was merely pointing out that Nate can be difficult to probe. He always has the upper hand."

"Good to know."

"And when he tires of you, he sends me the 911 text, and I come and rescue him."

The salesman cleared his throat. He had been standing behind her for the entire exchange, holding a hideous pair of cufflinks.

"He'll love those. I'll take them." Alex returned her attention to Emma. "Just a little thank you for him."

"Thank you?" Emma took the bait.

"An ex tried to make me leave a club with him last night. Nate stepped in."

Oh, she was good. In two sentences she had painted herself as a desirable woman, a damsel in distress, and the object of Nathan's attention. Emma wasn't fooled for a second.

"Here's the thing. When I first saw you, you were looking at bracelets, the cuff with the opal, I believe. It wasn't until you spotted me that you moved down to the cufflink case. Then you sought me out to tell your story. That tells me a lot."

Alex grabbed a thick strand of hair and ran her fist down the length of it. She was rattled. Good.

"Oh, really," she stalled. She needed to regroup.

"Yes. It tells me you're nervous."

She laughed. "O-ho-kay," she mocked.

"Please don't worry. I'm just here for the interview, then he's all yours. My only interest in Nathan Bishop is what he can tell my readers." Emma tried for sincerity, going for a truce. Kind of.

"Probably for the best. He doesn't do frigid." Direct hit. "See you around, Emma."

Emma felt like someone had let the air out of her tires. She couldn't let her win. She was being petty and competitive and even risky. And at that moment, she just didn't care.

"Alex?"

She swung back around with a cover girl smile and a raised brow.

"Yes?"

"He can't stand being called Nate. Everybody who's close to him knows that."

She froze in her spot, bags in her hands, that same perfect smile on her face. Emma spun and left before Alex could snap out of it and pushed her way out onto the sidewalk with a satisfied grin. Suck it, bitch.

Tox stared over Twitch's shoulder at the monitor as she replayed the video surveillance from last night.

"North's girl's got some moves."

"It's pretty standard self-defense," Twitch countered.

"Come on, Twitch. I know black belts who couldn't execute a takedown that well."

"Maybe she is a black belt. Or an instructor."

"You find anything like that in her background?"

"No, but that doesn't mean anything. People pay cash for lessons, or they're included in a gym membership. You're reaching on this, Tox."

"Okay, put a pin in it for now, but mark my words, she's up to something."

"Why do you say that?"

"Because I've known North a long time, and this woman . . . it's like somebody assembled her with his dream girl parts. Makes me itchy."

"Far be it from me to question an itch. I'll keep looking, but I don't expect to find much."

"We'll see."

CHAPTER NINE

Nathan's doorman gave Emma a suspicious once-over when she stood in his lobby that evening but relented after getting a second look at her. She was in torn jeans, Chucks, and a grey NYU sweatshirt, her hair in a high ponytail that trailed down her back. The strap of her pale pink bra showed where the neck of the sweatshirt had been stretched out from use. The whole Bergdorf's excursion had soured her on getting dolled up, so she went with comfort. After checking his computer screen, the doorman gave her a warm grin.

"Not a lot of gals visit Mr. Bishop dressed like that."

The doorman returned his reading glasses to the perch on his nose. He had a long scar that cut from his brow to his jawline on the right side of his face. Other than that, with his snowy hair and kind smile, he could have been a grandfather in a children's book.

"I'm special," she quipped.

"Oh, there's no doubt about that. He's expecting you. Go on up." He gave her a finger gun and indicated the elevator with a nod of his head.

"Thank you . . ."

"Leonard."

"Thanks, Leonard. I'm Emma"

"Have a good evening, Emma."

Leonard returned to his detective novel, and Emma stood in front of the elevator doors in a quandary. It could be hours before someone returned to this building to use the elevator, and even then, Nathan had the only apartment on the top floor. She hadn't thought this through. The doors slid open, and she stood frozen in place. They closed again, and she stared at her knotted fingers. When she felt a hand on her shoulder, she jumped and spun to face Leonard, who had appeared behind her.

"This way."

She followed him around a wide corner, and he entered a code by a door that he pushed open to reveal a stairwell.

"Better?"

"How did you know?"

"My wife. She was stuck in an elevator in the Chrysler Building for six hours when she was a kid. Hates the damn things." Emma gave him a grateful smile as he continued. "Go on up until you see the door marked ten. I'll watch you on the security feed and unlock the door remotely."

She walked past his extended arm and turned back to him.

"Leonard?"

"Yes, Emma?"

"Thank you."

"Don't mention it."

It was 3:58 when she pushed through the door to a broad, open hallway with the elevator doors to the right and the double doors leading to Nathan's apartment to the left. Between the two was a circular table holding a Kangxi porcelain bowl filled with floating lotus blossoms. The teak floors were bare, and the walls were papered in a subtly textured slate grey. The lighting was muted. The serenity of the space had her stopping to take a slow breath and compose herself. Emma was always late, usually by design. She was only ever prompt for her father because he would panic, and Caroline because she would pull Emma's hair if she made her sit somewhere alone. Everybody else could wait. With Nathan, though, she was the one who couldn't wait. She was excited for their date—she knew it was foolish, but in her mind, it was a date. There was no way around it. Plus, she got the distinct feeling people did not keep him waiting, and she wanted to please him. She knocked softly.

He pulled open the door without looking her way or halting his phone conversation. He walked purposefully into a large living room. The apartment was a Manhattan Classic Eight. A large center gallery opened to a bright living room. The space was distinctly masculine without being a bachelor pad. The chocolate suede couch and matching wingback chairs surrounded a coffee table made from a repurposed stable door. The Aubusson rug was a mix of rich gold and dark wine and stopped before two sets of French doors which led to a terrace balcony. Off in the corner, on a small pedestal, a Frederick Remington bronze depicted a raging bull. Nathan's voice was firm and infused with a current of anger that kept Emma in the doorway. He was wearing a suit, a gunmetal gray three-button number that looked like Tom Ford had tailored it personally, which puzzled her as he was working from home, but her unasked question was explained by his next utterance into the phone.

"I just met with my guys, and that's not their version of things." He paused listening. "All right. Keep me updated." He ended the call without pause and pinched the bridge of his nose. Emma wondered if he had forgotten she was there. Then he turned and looked at her. She tried to appear reassuring, smiled, shoved her hands into her back pockets and shrugged. Nathan just stood there and stared.

"Fucking perfect." He shook his head slightly with amused disbelief.

There was that word. *Perfect.* And for the first time, it filled her with something other than dread. She didn't look perfect, far from it, but she knew the second she saw him why he'd said it.

Under normal circumstances the term triggered something ugly; occasionally it almost made her physically sick. But the way Nathan had said it . . . . It wasn't a general declaration about perfection; rather, it was about Emma in this particular moment. He meant she was perfect for him. He picked up his phone.

"Greta, cancel Refuge. Have them send up two medium-rare strips with twice-baked potatoes," he glanced at Emma. "Spinach or artichokes?"

She gave him a raised brow that said, *are you kidding?*

"Artichokes. And that chocolate thing I like. Yes, that. About 6:30." He ended the call. "Give me five minutes." He disappeared down a hall, tugging at his tie. She tentatively took a step in.

"Make yourself at home, Emma." He spoke over his shoulder before turning a corner.

She took a few minutes to scan the room again. On her second sweep, she spotted it. She knew what it was the second she saw it, and her heart stopped. Her dad had a copy of it as well that he kept by his bed. Hanging on a wall in Nathan's living room was a montage of framed family photos. His oldest brother Henry's wedding photo, a picture of their family at Christmas, his brother James holding his Pulitzer Prize, a shot of Nathan with his uncle Charles, a former Secretary of Defense and CEO of K-B. Then there was *that* photograph. It was a picture of Nathan and Emma—correction, Nathan and *Emily*—almost completely from the back, one-quarter profile. Nathan was standing on the empty beach in Nantucket with her on his shoulders. She had just turned four, Nathan, nine. The sun was setting, and the sky was pure pink. Nathan was pointing to the ball of fire dipping below the horizon, making sure

Emily didn't miss the moment when it disappeared. With his other hand, he was holding her tiny, bare foot. Her head was resting on her hands that were nestled in his mop of hair. They were both utterly at peace. It was the most beautiful photograph she had ever seen.

Emma swiped at the tears streaking her face and tried, *tried* to get it together before Nathan came back and found her looking like a crazy person, a *nosy*, crazy person. Well, she was a reporter after all. When Nathan did emerge—exactly five minutes later—Emma had moved to the window and was staring out at what was no doubt a twenty-million-dollar view of Central Park and the Metropolitan Museum of Art. When she turned to face him, she had to catch her breath.

Grey thermal shirt, faded jeans, barefoot. Just wow.

"Wine?"

"Is that what you're having?"

"I'm having a scotch."

"Single malt?"

His brow quirked up. "Yes."

Emma hated wine—bad associations—and she had tasted single malt scotch once or twice. Her dad drank it. It was warm and spicy.

"I'll have what you're having."

This time when he said it, she could barely hear it. "Fucking perfect."

They sat next to each other on the couch and chitchatted for the next hour. This conversation was seamless. There were none of the awkward bumps and jolts from their first encounter. Emma stopped trying to lead the conversation and just let it unfold. They didn't force it. They didn't need to. She asked him about joining the family business. He told her about his four years in Naval Intelligence—what he could. His grandfather had insisted he have military experience—but not combat experience—before Nathan came to work for him. Nathan admitted he was apprehensive but felt compelled to serve. He said he almost considered a career in the military.

"I'm glad you didn't. I would have worried about you." She spoke the unconscious thought aloud. Nathan looked at her completely unruffled, almost pleased.

"That's a nice thing to say."

She thought about stumbling out some explanation, qualifying the comment, but the look on his face halted her. He didn't think it was weird or awkward, so she left it. He set his glass on the table, the single ice cube slowly disappearing.

"What you said the other night at The Gotham."

"I'm sorry for that. I was just so stunned."

"You had every right to be stunned. My behavior was, well, as you said, unbecoming."

"That was too harsh."

"I needed to hear it." He laughed to himself. "It took me hours to step back and see that from your perspective. I looked like such an ass."

"I guess that happens when you're irresistible."

"Ah, but you resisted."

"You seem to have recovered."

"I wouldn't be too sure about that." He gave her a weighty stare, and she nervously reached for her drink as he blew out a sigh. He scooted a bit closer.

"All I could think when you were on your way over today was that I had more work. I mean, I was happy you were coming over, but I just felt," he sighed, "out of gas. Then I opened the door to this." He grabbed her ponytail at her nape and ran his hand down to the end. "It's like you answered my prayers."

Her answering smile spoke volumes. As if he didn't want to betray her trust, he moved back a little and settled his hands on his knees, rubbing them gently over the worn denim.

"So. I'm an open book, Emma. Fire away."

"That's a horrible expression for a soldier to use."

"Sailor, not soldier. Okay, shoot."

She burst out laughing, barely swallowing a mouthful of scotch before it sprayed everywhere.

"Favorite flavor of ice cream."

"Peppermint, but it can't be green. It has to be white. Real. With crushed up red and white peppermint candies in it. There was this little ice cream shack on the water near my childhood home in Connecticut. My brother, James, used to walk me there when I was a kid. The. Best. Peppermint ice cream. Ever."

Emma remembered the place clearly—Half Shell. It was where they'd been headed the day she was taken. She didn't know if he saw something in her face, but his next comment stunned her.

"There are some photos . . . I don't . . . here, come with me."

Nathan took her hand and led the way into a spare room. Inside the sparse, clearly unused bedroom was a walk-in closet, and inside that were stacks of banker boxes: files from the look of them. He pulled a small box from a shelf.

"I don't want these used for the story, but it may help you . . . paint a picture. Be right back."

It was a true testament to the size of the closet that her anxieties hadn't kicked in. She started flipping through pictures thrown haphazardly into the box. There was no order to them at all, but she knew she would find photos of herself. They were together all the time as children; mainly because she was glued to his hip. She followed him everywhere, but he never seemed to mind. The thing Emma did find surprising as she moved through the box was the lack of photos of his father. Nathan's father had been the CEO of Knightsgrove-Bishop and a political kingmaker until his death two years ago. Emma once caught her own father muttering to himself about Henry Bishop, calling him an 'ugly drunk' despite the fact that they had been neighbors, and Emma assumed friends, for years. She had a vague recollection of peeking around a door in the Bishop house and interrupting Mr. Bishop shaking Nathan by the shoulders, but the memory wasn't clear. As a child, she'd just thought he was mean.

Nathan's mother, Seraphina, was the daughter of British nobles and looked the part. Emma thought she was a princess, and neither her father nor Sera Bishop herself discouraged the notion. She actually had a crown—well, a tiara—and sometimes she would let Emma wear it as she sat on her lap at her dressing table. She would try different pieces of jewelry on Emma and tell stories about meeting the queen or attending a royal ball. Emma loved her. She had no mother of her own, so she sort of adopted Seraphina. About two years after she was rescued and started her new life, Sera made the family's Belgravia home in London her primary residence while Henry remained in Connecticut. With Nathan's brothers out of college and Nathan away at boarding school, the time was ripe to flee a bad marriage. Nathan spent his downtime throughout college with his mother and even worked in London over the summer while in business school. Sera had this lovely lilting voice that Emma still remembered clearly. Occasionally in interviews, she could pick up just the slightest hint of the British influence in Nathan's upbringing. He never said "lift" or "telly," but if he was annoyed with an interviewer, he would finish a comment with a rhetorical—and slightly pejorative—question. *It's fairly obvious when you think about it, isn't it?* Very British indeed.

About twenty pictures in, she found one. He was fishing off of her family's dock in Nantucket. If you didn't look closely, you wouldn't even notice her. She was curled at his feet, playing with her toes as he focused on the water. She couldn't have been more than three. They seemed completely oblivious to one another, but completely content.

She gazed up at the ceiling of the closet to clear her emotions when another box caught her eye. It was sitting on a rack above a row of empty hangers and it read simply, *Webster.* The shelf was a white metal grid rather than solid wood. She stood and reached up through the squares of the rack that held it to try and inch it forward, her hands squeezing through the open squares. She was about to touch her fingertips to the bottom of the box when a large hand gripped her wrists. She turned, still tangled in the shelf and came face to face with a stoic Nathan. She looked up at her hands and her mind started to slip. She heard him say, "Are you snooping, Emma?" but he sounded far away. She blinked and saw his expression turn from amusement to concern as she drifted.

Two little hands poked through the top of a cage—like a dog kennel—and a man held them. Ah ah ah, little one. I will cut them off.

Her mind was flashing like a slideshow, and her body was shaking.

Her little hands reaching through the metal grid. A large hand squeezing them in warning, a tattoo on the soft skin between his thumb and index finger.

Then, nothing.

Emma looked up and realized she was sitting on the closet floor. Correction, she was sitting in Nathan's lap on the closet floor. He was stroking her hair, bringing her back. She stared up at him with unguarded emotion: fear, gratitude . . . love. He searched her face. Emma saw his relief. She felt calm. Safe.

"Where'd you go?"

Panic seized her. What the fuck had just happened? She had never had a flashback of her captivity. Never. She'd never seen a face that reminded her of anyone, a room that brought on anxiety, a smell, nothing. Being with Nathan had triggered something, and she needed to get the hell away. She pulled herself up and stood next to him. He looked up at her calmly, knees bent, palms flat on the floor behind him.

"I . . . sorry. I haven't eaten today. I think I just got dizzy."

"I know what that was, Emma. I've seen it."

She didn't want to engage in a debate or try to convince him it was a harmless dizzy spell. She just needed to go. She turned her back on him and spoke to the empty guest room.

"Can we pick this up next week? I'm sorry, I lost track of the time. I'm late for something."

"Emma."

She grabbed her bag and notes and moved calmly to his front door. She could hear him stalking behind her but keeping a safe distance. She turned and confirmed their next appointment.

"Wednesday, noon?"

He seemed to know she wasn't there, and inexplicably, he knew what she needed. He pulled the door open, stepping back a safe distance.

"I need to have Andrew drive you home. Okay?"

This was for him. He was calm, quiet, but he needed the reassurance that she was safe.

"All right."

"There's that word again," he muttered.

Despite her acquiescence, he seemed dismayed. He sent a text and walked beside her the ten or so steps to the elevator in his front hall.

"Wednesday at noon is fine."

"All right."

He almost winced at the robotic response. She knew she was freaking him out, but she was powerless to stop it. She stopped in front of the elevator and turned back with a look of pure desperation on her face. She had already revealed so much. Emma didn't know how he knew, or if he knew, but he stepped up next to her and said quietly, "Can I see you out?" She nodded, and he gently guided her into the elevator by her elbow. She peered up from staring at her feet to meet his emerald gaze and said the only thing she could think of.

"Thank you."

When the elevator stopped in the lobby, Emma forced a smile and told him she could take it from there. He nodded from the elevator and lifted his hand in a motionless wave as the doors slid closed. As she turned to make her way out of the lobby, she looked at her dangling hand and realized she still held the fishing photo from the box.

She sat in the back of the Range Rover uncharacteristically silent. She had been broken as a child, then glued back together and now, in an incredibly careless move, she had put herself in a position to be shattered.

She needed to call her father. She needed Caroline. And she needed to confront the sad reality that she had to stay away from Nathan Bishop. Her life wasn't real. It was invented, but she had no other option. And she was happy. Emma Porter was a comfortably well-off, attractive college graduate, living in the big city and cutting her teeth as a reporter. Emily Webster was an American tragedy; the daughter of one of the richest families in the world, abducted as a child and never found. She was the twenty-first century Lindbergh baby.

The thought of never seeing Nathan again made her feel sick. She was incomplete; she knew that, but what she didn't know was that something could fill that void. Being with him was like coming home; every ounce of her being was drawn to him. It was like her whole life had been a tornado, and Nathan calmed the winds. None of that mattered, though, if being with him was going to shatter her. She couldn't be Emma Porter with him, and she couldn't be Emily Webster because Emily Webster didn't exist.

Emma called Nathan's assistant and canceled their next two interviews. She didn't give an excuse. She planned on calling Farrell and seeing if he could finish the piece. Wildly unprofessional, she knew, but she would explain that Nathan was hitting on her or making her feel uncomfortable. That was shitty, but it would do the trick. It would be a huge slap in the face to Nathan to betray him by broadcasting his behavior at their first meeting, but that would be an additional sad but effective side-effect: he wouldn't want anything to do with her.

The thought turned Emma into a zombie. She crawled into bed wearing a camisole and yoga pants, the cornflower blue tie wrapped around her knuckles like a boxer's tape, and wailed, then cried, then sniffled, then slept. She recalled the vaguely familiar sensation from her childhood when Nathan went away to school. Back then, she had burrowed into a small space between his laundry hamper and the wall in his closet and hid; that was before small spaces did a number on her. She was different now, more complicated, but she still felt . . . desolate. She had once again been given that indescribable feeling of . . . *wholeness*, only to, once again, have it ripped away. It was all she could do to call *The Sentry* and leave a message that she had the flu. She texted her father the same thing. CNN had sent Caroline to Idaho to cover some sort of standoff between the feds and a cult. She was alone.

CHAPTER TEN

Hercules Reynolds sat on the threadbare sofa, took a long swig of his beer, and stared out the window. He was a stone's throw from his former home, Camp Lejeune. Six years as a jarhead—well, he supposed once a Marine, always a Marine, but whatever—and now he was considering a job as a mall security guard. He hadn't even told his grandmother that he was out. He wanted to wait and tell her when he had something positive to report: *Hey Mhamó, I left the service and got a job at a bank.* Or a car dealership, or a construction company, or an insurance agency, or a school. Just not a mall cop. He had been a Marine sniper, for fuck's sake. Hercules chuckled sadly then. He sounded like those pathetic alcoholics in movies who couldn't move past the achievements of their youth. He glanced at the photograph of his brothers-in-arms that he had printed but had yet to frame, his black hair and bright blue eyes broadcasting his Irish roots. He felt a pang of guilt for abandoning them, but snipers had short lifespans in the service for a lot of reasons. His was physical. He believed in what he did, and he was good at it, but after a bar fight got out of hand, Herc had ended up with a stab wound in his hand and a severed tendon. The injury didn't necessarily mean the end of his career, it meant rehab and retraining, but he knew a sign from Upstairs when he got one. It was time to move on. Herc didn't need a lot of money. He certainly didn't need fame. He just needed to respect himself. He wanted to be proud of the paycheck he earned. He just couldn't seem to think of any way to do it.

Just as he began, again, to troll the internet for jobs for which he was qualified, his cell phone rang. The tinny strains of "Highway to Hell" told him who it was before he glanced at the screen and saw his childhood best friend's gap-toothed grin.

"Hey, Billy."

"Herc, what the fuck? You get out, and you don't call?"

"How'd you know?"

"Daryl told me. He was bummed to see you go."

"I'm gonna miss those sacks of shit."

"Where you at?"

"Still in Jacksonville. Tryin' to figure some stuff out."

"Well, pack your bags, my brother. I've got your shit figured out for you."

"Oh yeah?"

"Yeah."

"And what exactly have you figured out?"

"Sweet union job with lots of perks, nice little house with my girl. Life is good, bro."

"That's great, man."

"I ain't callin' to brag, fucktard. Pack a bag. My supervisor said if I had any friends from the Corps, he needs a couple more guys. My girl's parents run a boarding house with a real decent room available. This is opportunity knocking, mutherfucker. Answer the door!"

Hercules thought for a minute. He never leapt before he looked. In this instance, however, he didn't have time to process all of his thoughts. Particularly what Billy had meant when he said the job had "lots of perks." There wasn't much for Herc to ponder. This wasn't an either/or scenario because he just had the "either." There was no "or."

"Savannah's five hours. Make it six in my piece of shit. I can be there by supper."

"Booyah! Get a move on, brother. The party awaits."

Herc raced around the small space to collect his few, meager belongings with one thought in mind: soon he would be able to call his grandmother with good news.

CHAPTER ELEVEN

The storms arrived almost on cue. For five days, Emma hardly left her darkened bedroom. Nathan called every day. She rejected the first few. When the doorman started calling up, she silenced her phone.

On Wednesday, when Caroline threw open the door, she winced.

"Okay, first of all, how long have you been in bed because your hair looks like birds are nesting in it? Second of all, I know you can't wash a dish, but the kitchen is spotless, so when did you last eat?"

Emma started to cry. Again. All the color drained from Caroline's face as she rushed to the bedside.

"Jesus, Em, what the fuck? I know it's not your dad because he asked me to check on you when I got back."

"I had a flashback."

"Oh no. Was it . . . ." she couldn't finish.

"No, no. Nothing horrible. Just a man grabbing my wrists. It . . ." she took a breath and steadied herself, ". . . it's Nathan. He's triggering memories."

Understanding dawned. "Oh."

"I can't see him anymore. It's dangerous for me."

"Are you sure what's happening to you with him is bad?"

"Yes. I can't go back to square one, Caroline. I can't become Emily Webster."

"But you are Emily Webster. You always have been. You're Emily Webster to me."

"That's not true. You knew the old me, but you are here with Emma Porter now. Your friendship now is with Emma."

Caroline scooted closer, her eyes filled with worry. Then she grabbed both of Emma's shoulders and spoke.

"Do you realize that I have never once called you Emma?"

"What?"

"I have always called you Em. When you became Emma, I just kept calling you Em. You have never changed to me. And I think this bizarre compartmentalizing you do where you are two completely different people is way off. You're one girl. You have always been one girl. The girl who hates peas but loves pea soup, the girl obsessed with thunderstorms and shipwrecks and finding the perfect blueberry muffin . . . ."

Turns out it is possible to laugh and cry at the same time.

"The girl hopelessly in love with Nathan Bishop. Call yourself Lady Fucking Gaga for all I care. You are one person. One person who had something horrible happen, but your life can't be about that one thing."

"That isn't all it's about. It's not," she insisted then relented. "And if it is, that's because it has to be."

"I think it's time to change that."

"Caroline, I can't just shed my skin and say to the world Emily Webster is back! God, just thinking about the attention. Plus, it's not safe."

"I know, but what I'm talking about is more of a change of attitude."

"How so?"

"I don't know exactly, but I think you need to say, 'fuck it.'"

"Elaborate."

"I'm not saying to stop being smart or stop being careful, but I think we need to lift this shroud of caution that covers everything you do. Yes, our apartment is owned by a holding company; yes, you have a different name, but you're the one keeping the Emily Webster that's in here locked up."

She touched her chest. Emma blew out a breath.

"Jesus, Em, how long have you been in bed? Cause that is morning, noon, and night breath."

She covered her mouth with her hand. "Sorry."

"Seriously? How long?"

"What day is it?"

"Wednesday."

"Since Friday night."

"Holy shit. What have you eaten?"

She focused on her hands twisting in her lap.

"Get in the fucking shower and clean up. I'm ordering Lorenzo's. Being heartsick is one thing, coming home and finding you dead is another."

Caroline mimicked a corpse frozen in a pose.

"Okay, okay, I get it. Get lost, and I'll jump in the shower." Emma needed her gone because truthfully, she wasn't sure if she could walk. Her stomach was cramping, and her hands were shaking. She put her feet on the floor and gingerly took a step forward. As she reached for the side table to steady herself, Caroline came back into the room.

"Do we like their chicken parm or veal . . . ." Her face went white.

"Jesus, Em, oh my God. Do you need to go to the hospital?"

"I think I'm okay. Could you run and grab one of those Vitamin Waters out of the fridge?"

Caroline turned and ran out without a word.

After a shower and a small meal, Emma was almost feeling normal. She and Caroline were sitting on the balcony listening to the rumble of thunder and the bark of an ambulance siren when the doorman called up to say they had a delivery.

"Please tell me you had cupcakes delivered."

"Why live in New York if you can't have someone bring you sweets at all hours of the night?"

A few moments later, there was a knock. From the balcony, she heard Caroline flip the deadbolt and open the door. Down below on the street, a cab driver was laying on the horn.

"We have coconut, chocolate, and what looks like lemon."

Emma peeked up as Nathan held the white bakery box, examining the contents with the curiosity of a child. Her heart stopped. Caroline joined him in his perusal. Her interruption gave Emma a moment to gather herself.

"I think that has a passion fruit filling. Bleh. When did cupcakes get so complicated? I'm chocolate. She's coconut." Caroline reached into the box.

"Nice to meet you, chocolate. Nathan."

"Caroline."

Nathan and Caroline had never met. Emma's and Caroline's mothers had drifted apart when Emma's mother fell off the wagon almost immediately after giving birth. As a small child, Caroline lived in Atlanta, and Emma saw her on family trips. Caroline came into her life in a significant way when Emma was returned from her capture, and her father moved them to Georgia.

Like their mothers, Emma's and Caroline's fathers had been friends since their college days and did business together often. Emma had a moment of anxiety that Caroline's last name, Fitzhugh, would ping with Nathan, but she, either inadvertently or by design, didn't mention it.

"Coconut, please." Emma smiled from across the room.

He reached in the box to retrieve the cupcake and started to turn his attention to Emma when he stopped. He took a sharp breath.

"Jesus, Emma . . . are you all right?" His concern was palpable. He wanted to come to her. She could see it in every coiled muscle of his frame, but he resisted the urge.

"You should have seen her an hour ago." Caroline retrieved a cupcake. "I nearly called an ambulance."

That did it. Nathan crossed to her in long strides and sank to his knees. He brushed her hair back from her face. Emma looked at him then. He had dark circles under his eyes, and his color was pale.

"You look like shit, too, by the way."

"I know that. I'm just not certain it's for the same reason."

It was the sweetest thing she had ever heard. He was worried about her.

Before she registered the movement in her brain, her hand was brushing his cheek. She gently felt the stubble. He closed his eyes and leaned into the touch. It was the most intimate moment Emma had ever had with a man. He returned the gesture, cupping her face in his large hand. He opened his eyes and pinned her with his probing gaze. Then he reached up and caught her nose between the knuckles of his index and middle fingers in a steal-your-nose gesture one might play with a child. *Exactly like he used to do when she was a child.* For a brief moment, he looked almost sad. She pulled back and glanced up to see Caroline leaning against the balcony doorway, arms crossed and staring unabashedly.

"Emma?" Nathan pulled her attention back to him.

"I'm sorry I quit, Nathan. I had a bad, um, reaction at your apartment."

"Emma."

She stood and paced the balcony, and Nathan moved from his catcher's squat to the ottoman next to her chair.

"Regardless, I shouldn't have just walked out."

"Emma."

"I understand if you want to cancel the interview. I can tell Farrell."

"Emma, stop."

The firm command startled her out of her shell, and she stared at him.

"I'm sorry, Nathan."

"You have nothing to apologize for." A warm smile spread across his features, and she relaxed instantly. "Now come back here."

She stepped in front of him, and he stood and smoothed a loose strand of hair behind her ear. Emma breathed him in and met his gaze, firm in the realization that this was her path.

"I'd like to continue . . . with this. It's a once-in-a-lifetime opportunity. I'd be crazy to walk away." The equivoque was lost on no one.

Out of the corner of her eye, Emma saw Caroline give a single firm nod and disappear into the house. She returned her focus to Nathan who was scanning her face from her forehead to her chin, a dozen thoughts seemingly racing through his head. His response distilled them all down to one simple word.

"Good." He returned to the bakery box and continued. "We're going to eat cupcakes, we're going to relax, and I'm going to tell you about the company in Kuwait I'm buying, and the family of ducks I rescued in college, and the time I hit back-to-back winning numbers at roulette."

He stood before her, the box of cupcakes between them.

"That is, if you're sure you want to keep interviewing me."

"I do," she said. "I really, really do."

With his attention on the treats, he nodded.

Nathan passed her the coconut cupcake, and her face lit up. She took a very unladylike bite, then licked the frosting from her lip.

"Jesus, you're beautiful."

"Thank you." It was like no one had ever said it to her before because Nathan was the only person who mattered. Setting the box aside, he took her shoulders and squared her to him.

"Don't do that again." Something in his grass-green eyes shattered her heart, and she nodded mutely. "Are we clear?"

She cleared her throat and nodded again.

"I need to hear you say it, Emma."

"I won't do that again."

He closed his eyes briefly and sighed.

"Right. Good."

Emma snagged a second cupcake with a devilish grin. "Suddenly, I'm starving."

The look on his face told her she wasn't the only one.

CHAPTER TWELVE

Dario Sava did most of his business at home these days. Located five miles outside of Parbo—the local abbreviation of the Suriname capital city of Parimaribo—the sweeping estate had once belonged to a governor, appointed when the Dutch reclaimed the trading post from the British in the late seventeenth century. The original home had been rebuilt after a devastating fire, but the current, and relatively young, 150-year-old structure still bore the Old World elegance of the original. Dutch seamen had nicknamed the estate Vuurtoren, *Lighthouse.* The property did still have a working lighthouse, but the name was a reference to the hilltop home itself, the bright white walls and red tile roof visible for quite a distance out to sea.

The home was comprised of a central structure with two massive wings extending back on either side. The center was the living space where Dario ate, occasionally entertained, and often sat at night listening to the surf and the breeze and the fading echoes of Tala's footsteps. She had died in this house ten years ago. The official cause of death was respiratory failure due to complications . . . blah blah blah. That wasn't what killed her. Dario knew this because the same thing had killed him years before Tala had succumbed. They were poisoned. Poisoned by the toxic mix of rage and grief and powerlessness and need. Strange to have so much in life yet feel so . . . void.

Originally, Dario had planned to take the American child. He was going to tell Tala that her parents had been killed in a car accident and the child had no family. He worried about having trouble embracing the child of Jack Webster, the man who had injured them so gravely, but Tala would be oblivious and regardless have had no such compunction. The girl would join them when they arrived at their new home in Parbo. Her light skin and hair could be easily explained—a genetic contribution from Tala's American mother—if anyone was foolish enough to seek an explanation at all. Dario had no interest in adoption, but this was different in his reasoning. At the time, the plan had seemed positively poetic. He would give his Tala her heart's desire, the one thing he had been unable to give her, and simultaneously bestow on Jack Webster a lifelong gnawing ache of never knowing what had happened to his child. Karmic justice dealt by an almighty hand.

But Dario had been young and had failed to plan for contingencies. Their move from Qatar to Suriname had been delayed by the sudden unexpected illness of Dario's uncle. It had stalled them for months. By the time that was resolved, and they were ready to proceed, the child had been rescued.

Jack and Emily Webster had disappeared. Well, Emily had at any rate. Jack would have been easy enough to find. He had almost no online presence, but some boots on the ground and some patience would have paid off eventually. What was the point? Dario had shown his hand. The opportunity to pluck the child from the hands of an enterprising nanny would not present itself again. So, Dario waited. Hoping, as Rigo promised, that this desire, no, this *need* for cosmic balance would resolve itself in other ways. It hadn't. And now with the clock ticking on his own life, the situation demanded resolution.

He would sell the Japanese instrument of destruction discovered by the Manchurian workers, kill the daughter of the man who had killed his, and live out his days with a sense of completion, with some notion of solace.

If there were anything for which to be grateful from the whole debacle, Dario thought, it was the invaluable lesson learned: *always have a backup plan.* Dario had not been left standing flat-footed since. As he became more adept at his craft, he'd even thrown in a few twists.

Five years ago, when he'd discovered a CIA informant in his midst, he hadn't simply flayed the man. Rather, he'd let him discover some very explosive intel that had left a U.S. black ops team standing in front of an empty cave in Afghanistan rechecking GPS coordinates like a father who had missed a highway exit on a family trip. Meanwhile, Dario had personally delivered the FIM-92 Stinger to a Somali warlord, staying for a meal of *tsebhi* and *injera* bread before returning to his home without incident. Then he had flayed the informant.

Dario had discovered, to his delight, that the best way to stay off the radar of international law enforcement was not to hide below it, but rather to fly above it. Dario was smart, and he was brazen—a combination of qualities that had yet to fail him.

Dario allowed his lips to lift at the memory—the ruse, not the flaying, which required patience and commitment and had been tedious—as he walked across the lush lawn to the outbuilding that housed the lab. He entered without knocking to find his scientist, Fyodor, sitting in a recliner, watching a game show, eating a plate of pancakes doused in syrup, and drinking a Coke Lite. He rose, using the recliner's throttle to assist in propelling him from his seat.

"Good evening, sir."

"You have what I asked for."

"Of course. My sister-in-law ordered most of it from Amazon," Fyodor chuckled.

Dario joined him. "Very well."

Fyodor bent down and scooped up a silver case that looked like a small, hard-sided suitcase. He flipped the clasps and opened it to reveal a hard foam interior with a cutout in the center. Dario nodded his approval and walked to a standing safe with the heavy door slightly ajar. He pulled it open fully and scanned the shelves. He retrieved the sealed test tube from a rack, along with the metal containment canister, and returned to Fyodor's side. He held the test tube up to the light and tilted it, watching the brown viscous liquid climb the sides. He glanced at the items scattered on the lab table and raised a brow to Fyodor, who shrugged in response.

"Sometimes the simplest solution is the correct one."

"Indeed," Dario concurred as he slid the test tube into the protective canister and nestled it into the foam. He clicked the case shut and spun the small cogs of the combination lock at the center.

"Rigo will be by for it shortly."

Fyodor nodded and returned to his recliner meal. On the television, a woman spun a giant wheel and jumped up and down. Dario turned back as he reached the door.

"Fyodor."

The scientist looked up, plate in one hand, remote in the other.

"Next time something a bit more challenging, I think."

Fyodor smiled at his boss. "That would be wonderful, sir."

Dario nodded and left.

Jack Webster glanced at the weekly email report on his phone as he strolled through Amagansett. He hated this time of year when New Yorkers flocked to the chic beach village; suddenly, there was no parking, and his favorite lobster salad was eighty dollars a pound. The calmer times of year more than made up for it, though. So, Jack tolerated the hedge fund robber barons and the college students crammed ten to a rental house and the sticky, sandy children and waited for the storm to pass. He continued to scroll through the report JT had sent. He wasn't upset by Nathan Bishop's sudden reappearance in his daughter's life; if anything, he was pleased. Perhaps it was inevitable. The ember of the romantic in him still glowed, he supposed. What concerned him was how to handle it. Nathan was a trained intelligence gatherer with a team around him that rivaled the NSA. Jack needed to get everyone on the same page before false assumptions and miscommunication created a problem for his daughter. He was looking for a controlled detonation rather than an all-out explosion.

Jack texted his driver and arranged for the unscheduled visit to Manhattan. Perhaps he would take the girls out for dinner. He was so preoccupied with his mental to-do list when his driver pulled up to the curb, he failed to notice the paunchy man in the nylon Mets jacket slip into the innocuous blue sedan and follow him.

CHAPTER THIRTEEN

The next afternoon Emma was sitting on her balcony organizing her notes from their interviews. Okay, she was daydreaming about Nathan. The evening had ended abruptly when Nathan had received what Emma realized was an urgent, and upsetting, phone call. He had quickly cupped his hand over the bottom of the phone, told her he would see her soon, kissed the top of her head, and slipped out. With her iPad on her lap and a coffee in her hand and her mind in the gutter, her phone buzzed.

Mr. Wonderful: *I'm downstairs. Come as you are.*

Emma almost burst into flames. She leapt off the lounge chair, pulled the hair elastic out of her hair, and raced through the apartment, grabbing flip flops and a bag as she typed a response.

Emma: *Coming.*

She texted JT as she flew down the stairs and was tossing her lip gloss into her bag when she pushed open the door to the lobby and caught Nathan getting the stiff arm from the weekend doorman, Ray. Nathan was wearing faded jeans, loafers, and an untucked white Oxford. He looked edible. And annoyed.

"Hi, Ray; this is Nathan. I'm hoping we'll be seeing more of him around here, so try not to injure him."

Nathan huffed at the idea of the scrawny nineteen-year-old inflicting any sort of injury on his six-foot, two-inch frame, then he realized what she had said, and his gaze found hers. He raised his brow in pleasant surprise and then sidestepped Ray and stood right in front of her. He kissed her on the cheek with ingrained politeness and soft heat.

"Right. Let's go."

"Where are we going?"

"It's a surprise."

"Nathan?"

"Yes."

"I hate surprises."

"Then you have been improperly initiated into the surprise process."

"Understatement of the year," she mumbled.

"Hmm?"

"Okay, then. Show me a good surprise." She texted JT without taking her phone out of her purse and told him to stand by. She looked up to find Nathan staring at her with an unreadable expression. "Chop-chop, mister. Every minute that ticks by, my expectations increase."

"Christ, well now I'm going to cock it up."

Emma laughed. "Sometimes your inner Brit leaks out."

"Sometimes." He winked. "Come on, the longer I build it up, the more chance you'll be disappointed." He headed for the front doors, but she pulled on his forearm with both hands to stop him.

"Somehow I don't see that happening."

"Where the hell have you been hiding?"

In plain sight, she thought but didn't say.

He didn't expect an answer. "Come on."

The surprise was an Italian street fair. Her SoHo apartment was just above Nolita and Little Italy, so it was a short walk down relatively quiet streets until they came upon the chaos. Sounds of music and the smells of food filled the air. Children ran around laughing and munching zeppole. It was perfect. They wandered from stall to stall and ate and browsed the odds and ends for sale. Nathan had his arm slung around her shoulders, and Emma held the back of his shirt in her fist. She never wanted to let go. If she started to analyze it, she would have gone crazy ticking off all the reasons why they should or should not be strolling through Lower Manhattan arm-in-arm. So, she didn't. It was like it had been when she was a child. And totally different. She somehow just needed to touch him. They just were.

People were milling about, music from an Italian folk band lilted through the air. Vendors called to passers-by, luring them to examine their wares. About an hour into their little adventure, Nathan bristled. He tossed his Italian ice into a trash can, and his grip on her tightened. He wasn't obvious about it, but something had triggered his military awareness. He squeezed her hand, released it, then put his arm around her and pulled her into the circle of his body.

"What's going on?"

"Huh? Nothing."

"Nathan, you look like you're poised for battle."

"Sorry. Old habits. It's just there's a guy behind us. Moving through the crowd at our pace, trying not to be seen."

She knelt, ostensibly to fiddle with her shoe, and glanced behind her. When she caught a glimpse of JT's hulking form, she rolled her eyes. She slipped her free hand into her purse and texted JT: *btfo*. It was their code that she was fine, and he was being too obvious: *back the fuck off.* Nathan moved to the next booth. JT waited thirty seconds, then made a slow about-face and headed the other way. Nathan visibly relaxed.

"It's okay, false alarm."

"He's probably tailing some mob boss."

"Maybe. Sorry. This business makes you paranoid. I've seen a lot of kidnappings."

Her knees buckled and Nathan caught her. He saw the unmasked look of distress on her face before she reined it in.

"Emma?"

"Shit, sorry. Low blood sugar I guess." *Why do I keep using that stupid excuse?* She joked as she took a generous bite of lemon Italian ice and instantly gave herself a brain freeze. She smacked her palm to her forehead. It turned out to be the perfect distraction.

"Press your tongue to the roof of your mouth." Nathan held the back of her neck and turned her by her shoulders to face him. She immediately obeyed and the pain subsided. He stroked her face, looking puzzled. Out of the corner of her eye, she saw the display at the stall next to them. Tiny charms of all shapes. They weren't expensive but one immediately caught her eye. As she reached for it, his big hand brushed hers. She knew he was reaching for the same one, and she knew why. She withdrew her hand, and he picked up the tiny lighthouse.

"My family . . . we had a place on Nantucket. My bedroom looks out on a lighthouse. Our neighbors had the same view and we used to play this game . . . ." he trailed off, but she knew the story he was going to tell. It was her bedtime entertainment. It was a game he used to play with her.

They would appear at a window as the light swept the harbor and then duck and move to a different one in the intermittent darkness. They would try to spot each other each time the beam began a new rotation.

"I love that lighthouse." He looked at Emma.

"Me, too," she said dreamily. "Um, I mean lighthouses in general."

"I don't imagine you see a lot of lighthouses in rural Georgia."

The veiled suspicion in his voice put her off, but her lie was seamless. She was prepared for any scenario.

"Spent vacations in Sea Island growing up. There's a lighthouse there that's . . . special." She hated that lie. It tasted awful in her mouth. She wanted to say *Yes! That's our lighthouse! We both love the same place.* Instead, she just stared wistfully at the little charm. Nathan bought it and carefully attached it to her keychain.

They left the fair and walked through Tribeca, wandering toward SoHo. He reached for her hand, and she took his without a thought, twining their fingers. He sighed, calm and happy. When they got to her building, he stopped her short of the front door and backed her gently up against the wall. He buried his face in her neck and ran his hand up the side of her body, brushing the outer curve of her breast in the most intoxicating way. It was an odd mix of comfort and lust—seeking solace and barely leashing this *need*. She involuntarily arched into his body. Her breasts pressed against his unyielding chest, his erection massive and solid against her hip. Then he kissed her.

Such a strange thing, a kiss—the action so simple, the meaning so complex. Nathan's lips moved over hers, the perfect blend of passion and finesse. It felt like home, but certainly no home Emma had ever known. At once familiar and foreign, cementing and shattering, tranquil and thunderous. She parted her lips, and Nathan responded, deepening the kiss, pulling her into him. When they pulled apart, Nathan ran his nose up and down the length of hers.

"I want to go upstairs and do unspeakable things to you."

The reality of her inexperience crashed down on Emma. She stiffened but it felt so good to be near him. She just didn't know what to say.

"I . . ."

She was spared from forcing herself to give him some go-to catty brush off by Ray, the doorman, who cleared his throat loudly behind Nathan.

"Ms. Porter, sorry to interrupt, but, um, your father is here."

"My father?" Of course, he would show up. No doubt, he had received word that she was working a bit too closely with Nathan.

"Yes, miss. Mr. . . ." he stopped himself, knowing, and being very well compensated for, her father's insistence on anonymity. "He's upstairs."

Her father was careful to protect her identity. The doormen, and the few people in Emma's life who knew him, knew him as Mr. Webster—a common enough thing to have a daughter with a different last name. His small circle had long ago moved on from her tragedy. Once, while they were having dinner, they had run into a colleague of her father's. Without missing a beat, Jack Webster introduced her as the daughter of a friend. Beyond some salacious speculation about why he was dining with a woman half his age, not an eyebrow had been raised.

"Okay, thank you."

Nathan smirked. "Well, that changes things. Should I meet the old man? Declare my intentions?"

Emma blanched. He already knew "the old man." Nathan noticed, but her hand on his chest distracted him and she laughed.

"I guess this has to be a G-rated date. A kiss on the stoop before daddy comes out with the shotgun." She let a hint of her 'accent' show.

"I'll take what I can get." And with that, he kissed her senseless. When they reluctantly broke apart, she ran her index finger over the scar on his lip. His hands slipped from her shoulders down her arms and he pulled back.

"In the spirit of full disclosure . . ."

"Yes?"

"Off the record?"

"Sure."

"I did split my lip open in a motorcycle accident, but it was technically *reinjured*. There was already a scar there."

"Oh?" She didn't want to appear too exuberant about his declaration, even though she was bursting inside.

"Yeah. Fell off a pool slide when I was a kid, acting like an idiot. You can see why I prefer the motorcycle story."

She didn't know what to say, so she threw her arms around his neck and kissed him like she meant it.

"How did you know?"

"Know what?" she asked, nuzzling his neck.

"When I told you that motorcycle story, you seemed skeptical."

"I don't know. A scar from a motorcycle? It just sounded . . . like a *guy* story."

"I am a guy."

"I know," she sighed. *Boy, did she know.*

"I like kissing you out in public. I can chase away any of your stalker boyfriends."

She laughed. "Not to worry. None of those out here."

"Stalkers?"

"Boyfriends."

"None?"

"Nope . . . not at the moment . . . I don't . . . nope." Her lack of clarity on what to confess made her stumble. Should she admit her astonishing dating history, or lack thereof, or should she simply gloss over it?

He sensed her disquiet and deftly lightened the mood.

"Well, in keeping with this G-rated date, I think I should ask you out again, Ms. Porter."

"Oh really, Mr. Bishop?"

"Really. I've actually been meaning to bring it up all day, but you're distracting."

"Good distracting?"

"Very."

"Good."

"So, Fourth of July. K-B has this big event . . ."

"A defense contractor and fireworks? Seems fitting."

"You're actually the first person to notice that. Most people think patriotism."

"Patriotic explosions," she quipped. He chuckled, a dimple on his left cheek making a rare appearance.

"Exactly. Anyway, I could say it would be good for the story, but the truth is I want you to come with me . . . as my date."

"I'd love to," she beamed.

"You would?"

"Yes. Can't you tell?"

"I think so. You're hard to read. And I specialize in reading people like books."

"Well, I have a lot of chapters."

"That much I can tell." He pinched the bridge of his nose and then looked at her with earnest eyes. "Listen, Emma, I wanted to say something." He was struggling, so she let him take his time. "Honestly, this may be premature, but as you have pointed out repeatedly, I have a rep." He air-quoted "rep" and rolled his eyes. "I want to make the parameters of our relationship very clear, so there's no misunderstanding." *Oh no.* She braced herself. "I want to spend time with you . . . to the exclusion of other women." He laughed to himself. "I almost said to the exclusion of all other people but that would sound a bit crazy, wouldn't it?" The faintest hint of his British lilt leaked out. "What I'm trying to say is . . . ." He looked to the sky for inspiration.

"You want to date me. And you don't want to date anyone else."

He laughed then.

"Yes. Exactly. Thank you."

"Was that so hard?"

"Well, I've never done it before."

"Voiced your intentions?" she asked.

"Had intentions," he confessed.

"Oh." That shut her up.

"Don't look so delighted—not all of my intentions are honorable."

She gasped and he smirked.

"Good."

His turn to gasp. Her turn to smirk.

"So, *eh hem*. I was hoping you were feeling like this was . . . I mean I'm not really . . . I'm not sure I'll be any good at this, but, you've . . ."

"Okay."

"That's it? Okay?"

"Yes. That's what you want to know, right? If I want the same thing?"

"Yes."

"Then, okay."

"Why are things so easy with you?" He shook his head as if he couldn't believe it.

"I'm not sure," she laughed. "I think most people think I'm difficult."

"Well, to me you're easy. I mean, not easy. I just mean . . . fuck." She pulled his hand from his hair and squeezed it.

"It's okay. I knew what you meant."

"I'm usually more eloquent, you know."

"That's what makes this so special."

For a minute they just grinned at each other like idiots.

"So, back to business, I will see you Wednesday. Come to my office. And no funny business when we're at work." He winked. "I had a security pass made for you. You now have clearance to get to my office."

"I'm honored. Thought you would need to collect my DNA for that kind of access."

"Oh, I got it."

She laughed. He had to be kidding. Right? "Okay, then."

He started to step away. Without thinking she fisted his shirt at the waist. "Nathan?"

"Yes?"

"Kiss me again."

"It would be my pleasure."

CHAPTER FOURTEEN

Her father was concerned. An unplanned visit from him was highly irregular. They had an established, secure routine: Jack Webster would come into the city for his monthly visit to The Union Club. He would check-in at the front desk of the exclusive members-only establishment and ask for any messages from his "assistant." If Emma had a rare unexpected conflict, she would leave a message saying his 4:00 p.m. meeting had been rescheduled. If all went according to plan, Jack would slip out a back exit and meet Emma at one of the bustling midtown delis they rotated through. This spontaneous visit was understandable, of course. He had spent more than a decade hiding her, turning Emily Webster into Emma Porter. Making sure she was safe.

Her abduction was still unexplained. The feds at first suspected kidnapping for ransom, but a demand never came. Then they explored the idea of revenge. Her father had grown his family fortune mainly as an investor in both fossil and alternative fuels. He had also served briefly as the U.S. Ambassador to Qatar until an illness forced him back to the States. It seemed farfetched to think that someone who ended up on the wrong end of an oil deal would target one of dozens, maybe hundreds, of investors, and he wasn't in the Middle East long enough to make a diplomatic impact. So, revenge was back-burnered. The feds explored black market adoption and trafficking, but nothing panned out. The information was incomplete, but from what they gathered, the people who took her had simply taken her. Nobody seemed to know why.

Every enemy, business or personal, had been investigated down to the smallest detail. Nothing turned up. One thing was clear, however. A considerable amount of planning and expense had gone into the abduction. That's why the danger was ongoing; someone had paid dearly for their treasure and apparently wasn't willing to let it go. Someone wanted Emily Webster, specifically. That was the best explanation they could come up with as to why. What else could it be? What little information they were able to get in order to piece together this theory came from a partially fried hard drive found at the scene of her rescue—a rescue that had come about through little more than dumb luck.

An older woman in an upper-middle-class section of Baltimore had just watched a segment on her favorite television news magazine about terrorists and drug cartels smuggling contraband and weapons into the country in everyday items like coffee and sporting goods. It was then that she'd noticed two Middle Eastern men bringing stuffed animals into a neighboring home with no children in sight. The woman immediately suspected a terror plot involving explosive-filled teddy bears. After observing their behavior for two days through the lace curtains in her breakfast nook and using her birding binoculars, she'd determined their behavior to be quite suspicious and called her FBI-agent nephew. Now the nephew, on any other day, would have dismissed this as yet another cockamamie call from his eccentric relative, but it just so happened that on that day, he was involved in a manhunt for two bank robbery suspects who matched the descriptions his aunt gave. The subsequent stakeout and raid did not produce the agent's bank robbers; it did, however, produce a violent member of a Russian syndicate, two Middle Eastern men, a damaged laptop, a smattering of recreational drugs, and Emily Webster.

The kidnappers were now all dead: one was killed in the rescue mission, and two others were stabbed in prison. The two prison murders confirmed the FBI's suspicions that whoever had orchestrated the kidnapping wanted to silence any potential informants and had the means to do so. FBI analysts made note of carefully masked data searches about Emily Webster over the years, and a disturbing file that turned up four years ago that contained an age sequencing of her eight-year-old photo that was, thankfully, fairly inaccurate. Her father and the men assigned to her case were convinced that she had become, if not an obsession, a person of interest to someone who was not easily dismissed. It wasn't a Helen of Troy scenario; the person or people involved were not launching troops to retake her, but it was clear someone was still putting out feelers.

After Emily was rescued, her father moved them to an estate in a remote part of Georgia and Emma Porter was born. It was her father's own private-sector version of the Witness Protection Program and equally as effective as the federal system. She attended the local public school and spent her limited free time with Caroline, who lived nearby. She had become Emma's best friend during the exile and even spent entire summers with Emma under the pretense of going to camp. Caroline was the daughter of her father's closest friend, and they were the only outsiders who knew the truth. Emily Webster wasn't officially dead, but she was missing: a cold case. Only her father, the FBI, Caroline's family, and the person who'd masterminded her abduction knew she wasn't dead or still a captive. Well, she was still a captive, but not in the way people might have thought. And in truth, she really didn't think about it that way until she got older. It was simply her reality; she didn't know anything else.

As time passed, however, Emma started to realize how trapped she really was, and the more tiny tastes of freedom she got—driving, travel, financial independence—the more she wanted. When she turned eighteen, she had a choice, and her father was prepared for her decision. She told him she would rather risk her fate and live a normal life. He reluctantly agreed, and with Caroline by her side and JT at her back, off she went to NYU.

In retrospect, "normal" may have been an exaggeration, but as far as Emma was concerned, it was close. She didn't know if her decision had been a risky one. She didn't really comprehend the threat because she had no memory of being taken the first time. She hadn't known where she was, where she'd slept, what she'd eaten. She couldn't picture the room or the people. Apart from that brief flash in Nathan's closet, it was like her mind went from the moment before she was taken to the moment she was safe without skipping a beat.

It had happened when she was eight. Emily was walking with a nanny to the little seaside ice cream shop in Greenwich that Nathan had reminisced about. She had been wearing a blue sundress that tied at each shoulder and glittery flip-flops. She could remember finding a stick bug on the concrete and moving it to the grass. The nanny had grabbed her hand and pulled her back to the sidewalk. They rounded a corner, and a van pulled up—it was a big white van with writing on the side and a cartoon picture of a man in overalls with his hands on his hips smiling broadly. The door slid open with a metallic groan, and the nanny shoved Emily toward a skinny, smiling guy inside without a word. Emily remembered thinking the man smelled like a closet and had tattoos on his arms: a mermaid and a sword and other things. She remembered the fear. When the big door of the van slid shut, so did a door in her mind.

Her next memory was being in the back of a large SUV. Her father was holding her, and she was wrapped in a crinkly silver sheet and wearing a huge gray FBI T-shirt. She had been missing for one hundred and forty-three days.

Her mother had died from a drug overdose when Emily was three; she had never been a part of her life. Her mother was the wild child black sheep of a Palm Beach society family and had partied her way up the East Coast. Her father had been mesmerized by her—she was a free spirit and a beautiful one at that—but he hadn't realized the depth of her darkness until after she had gotten pregnant. He married her out of obligation, kept her sober for the duration of the pregnancy, and tried to get her treatment. She left when Emily was two and was dead by her third birthday. It had been Emily and her father for as long as she could remember. Despite the lack of a mother, Emily had been an exuberant child: bright, happy, curious up until the day she had been abducted. She was never morose or despondent—with the exception of those times when Nathan had gone away. She was a generally cheerful child, but after the kidnapping, Emily was focused, studious, and private. Emily Webster had become a different person. She had become Emma Porter.

Her father was the best man she knew. He was kind and smart and encouraging. Emma knew his life had been filled with stress and paranoia for the last fifteen years, but he was resolute. He carried the burden of two unsolved mysteries: who had planned the original kidnapping, and who was the person who still seemed fixated on her? Her father's sole focus was her safety. Emma loved him.

"Em . . . ." Her father stared out the window, the sheer curtain in his hand pulled to the side.

"He doesn't recognize me. He hasn't seen me since I was eight."

"You were striking then, and you're more so now."

"Dad, there's not even a flicker of recognition." Well, that wasn't totally true, but she got the sense that the occasional glimmer she saw in his eyes wasn't about the little girl who'd lived next door.

"He was an elite soldier, darling. He's trained in ways you cannot imagine."

"I can imagine." She had been trained too. Her father chuckled.

"True." He took out a handkerchief and rubbed it across his upper lip under his nose. "If you're sure."

"I'm sure. And it's only for six weeks." She hoped it would last forever, but she wasn't going to admit that to him, or to herself. "I'm just an annoying journalist to him, trying to get a break."

"You and I both know that's not the case."

"Too far?"

"Just an inch."

"Dad?"

"Hmm?" He was glancing out the window at a fire truck squeezing by.

"Something strange happened." He blanched, and she spoke quickly to allay his panic. "A flashback, I think."

His brow furrowed. "You've never had one before, correct?"

"Never. I remembered," oh God, this was going to be hard, "a cage, and a man holding my hands when I poked them through the grate." Her father looked desolate, so she hurried to the pertinent information. "I remembered a very small tattoo. Here." She pinched the soft flesh between her thumb and index finger. "I think I could maybe even draw it." She went to him and wrapped her arms around his waist, but he didn't return the hug. He was normally very affectionate—surprisingly supportive and functional for a titan of industry—but he seemed paralyzed. "Daddy?"

"Have you called Neil?"

"I will tomorrow." He was right. Her therapist should be the first one to know she'd recovered a memory. He put his arms around her then, like he had forgotten to do it.

"Good." He sighed heavily. "I guess this is good news, sweetheart. I don't know."

"I think it is."

"It's because of Bishop. He's triggering memories from your childhood."

"I know."

"I'm concerned that it's all . . . too much for you."

"It's not. I swear it's not." He picked up on her overly emphatic tone.

"I'm not sure you're in a position to judge."

"Let me do the story. I'll be out of his world by August."

"Okay, sweetheart. I trust you. Nathan's a good man. Truth be told, I trust him too."

"Me too, Dad."

He paused, looking down at her for a moment. He tweaked her nose with his knuckles, the benign gesture belying the serious look in his eyes.

"He contacted me, you know."

"Nathan?"

"Yes. Many times." He squinted up at the ceiling, recalling. "On your ninth birthday—that would have been his fourteenth, you were still missing. Then again about six months later."

Emma thought he was finished, so she stepped away, but he kept going.

"Then, every year on your birthday. Though he stopped calling when he went into the Navy, and just sent emails."

"What did he say?"

"He used to want to leap to action. Asked what he could do, what was being done, that sort of thing. Eventually, I stopped taking the calls, and he would just leave a message with Janine. The emails, well, they were different, more resigned. I can forward them to you. They are mostly just well-wishes."

"He gave up." She didn't know why the thought broke her heart.

"Hardly. I think he may have . . ." He stopped himself from finishing the thought. "I think he thought I would contact him if I received any new information. I don't think he had given up hope."

"I don't know why, but that makes me feel so . . . relieved."

Her father smiled. He knew why.

"I regret not telling him the truth, but I had to draw a line and his father . . . I hated to punish Nathan for Henry's behavior, but I just couldn't risk anyone else knowing."

"I understand, Dad."

"It may be time to expand our little circle of trust."

"You'd be okay with that?"

"Yes, but think long and hard about it. You can't unring that bell."

"I will. I promise."

"Good." He gave Emma a probing look but kept his thoughts to himself. He was about to say something else when the sound of the key in the door stopped him. Caroline came through the door with a small, black French Bulldog on a leash.

"Don't ask. Oh, hey, Mr. Web. What brings you by?" She held up a hand. "Kidding. I just won a bet with myself. I had you showing up sometime between her second and fourth interview with Nathan." She gave Emma's dad a hug, still not acknowledging the dog.

"Caroline, you look beautiful as always. How are things at CNN?"

"Eh. Can't complain. For every day I have to take my producer's dog to the acupuncturist, there's a day I get to interview Clark Rhodes."

Emma poked her head into the fridge and retrieved a bottled water.

"I take it today is an acupuncture day."

Caroline nodded her head in big deliberate moves, urging Emma to process to the rest of her comment.

"Wait. You seriously get to interview Clark Rhodes?"

She squealed so loudly the dog winced. "He hates Christine because, on the *Black Dawn* press junket, she basically told him his wife left him *during* the interview. His manager told Frank he wanted a completely non-confrontational interview with someone new." She brushed her hands down her body from head to toe in a *that's me* gesture.

Jack looked at Caroline with a raised brow. "Is non-confrontational a good quality in a reporter?"

"It's good that's how they *think* of you. The scariest shark is the one you don't see." She winked at Emma's father, and he gave her an uncomfortable smile. He knew the truth of that statement all too well.

"I thought you hated Clark Rhodes."

"You know our love story, bitch. Sorry, Mr. Web. At first, I loved him. In tenth grade, I wanted to invite him to winter formal. Actually, Mr. Web, you were the one who pointed out that a twenty-nine-year-old man might not look too good going to a school dance with a sixteen-year-old girl."

"Not to mention, I was a little concerned he would accept." He winked back.

"Then, when he attacked that bartender in the Meatpacking District, I hated him. I mean of all the spoiled temperamental things."

Emma chimed in, needing her to hurry up the story. She had heard it a dozen times and was actually surprised Caroline was giving her father the edited version. There were at least three more bouts of love and hate in the full story. "Land the plane, Caroline."

"Right. Anyway, since I started at CNN . . . I mean, not Clark Rhodes specifically . . . I've just learned things aren't always as they seem. We can't judge a situation unless we know the whole truth."

The whole truth. Emma stared at her dad. The truth was practically a stranger to her. Her dad loved her, and he was doing whatever it took to keep her safe, but he was also keeping her from having any meaningful connection to another person. How could she even contemplate a relationship when she wasn't even a real person?

"Stop spinning out, Em." Caroline knew the look on her face all too well. "Your situation is . . . unique."

"I'm not truthful."

Her father checked his phone.

"You're not a liar, either. You're like a superhero with a secret identity." Her eyes lit up. "You're *Incognito!*" Emma rolled her eyes at Caroline's proclamation, so Caroline continued. "Just stop whining or I'm changing it to *The Incredible Sulk.*"

Jack Webster chuckled and finally acknowledged the dog who was currently chewing on one of Emma's stray flip flops.

"Can that beast survive an hour on his own so I can take my two best girls out for dinner?"

As if understanding the question, the dog moved to the couch, curled into a ball, and stared at a pigeon perched on the sill outside. Emma plopped next to him and scratched under his collar. He voiced his approval with a contented grumble.

"His name's Wendell. I just have to drop him at the place. The trainer is picking him up."

Her father rolled his eyes. He was one of the richest men in the country in his own right, but even he could see the absurdity of extravagance. That, and he disapproved of substituting money for hard work. "That dog needs a ball and a park."

"I know, Mr. Web, but I'm just a lowly newbie. All I can do until I climb the ladder is smile and nod."

"Come on. I'm starving." Emma gave Wendell a parting pat and pushed up off the couch.

"How 'bout that burger place on Mott?" her dad asked.

"Perfect," she and Caroline chorused.

⚓

"Jesus, finally."

Mac Ferguson thought he was at the point in his career, and certainly his life, when the down-and-dirty private detective crap was behind him. He had flunkies to do this shit, but the client, more precisely the client's money, had been too enticing to hand this job off to a subordinate. Once again, his instincts had paid off. He stepped into the doorway of a rundown apartment building and placed a call.

"Yes?"

"I found her."

"You're sure."

"I'm sure. Told ya, the key was the father. It's like WITSEC. Eventually, they all break routine or do something dumb. Unless he's got a thing for much younger tail, Daddy just paid her a visit. Man, she's a looker."

"My employer will be quite pleased."

"Yeah, well, if that gal's your employer's ex-wife, I'm the Pope, but as long as the money's green."

"Black on one side, green on the other, Mr. Ferguson."

"I'm going to stay on them for another hour or so. I'll meet you at the coffee shop by your hotel at, say, 10:00 p.m. I'll give you the pertinent information."

"The alley just beyond. We don't need a nosy waitress monitoring our actions."

"Agreed."

After dinner, the three of them walked off their cheeseburgers window shopping on Spring Street. Her dad groaned.

"Good thing I'm only allowed one of those a month. I'm about to fall asleep. I was hoping to get some work done on the drive back."

Shortly after Emma was rescued, her father had sold the Connecticut house where they lived and moved them to the estate in Georgia where she spent the rest of her childhood. He also bought a large but less imposing home in Amagansett in the Hamptons, so he could take her inconspicuously by helicopter to the beach—well, as inconspicuously as one could manage, traveling by helicopter. He kept the Nantucket house for eleven years, in the hope that the man or men pursuing her would be caught or killed, and they could go back one day. Then unexpectedly, on her twentieth birthday, he'd sold it without remorse or regret. It had broken her heart a little. Nathan's father had sold their place on the island when Nathan's mother left him. Selling the Webster home closed the book on a very happy chapter in Emma's life. In any event, her father now divided his time among the Hamptons house, a London brownstone, and a house in Bermuda that she had never seen.

"You'll wake up. It's only 8:30. Do you want me to grab you a coffee?" She tilted her head toward a corner Starbucks.

"Actually, yes, Beauty. A half-caf."

"Be right back."

Caroline pulled on Jack Webster's sleeve. "Oh, Mr. Web, come look at this tie in the window at Thomas Pink. I thought Dad would love it for Father's Day."

Emma heard her father grouse as they rounded the corner, "You're actually going to give him a tie?"

Emma walked right up to the counter of the nearly empty coffee shop where a still perky barista greeted her. She placed the simple order and waited while the teenager poured the drink. She glanced through the glass and caught sight of a man. Standing across the street, he was wearing a cheap Mets bomber jacket and just staring into the coffee shop. He creeped Emma out, but he was so unabashed about his staring that she took him more for a deviant than a threat. She took the coffee and headed outside.

Joining in the debate over acceptable Father's Day presents, they made their way back to the apartment.

Upstairs, after hugging her father goodbye on the sidewalk, Caroline and Emma both changed into sweats and T-shirts and plopped on the couch for some bad TV and good girl talk; the man outside the coffee shop was completely purged from her thoughts. A perfect night.

At 10:00 p.m. sharp, in an alley that smelled of rotting garbage and piss, Mac Ferguson handed over a food-stained paper file containing his findings. He was so focused on the envelope of cash in the other man's outstretched right hand, he didn't notice the syringe in his left.

CHAPTER FIFTEEN

Neil Tyson's office should have been the most relaxing place on earth. The walls were a soft sage, and photos of long grass blowing in a meadow decorated the walls. A small water sculpture gurgled in the corner, and the chairs, couch, and loveseat were an inviting taupe suede. It was all so soothing. Emma imagined most of his patients fell asleep mid-session.

Emma was a nervous wreck.

She sat in the corner of the big couch with her legs folded underneath her and chewed on a cuticle. Neil made a note on a yellow legal pad and then placed it under the iPad on his lap. She idly thought she must have so many issues he needed more than one way to take notes.

"Care to tell me what's going on, Emma?"

Neil had been her therapist since she'd gone away to college. He was a specialist in abduction trauma and had been thoroughly vetted by Jack Webster. He knew everything and was loyal not only out of professional obligation but also because of a sincere concern for Emma's wellbeing.

"Well, lots." She knotted her hands in her lap. "I'm interviewing Nathan Bishop for a series of articles for *The Sentry*."

"I see. And how is that going?"

Emma met his gaze then, and, with a surety that she felt in her soul, she said, "I love him."

Neil sighed and smiled kindly. "I know you do."

"Not like that," she protested.

"Elaborate."

"I'm in love with him."

"How much time have you spent with him?" It was an innocent question.

"Um, a few interviews and a couple of dates, I guess?"

"You guess?"

"He came to my apartment once, and we went to a street fair."

"Really?" He seemed pleased.

"Yes, he surprised me."

"Any anxiety about that?"

"Not really. I told him I hated surprises."

Neil cocked a brow.

"What?"

"I'm just gratified you were so forthcoming."

Emma guessed that qualified as forthcoming for her. She shrugged.

"Emma, I want to choose my words carefully here. There is not a doubt in my mind that you love him, are *in love* with him," he amended. "I also don't doubt that Nathan could have deep feelings for you. Even as children, you seemed to have an indescribable connection." He paused and set the things on his lap onto the table next to him, then leaned forward on his elbows. "You've spent years guarding your identity, but you've never had to guard your heart. Frankly, I've always been a little relieved that your romantic life hasn't added another complication to your recovery." He rubbed a hand over his bearded jaw, like what he was saying wasn't coming out right. "I guess what I'm trying to say is that at some point you were going to have to risk your heart, and while I absolutely want you to have those experiences, I also worry."

"I'm sure about him, Neil."

"I'm glad. You're a strong woman, Emma, but parts of you are very fragile. I want to ensure those continue to mend."

"I'm hoping Nathan can help there too."

"How so?"

"I had a flashback."

Neil's face revealed nothing, but his shock was palpable.

"Go on."

She described the scene to him. The cage, the man, the voice, the tattoo. He diligently wrote down everything she said.

"This is wonderful news, Emma."

"It is?"

"Yes. Your mind is letting you know you are ready to handle memory. In the flashback, do you recall how you felt?"

"Um, physically?"

"Either physically or emotionally. Do you recall any feelings you had?"

"I wasn't afraid. I think I was curious."

"Curious?"

"I don't know. I think his accent and his tattoo and his clothes made me curious. I'm sure I hadn't seen anyone like him before."

"His clothes?"

"Hmm?"

"You said his clothes."

The color drained from her face and recognition dawned.

"In my mind, I was thinking *why is a man wearing a dress?* Neil, I think he was wearing a dishdasha."

After her session, Emma walked out onto 57th Street and ducked into the corner bodega. Inside the store, she maneuvered past boxes of breakfast cereal and toilet paper and around a mop and a bucket, to the cooler in the back where she found the Fiji Water and grabbed two bottles. She also clipped a bag of the caramel corn Caroline loved and a copy of *Business Week* that had a picture of Nathan on the cover. She had resisted buying it the day before because she didn't want to read another interviewer's take on him. In the photo, he was behind a desk taking a monster bite out of an apple. He was staring directly at the camera, his emerald eyes in sharp contrast to the red of the apple skin. Various red items caught the reader's attention: a partially obscured file marked 'Top Secret' on the desk, the ribbon of a military medal tossed to the side, and in the periphery, barely visible on the floor, a red-soled stiletto. In bold letters across the bottom of the page read the headline: *When Does Nathan Bishop Sleep?* Okay, maybe there was another reason she didn't want to read it. Nevertheless, she folded the magazine under her arm and carried the items precariously as she rounded the corner to the register and immediately slammed into a man holding a shopping basket. The water bottles and the magazine hit the floor as she snagged the popcorn in midair. They both immediately squatted to retrieve her things.

"They need a traffic light here," the man quipped in a cultured accent.

"Sorry about that."

"My apologies, I'm new to the neighborhood and still finding my way around. That includes the local market."

She quickly grabbed the things and moved to walk around him. This man was older and unthreatening, late fifties she guessed, and impeccably dressed; still, casual encounters, no matter how benign, made Emma wildly uncomfortable.

"Have a good night."

"You, too, little one."

Her blood ran cold at his endearment. She turned to look back at him, but he had already disappeared down the aisle, continuing his shopping. She immediately shook it off. Her shrink had told her countless times not to see a threat around every corner. It was the surest way to drive herself insane. Neil and Emma agreed it would be impossible for her to trust her instincts if every little thing set off alarm bells, so she paid for her items and left the store.

CHAPTER SIXTEEN

Caroline, Farrell, and Emma sat discreetly tucked into a corner table at 21, the former prohibition speakeasy and iconic New York restaurant. Technically, they were "on assignment." Farrell was convinced that the mayor was strong-arming the president of the sanitation workers' union into an unfair contract with the city. It was the fodder of eighties action movies, and Caroline and Emma loved it. So, when Emma got the text, they were quick to throw on their best little black dresses and provide some cover for Farrell, in exchange for an expensed meal. Occasionally, Farrell got recognized, but in his barely presentable tweed blazer, with two attractive women, he looked more playboy novelist than newsman.

Caroline sipped her red zinfandel and whispered loudly. "It looks like the mayor is the one getting the thumbscrews, not the other way around." The mayor was looking at a bunch of photos the other man passed him. He had visibly paled.

"I'm going to see if I can peek over his shoulder." Farrell scooted back and pretended to wander past the extensive wine collection that lined the walls, glancing at bottles. Caroline giggled and leaned into Emma. "I love being on a stakeout. We should have brought huge sunglasses and floppy hats," she beamed. She continued talking about possible disguises, glancing over her shoulder at Farrell's ridiculous attempt at subtlety, when Emma's breath was stolen.

Nathan had come into the very small, very intimate bar holding the arm of a striking brunette. The waiter opened a prearranged bottle of Cristal upon their arrival and placed a flute in front of each of them. With her wavy shoulder-length hair and candy apple lipstick, she looked like a forties pin-up girl. Their fingers were intertwined on the bar, and Emma's stomach churned. When he leaned over and started nibbling her neck, Emma rose to her feet. Rage and confusion propelled her steps. The woman saw her coming first. As she got closer, she saw that she was older than Emma had first thought—doing a damn good job of masking forty. She watched Emma approach with a satisfied gleam in her eyes. Nathan noticed her lose focus and detached from her earlobe.

"Hi," she said quietly.

"Emma." He seemed panicked for a second, but it wasn't the panic of a man getting caught. Emma wasn't sure, but she thought he looked . . . afraid. "What are you doing here?" The woman turned to the bar to sip her drink and check her phone.

"Having dinner with Caroline and Farrell. What are you doing here?"

"Emma, you need to excuse us." He grabbed the woman's hand and kissed it. "It was nice seeing you, but I believe I made the *parameters of our relationship clear*." He kissed each knuckle of the woman's hand and let the words sink in. 'The parameters of our relationship.' That was the awkward term he had used to explain wanting to date her exclusively. He was sending her a message; whatever this was, it wasn't what it seemed.

"I will see you in the office." His arm circled his date's waist and he gave Emma a pleading but firm stare. Whatever was going on here, she needed to make this look good. Watching him fondle this woman was making her blood boil, but she certainly wasn't going to make a scene, not when Nathan was silently screaming that there was an explanation.

She brushed down the front of her dress, glanced up at him, and shrugged. "Sorry to interrupt." Her voice cracked, and she cleared her throat to cover it. "We were just leaving." She nodded in deference. "Mr. Bishop."

The brunette cooed, "Ooh, *Mr. Bishop*, I like that." Emma ground her teeth together and glared at her as she turned away. "Nice meeting you," the older woman purred. So, this was what getting the brush off felt like. No. This was what getting the brush off from Nathan felt like. Awful.

She rounded up Caroline and Farrell, and they made their escape. As they exited the room, three suited men clogged the doorway, smelling of cigars. Emma was shoulder-to-shoulder with the first man in the group, facing out while he was facing in, scanning the room. The man stilled, and the stem of his wine glass snapped in his hand. Emma couldn't see his face, but his body simmered. She could guess what was in his sightline, but all the speculation was giving her a headache. All she really knew for sure was that Nathan was in a dark bar fondling another woman.

She couldn't explain her heartache in front of Farrell. She knew there was more to the story, but that didn't eclipse the fact that Emma had to sit there and watch Nathan make a meal out of another woman's neck. Turned out she didn't need a cover story. Farrell had been oblivious to the exchange and regaled them with the story of the photos he had spied the union chief trading with the mayor.

"They were shots of the mayor capturing all his worst attributes." He grabbed his flat stomach and moved it up and down mimicking a beer belly. "He wants the mayor to try this diet drink he sells. It's a meal supplement, you know, one of those pyramid schemes." He cleaned his glasses with the tail of his shirt. "Actually, I should look into that. Talk about a great way to launder money." He prattled on as what would surely be his latest conspiracy theory took root. Caroline squeezed her hand soothingly. Emma forced a smile. When they got to Hell's Kitchen, Farrell insisted on putting the women into a cab—he liked to think the now upscale area was as dangerous as its name. JT was behind them in the Suburban, so Emma explained that she had called for an Uber and that it was pulling up. Satisfied, they went their separate ways.

In the back of the car, Caroline unleashed. "What the fuck was that?"

"I don't know."

"It seemed fairly obvious, Em."

"I know this sounds crazy, but I think there's an explanation."

"Em, he's like a fucking NBA player—of course he has an explanation! His dick fell out of his pants and got stuck in her."

"I think he was giving me a signal."

"Yeah, a get-out-of-here-so-I-can-fuck-my-date signal."

"Look, we're journalists. We're not supposed to judge until we have all the facts."

"Yes, and we are women. We are not supposed to live in denial when our significant other has his tongue down someone else's throat."

"I know."

"Come on, let's get a slice. You didn't even let me eat."

"I'm not hungry."

"Oh, hell no. I am not letting Nathan Bishop steal your appetite along with your heart."

"Fine."

Caroline called it a night after two slices and two episodes of a plastic surgery reality show. It was after midnight, but Emma was nowhere near sleep. She sat on the balcony and stared at the night, the growl of traffic dimmed only slightly by the ten stories between. Her phone buzzed across the end table.

Mr. Wonderful: *Let me in.*

Emma: *I did let you in and you abused the privilege.*

Mr. Wonderful: *It was absolutely not what it looked like and I think you know that.*

Emma: *Yes.*

Mr. Wonderful: *Go out on your balcony.*

Emma: *One step ahead of you.*

Mr. Wonderful: *As usual. Look over the edge.*

Emma stood and crossed to the edge and peered down to the sidewalk. Nathan was standing there, arms spread, tie loose, shirt untucked. He looked winded, like he had run there from midtown. In his fist, he held a bouquet of awful flowers. His expression was pleading. And adorable. She shook her head and disappeared back into the apartment as she texted.

Emma: *You have five minutes.*

She called down to let the doorman know Nathan was expected. A minute later, the doorbell rang. She had barely cracked the door when Nathan burst through. Without preamble, he grabbed her and kissed the shit out of her. Any normal person probably would have rejected him, slapped his face, yelled, but Emma understood. He needed to feel her. She needed to feel him. She gave him a minute to settle. He stroked her face.

"Don't disappear on me," he pleaded.

"I'm right here."

"That's not what I mean, and you know it."

"I'll try."

"Thank you."

He pulled her to the couch, but before he sat, he said, "Do you have anything to drink? I don't allow myself alcohol in situations like that, and I could really use it."

Situations like what?

"Um, I have some scotch I keep for when my dad comes, and I think there is some beer in the fridge."

He poured himself a generous glass of Glenfiddich and downed half of it before he sat. "You understood, didn't you? My code?"

She eyed him warily. "I think so."

"Good." Another gulp. "Okay, Emma, I'm telling you this as my girlfriend, not my interviewer, just so we're clear."

"Understood." *Girlfriend.*

"That was business." She arched a brow, but he plowed on. "I can't go into detail. Everything is extremely sensitive, but let's say I owned a candy company."

"I think I would prefer that."

"At times I would too. Now pay attention." He tapped her nose with his index finger.

She sat up straighter and met his gaze.

"My candy company wants to buy this new candy product from a supplier who is making big claims, but there are a couple of problems. One: the man who has the candy doesn't want to sell it to me. He wants to auction it off to the highest bidder. Two: the other potential buyers and I don't know exactly what the supplier is selling yet. Is it a hybrid cocoa bean? A new flavoring? A recipe? A method of transporting candy?"

"Seems like information you'd need to make an informed purchase."

"Exactly. The woman in the bar is the wife of the owner of a rival candy company that also wants to purchase this new product. And because of his reputation as a frequent buyer of all different sorts of candy, I thought he might have more information about this particular product than is generally known. I'd met her before in past, *eh hem*, candy negotiations, and she had made her interest known. So, I decided to use that to find out what her husband knows."

"And she'd tell you because you're hot? I don't think I understand the candy business." Nathan just shook his head.

"The owner of the chocolate factory isn't an honest businessman. He buys his beans from sketchy people and sells his chocolate to even worse. We needed to use every tactic available to get information on this . . . candy."

"I guess I never really realized that your business, *the candy business*," she amended, "could be so, I don't know, covert."

"It's not usually so cloak-and-dagger. This particular transaction is an exception."

"A very glamorous exception."

"Emma, that was all for appearances."

"Did she know that?"

"Sort of."

"And she was okay with that?"

"Definitely. I think she enjoys pissing off her husband."

"Did you discover anything interesting about this candy?"

"Possibly. Anya, that's her name, said her husband had a secret meeting several weeks ago and was muttering about it after. She said she asked him if everything was all right, and he assured her that it was, that the information was unexpected but useful."

"So maybe it's not the kind of candy you think it is."

"Or maybe it isn't candy at all."

"And she just volunteered this information."

"Quite."

"How?"

"I'm really quite charming when I want to be."

"Did you sleep with her?"

"*What*? Emma, no. It was a job. Tox and Chat were outside in a car listening to the whole thing. You probably walked right past them when you left. I meant what I said. If I didn't want exclusivity, I wouldn't have asked for it. And I expect the same of you."

"Okay." She blew out a breath.

"Okay?"

"Yes. Okay."

"That's it?"

"What else is there? I either believe you or I don't. If I don't, we are over, and if I do, it's forgotten."

"And the verdict?"

"I think you know."

He pounced then, kissing her with relief. She laughed into his mouth.

"I don't know why you're so relieved. It seems like a lot of people trust your word."

"You just don't get it, do you?" He brushed her hair out of her face. "It's *your* belief in me that matters." She kissed him again, but then pulled back.

"One thing, though."

"Anything."

"If you ever suck on another woman's ear again, work or not, I will not be held accountable for my actions."

Nathan couldn't hide his elation at her possessiveness.

"Understood."

Nathan and Emma sat cross-legged on the floor of his office, the remnants of Carnegie Deli pastrami sandwiches between them. Nathan had just finished telling her the story of his Bronze Star, under the proviso that Emma did not include it in the story. She hadn't taken notes, just sat and listened, rapt, as he told the story of how, from ten miles away using comms and satellite maps, he had guided a SEAL squad out of an ambush in Afghanistan. The SEALs had just rescued a group of captive women and were about to be surrounded by hostiles. Nathan calmly and carefully led them through mountain passes and cave systems to the exfil site. It was how he had earned his call sign "North." He had been their compass.

"I ran out to the helo to help with the women. They were dazed, probably drugged. I started pulling off their headscarves and they were terrified. Some were western. Some were . . . young."

"Why were you pulling off their scarves?"

"To show them we weren't like their captors. The scarves weren't meant as a religious observation—they were to conceal them. These women were slaves, Em, I was trying to show them we were getting them to safety." He paused for a moment, lost in thought. "Also, I was looking . . ." he changed tack, and they both knew it, ". . . to see if they were injured, if they could travel."

She chewed on the end of the pen and looked up into his haunted green eyes. He was just staring at her. *Tell him.* The thought gnawed at her.

"Come here."

"Whatever for, Mr. Bishop?"

"Em, come here."

She started to crawl over to where he sat. It was sexy as hell. She prowled onto his lap and looped her arms around his neck.

"I thought you said no hanky-panky at the office."

"No, I said no funny business at the office. Hanky-panky is within my discretion."

"And what about shenanigans?"

"Absolutely."

"Dipping your pen in the company ink, Mr. Bishop?"

He kissed his way down her neck. His hand gently cupped her breast, and when she didn't pull back, he squeezed, sending a jolt of arousal right between her legs. She arched into him.

"Technically, you're not company ink, but I have every intention of dipping my pen. Although come to think of it, 'pen' is rather insulting."

He paused for a moment and brushed the backs of his fingers on her cheek. "Do you remember me?"

She nearly passed out.

She wanted to scream *yes!* and hug him and tell him what had happened to her, but she had been trained to be careful, to never show her hand.

"Remember you?"

"I saw you once. A couple of years ago at a bar. I thought maybe . . . I'd made an impression. You certainly did."

Emma felt a stabbing sadness at the misunderstanding and having missed a moment with him. When her gaze met his, it was clear, and her smile was bright.

"Sorry. I go into defense mode at bars sometimes. I don't like handsy guys. Present company excluded"

"Understandable. You are beautiful. And I don't mean on the inside. You're beautiful on the surface where it counts." Emma laughed, and Nathan returned to kissing her neck.

"Then we're not even. You're beautiful on the inside and the outside. I'm a mess on the inside." His hand ran over her breast and she stiffened. He stilled.

"First of all," he paused to brush her hair from her face, "I'm not as pristine on the inside as my widely exaggerated tales of naval valor might suggest. Secondly, why do you say you're a mess?"

Emma felt the need to, if not confess, at least prepare him for the minefield that was her inner life. She didn't pause, didn't hesitate. She went against every bit of training she had ever gotten, rested her head on his chest, and said, "Something happened to me."

He didn't say a word. He just stroked her back. Tears were sliding effortlessly down her face and dripping onto their jeans. She had never confessed this, even the small part she was admitting, to anyone. "When I was very young, something bad happened to me." He firmed his hold and continued to soothe her. "I don't remember much, but . . ."

"It's okay, Em."

"It's why I don't, um, date much. Or notice guys in bars. Then the one time I actually got up the nerve to date a guy . . ."

"What?"

She could feel his body locking tight, tamping down anger. She thought better of dumping another tale of woe on him.

"Nathan?"

"Yes?"

"Will you kiss me again?"

He answered the same way he did the last time she'd asked.

"It would be my pleasure." He held her face in both hands. "Even if it is to distract me."

End of discussion.

They traded some college stories, and she was learning some more about his business school years when his phone behind his desk trilled. His brow furrowed when he glanced at the screen.

"Em, I have to take this. Can we talk later?"

"Sure, I'll get out of your hair." He was too distracted to kiss her or sign off, so Emma gathered her things and headed to the door. She only heard him say one thing before the door shut behind her: *copy that, standing by for Cerberus.*

CHAPTER SEVENTEEN

Cerberus tugged on the leashes guiding the three Belgian Malinois around the corner onto the quaint strip of Main Street. Bruno had been blinded in one eye. Petrol was missing his right back leg, and Daisy—well, physically Daisy was fine. Mentally, not so much. His wife, Maggie, called her Crazy Daisy and threatened to leave him if Daisy destroyed another piece of furniture in a thunderstorm or attacked another visitor.

He ducked into the small public park and, after seeing he was alone, let the dogs off-leash. Mrs. Baker at the B & B across the street would give him an earful if she caught him "letting those attack dogs run wild." She didn't seem to care that they had served their country as bravely as any soldier. Daisy stayed by his side, but Petrol and Bruno took off after a wayward seagull. He sat on a slatted wooden bench and pulled a section of the print version of the local paper out of his jacket pocket. Keeping the paper folded in half, he glanced at an article on lead levels in the drinking water in a nearby county. He didn't care about the article. Ten minutes later, a smartly dressed woman walked briskly toward him. She perched on the bench and pulled out her phone.

"You're showing your age, my friend. This isn't how it's done anymore."

"Maybe it should be."

"Well, you certainly make a point, considering recent events. I'll give you that."

Cerberus snapped his newspaper to straighten it.

"You asked to see me. The dogs needed a walk."

The dogs had returned to his side without their quarry. He withdrew a bowl and a canteen of water from the cloth bag he carried and poured water for the dogs.

"Living out your golden years feeding pigeons in the park, is that it?"

He chuckled. "If Maggie had her way."

"Our man inside got a look in the lab. Not a good one, unfortunately. Not too much to see. One scientist who was," she quoted directly from the report, "'eating fried plantains and examining something under a standard microscope.'"

Cerberus waited, scratching Daisy on the small black patch of fur on her chest.

"Something's off."

"You mean what he didn't see more than what he did."

"Exactly. No protective gear, no clean room."

"Could be a fairly stable toxin. Or it needs to be combined with another component."

"Maybe he discovered it's no longer viable." He withdrew a gnawed tennis ball from his pocket and tossed it across the grass. Petrol and Bruno took off after it.

"He's lining up buyers. He has something of value."

"Anything coming out of Pingfang is a top priority."

"Agreed."

"The construction workers who discovered the remains and the package, are they still breathing?"

"I assume so. After they handed over the package to the imposters, they went about their business."

"I want to send North over to talk to them."

"Why?"

"Because we are making a lot of assumptions, and it would be nice to have some facts when potentially hundreds of thousands of lives are on the line."

"I think it's unnecessary. We know it's a weapon. We know it's from Detachment 731. It has to be a bioagent of some sort."

"But what sort? There's no such thing as too much information."

"True. All right, let me know if he discovers anything useful." The woman stood, pocketed her phone, and walked back toward an idling SUV.

CHAPTER EIGHTEEN

The next morning, Emma woke to a text sent at 3:30 a.m.:

Mr. Wonderful: *I need to cancel Friday. Will resched if I can.*

It was so formal it left a pit in her stomach.

Emma: *OK. Hope everything is all right.*

He didn't reply.

By Sunday afternoon, Emma was starting to worry. Yes, Nathan Bishop was a player of epic proportions. Yes, he once famously woke up on the skating rink in Rockefeller Plaza surrounded by cops and several *Today* show cameras. (He had simply smiled for the cameras, shaken hands with the hosts, and asked the weather assistant for a date, which she accepted.) Yes, he did stupid, dangerous things every day and seemed to emerge unscathed, but something told her this absence merited concern.

Emma busied herself by going over her notes. Something Caroline had said at the bar the other night struck a chord: *you can rock climb anywhere.* Why Morocco? Something scratched at the back of her mind, and then she remembered the whiteboard in Farrell's office. Tucked in a corner next to a detailed photo spread on how the government faked the moon landing. *White Hat Black Ops.* Could Nathan really be doing covert paramilitary work? She wanted so desperately to believe the tabloid manwhore was a façade, but even she realized, as she clacked away on her laptop, that this was extreme. Masking some hidden pain of a damaged youth with booze and women? Sure. But Batman? She checked the long list of daredevil adventures Nathan had chalked up. Yes, they were all in or near hot zones. Yes, news stories coincided with his trips, but nothing stopped her dead in her tracks. It wasn't like Nathan was hiking through Syria when a local terrorist leader had been assassinated. There were all kinds of things happening in that part of the world all the time. Nathan's presence or lack thereof didn't seem to be a factor . . . until she noticed one particular coincidence. It was a story from Ukraine, about two years old. A school bus of children from a small village near the Romanian border had been taken by Chechen rebels. A child was being executed each day until the government met the rebels' demands.

As that was occurring, Nathan and a small group of "outdoorsmen" had gone on a rock climb in the Carpathian Mountains and then partied on a yacht in the Black Sea. Two things struck her about the trip: in the interview, Nathan described the trip as "last minute," and, while the children hadn't been rescued until days later—Nathan was already being photographed at sea with a topless Miss Moldova—the Ukrainian rescue force reportedly met with no resistance during the operation, and no children had been harmed.

The biggest mistake a researcher can make is trying to force the facts to fit their theory. It was a notable piece of information, but if she wanted proof that Nathan was some sort of, she didn't know, vigilante? Superhero? This wasn't it.

It did go a ways toward confirming her theory that Nathan liked having these "playboy pics," as she had come to call them, and the reason wasn't to feed his ego. If nothing else, her investigation was a time-consuming distraction.

By 2:00, she was pacing her apartment.

At 2:30, he texted.

Mr. Wonderful: *My place, 1500*

His use of military time pinged in her brain, but she was so relieved and frantic to get to him she didn't dwell. She threw on the fastest, flirtiest thing she could find, a breezy lavender sundress with flat sandals, and texted JT where she needed to go. She raced into his lobby at 2:57 p.m.

Leonard glanced up over half-glasses and smiled.

"Hello, Emma. He just walked in himself."

"Oh, good."

"You can go on up. His floor is unlocked. He'll probably be in the shower from the look of him."

With that curious comment, she opened the door to the stairs that Leonard had buzzed open and headed up.

Nathan's door was ajar, and she heard water running in the kitchen. As she rounded the corner, she saw his broad back under a soiled T-shirt bent over the sink, his hands resting on the counter on either side.

"Busy week?"

He turned and looked at her and time stopped. His cheek was scratched as if he had fallen on pavement. There was a butterfly bandage on his scalp and his knuckles and forearms were cut. But the thing she couldn't look away from was his gaze. His clear green eyes were relieved and needy, and she didn't hesitate for an instant. She ran to him. He met her in the middle of the kitchen, and they exploded.

Emma had never felt anything like it. Her legs wrapped around his waist, hands snaked around his neck, and he held her up without breaking the kiss as he set her on the counter.

"I need you."

"I need you, too."

He kissed his way down her neck to the swell of her breast while his hands deftly dropped her zipper. The dress pooled at her waist. She unclasped her pink bra and freed her breasts as Nathan sucked the berry tip into his mouth. She groaned with pleasure. He cupped and squeezed her breasts as he explored them with his mouth. Nathan was at her like he was parched, and she was a pool of cool, clear water. She didn't think. She didn't analyze. She didn't spin out. She just felt. She tangled her fingers in his chestnut hair as he kissed his way down her middle. When he got to the fabric of her dress, he dropped to his knees and began a ground assault. Her thighs parted.

He snapped the elastic of her thong and pulled it from her body like a man possessed. Then he pushed his face between her thighs. For a long moment, he didn't do anything but breathe her in. She bunched up the fabric around her waist as much to have something to hold onto as to see him. His expression was worshipful; it was almost as if words would shatter the moment. He held her gaze as his tongue ran through her folds. When he began to focus on her clit, Emma saw stars. She clenched her thighs, and Nathan pushed them apart with his big hands, holding her open. She was melting and throbbing. When he sank a long finger into her, then two, she cried out. Even his fingers were a tight fit, but he felt so right, inside of her. He curled his fingers gently as they fucked her, and she was lost to sensation. She was wanton, greedy. She tilted her hips, pushing toward his hungry mouth, urging him on. When he pulled the pearl between his lips and sucked, the orgasm hit her like a freight train. She shouted his name incoherently and pulled his hair. Her body was on fire, electric, as wave after wave of heat and pleasure shot through her. She bent forward, struggling to catch her breath and met the top of Nathan's head as he continued to lick and kiss, gently bringing her down from her very. first. orgasm.

Holy mackerel.

Nathan kissed his way back up her middle, giving a quick suck and soothing lick to each nipple. She grabbed his head with both hands and pulled him to her mouth. He tasted sweet and salty. Her body stirred.

"You taste good."

"Yes, you do." He winked.

He lifted Emma into his arms and walked into his bedroom. She was blissful, but when he set her on his bed, she felt a wash of panic. She placed her hands flat on the comforter to mask the shaking. Nathan wasn't fooled for an instant.

"Em, look at me."

"I'm okay."

"Em."

When she finally met his gaze, everything settled.

"Now I'm okay."

"There she is."

He sat next to her on the bed, but his eyes never left hers. His hands slid up her bare legs and rested on her hips when the thought occurred to him.

"Emma?"

"Hmm?"

"Have you done this before?"

She was relieved by the way he worded the question. Because she didn't ever want to lie to him—well, aside from the glaringly obvious. If he had asked if she was a virgin, well, that was complicated, because honestly, she didn't know. But this? *This* she had definitely never done.

"No."

He was thoughtful for a moment. She could see him thinking about all their interactions. The implications of her words regarding her experience with men.

"And that?"

He nodded his head back and to the side toward the kitchen.

She looked at him, and she was completely exposed. She had never felt safer. She grinned.

"All new. *All* of it."

He let out a slow breath. "Okay."

"Soooo, thank you for that." She touched her forehead to his.

Nathan chuckled. "No, thank you."

"Nice to finally know what all the fuss is about," she shrugged. He brushed her cheek with the rough pad of his thumb.

"You are a fucking miracle."

"What now?"

"That is the question I am currently pondering."

"Let me help you reach a conclusion." She started nibbling his neck. He was sweaty and dirty. He tasted like heaven.

"How on Earth does someone like you . . . ." He didn't finish the thought. He just shook his head. "Jesus, Em."

"I've been taught not to trust people, and I've learned from experience not to trust them. I've never felt this way before. Nathan, I trust you. Completely."

"Why?"

She didn't answer. There was no explanation for it. There never had been.

"Come with me."

She stood quietly and took his hand. The dress slipped from her body as she led him to his bathroom. Nathan's sharp intake of breath and muttered curse told Emma he liked the view. She smiled.

She examined every cut and scrape on him. After locating a first aid kit under the sink, she parked him on the broad edge of the immense marble tub and set to work. He winced as she dabbed a particularly deep cut near his ribs.

"Hang on. Something is catching the cotton." She retrieved a pair of tweezers from the case and carefully got a firm grip on the small pro-trusion. Gently she pulled out a metal splinter and, without a word, wrapped it in a tissue to throw away. She returned to his injuries with a concerned perusal.

"Aren't you going to ask?"

"Nope."

"Why?"

"Three reasons. One: if you lie and tell me you were off-roading with a bunch of college buddies, I will cry. Two: I know you well enough to know it's probably something you can't tell me, which is okay. Three: If you could have told me, you would have by now." She started to dab a new cut, but he cupped her face in both his hands, stealing her attention.

"I . . . ." He just stared at her, and it was everything Emma was feeling. Exactly.

"Me, too." She smiled.

CHAPTER NINETEEN

Emma hated the Fourth of July. She wasn't un-American or anything, but this holiday blew. Red, white, and blue looked awful anywhere but on the flag. Fireworks scared the shit out of her. Sticky little kids running everywhere unchecked. The crowds, the noise, the patriotic music . . . ugh.

This Fourth of July, however, she was feeling very *Stars and Stripes Forever.*

The River Club was one of the most exclusive private clubs in Manhattan. It sat on the East Side, just north of the United Nations Headquarters and overlooked the river. A logical deduction would be to think that the club housed a marina for New York's seafarers, but no, this was more of a sophisticated après-boating spot. There was a large reception area for the occasional wedding or anniversary party, a cozy lounge for drinks or an intimate meal, and a long, narrow brick balcony, where she currently stood, that was the perfect viewing spot for several waterfront firework displays.

Nathan was running late, but she knew he'd be there. After the other night, their attraction had grown into a need. Emma felt his absence like an injury. It was strange to think she had always missed him like this. When he went away to boarding school years ago, she was inconsolable. She couldn't eat, couldn't sleep. Nathan's mother had brought over a few things from his room to get her out of her funk—a Derek Jeter jersey and an old iPod with his playlist. She was just starting to adjust to his absences and look forward to his homecomings when she was taken.

This time though it was different. She was standing on the deck at The River Club overlooking the surprisingly bucolic setting as evening descended on the city. Her white halter sundress was billowing, and she shifted nervously from one nude Gucci sandal to the other. She was on her third glass of champagne, which was buckets for her, and it was doing nothing for her nerves. They were going public. They were going to take things further physically—much, much further. They were unlocking some dark memories in both their minds. Oh, and small detail, she was in love with him, hopelessly, irretrievably, uncontrollably in love. And unlike the soothing, safe calm she felt in his presence as a child, this feeling was . . . incendiary.

Emma made small talk with a few of the K-B executives. Most were initially suspicious of a reporter from her organization, but they warmed to her quickly. She fit in and they knew it. She was, as they say, to the manner born.

She should have eaten something, but the promise that this night held had Emma chewing on her nails, not the shrimp puffs. The band broke from their USA-themed repertoire and started to play "Fly Me to the Moon." The wind kicked up, and she felt him, almost as if Nathan's presence had caused the gust. She stepped inside the buzzing room and spotted him at the bar. He was holding a bottled beer and kissing an older woman on the cheek. He stood out in a sea of red, white, and blue, wearing a dove-gray blazer. Emma could see the streaks of auburn in his chestnut hair. He turned his head, and their eyes locked. He gave Emma an intense assessment, set his beer on the bar, and turned to walk the length of the dance floor. Emma waited like a girl at an eighth-grade dance, which in some ways she guessed she was. That's when she saw it. He was dreamy from head to toe, tousled hair, white button-down, his hands shoved carelessly into his pockets. And around his neck, a cornflower blue tie. *The cornflower blue tie.* The identical tie to the one she had held the night she had been drugged on a date. The same tie she had stashed in her lingerie drawer. The people in her periphery started to blur as she stared at the tie the mysterious stranger who rescued her had worn. She started to see spots. The tie she refused to let go of, even unconscious. She swayed on her feet. Nathan had saved her that night. The room spun. In a final, long stride, Nathan stood in front of her. His cocky smile of affirmation turned to panic, as, once again, Emma grabbed onto that tie like a lifeline.

And passed out.

Again.

Her eyes fluttered open, and Emma was lying on a couch in a quiet room. Nathan was sitting over her, pressed into the crook of her side, holding a cool cloth to her forehead. She beamed at him and his answering smile was one of relief.

"Is it the tie?"

Emma burst out laughing and grabbed onto it, pulling him in for a kiss.

"I still have the old one." That surprised him. "I hold onto it when I get anxious. It calms me down."

"It was my favorite tie, and some passed out blonde wouldn't let go of it."

"I should give it back to you."

"Hey, if you play your cards right, I'll give you this one too."

"You hang onto it. Somehow I think you may have more inventive uses for it than I would."

"Oh, Sunshine, you have no idea."

"Take me to your place."

"With pleasure. Can you walk?"

"Yeah, I just got a little light-headed. Happens a lot around you."

"I have been known to have that effect on women."

"You should list swooning as one of your special skills."

"Nope. You swoon. I, I don't know what I do."

"You save me."

He let out a weary sigh and pinched the bridge of his nose. "When I think about what could have happened that night . . . ."

Emma shuddered, and he pulled her into his lap. "I couldn't think clearly. I just needed to get somewhere safe." She wrapped her arms around his neck. "I guess I found it."

"I will keep you safe, Em. I'll do whatever it takes." A wave of anger surged through him, and she remembered something.

"That guy, Tom?"

Nathan stiffened, not from nerves but from rage. He ground his teeth.

"What about him?"

"They told me he got mugged walking home from a bar a couple of days after my . . ." she didn't know what to call it, ". . . incident."

"Incident." Nathan rolled the word around like it was the last word he would ever use to describe what had happened.

"He broke his arm, ruptured his spleen, and had a skull fracture."

"He got off easy."

She squinted at Nathan, and his face went completely blank.

"Do you know something about that?"

"I know something about karma."

Boom. The crack of the first fireworks exploding in the sky made Nathan flinch, but he quickly recovered.

"You okay?" He brushed a honey-colored curl from her face.

"Yes. So okay, you have no idea." She kissed him softly as another firework blew.

"Not my favorite sound." He squeezed his eyes shut on a long blink.

She held his face and kept his lips close to hers.

"Nathan?"

"Em?" he mimicked.

"I have a confession to make." Nathan paled as though he expected her to drop some huge bomb . . . as if he knew she was hiding a big secret. He remained silent.

"I hate fireworks." When the next one sounded, she clamped her eyes shut and wrinkled her nose. "Too loud."

Everything faded but the sight and sound of him laughing. He laughed with relief and joy and, yes, love. She saw love in his eyes as clear as his bright green irises. And then he kissed her like he meant it.

"Come on."

"Where are we going?"

"Well, we are two people who hate fireworks, so this time I'm taking you home with me. In the future, we should consider leaving the country on the Fourth. The Caribbean or Greece."

He tugged on her hand as he pulled her quietly from the room, the words *home* and *future* fizzing in her brain like champagne bubbles. No one noticed as they slipped out, their attention on the sky. Emma squeezed his hand, and he squeezed hers back, keeping his eyes forward, a hint of a smile dancing on his lips. As she walked to Nathan's car with him, she imagined being together in a year, escaping to some tropical island to be alone, and she felt the best thing she had ever felt, deep in her soul.

Fireworks.

Two days later, Emma stood in the lobby of Knightsgrove-Bishop. She and Nathan had had a fairly businesslike interview, if you ignored the fact that she was in his lap for most of it, which ended abruptly when a giant of a man opened the door without knocking or speaking. A petite freckle-faced redhead stood behind him, holding a laptop, and staring down at her bright pink Converse high-tops. Nathan stood them up without embarrassment, kissed her on the lips and said he'd call later. The giant blocked the door for a moment, giving her a probing look filled with suspicion before moving to the side to let her pass.

Tox marched up to the desk and tossed a paper file in front of Nathan. Still lost in an Emma fog, Nathan glanced at it absently.

"What's this?"

Tox leaned forward onto his fists. His expression was equal parts anger and sympathy.

"North, you're being honey-potted."

Down in the lobby, Emma shot a text to Caroline confirming lunch and shopping. Caroline was leaving for LA the next day and felt the need for some seriously unprofessional outfits. When Emma got Caroline's 'thumbs up' emoji, she glanced through the glass and spotted JT contemplating the souvlaki cart on the corner. He saw her waving and turned her way. She mimed eating and he nodded, relieved. Across the street, a jogger was running in place at the intersection. A lean, well-built guy, maybe thirty, probably scrolling through his playlist. She wouldn't have thought anything of it, but the light had changed twice, and he remained as pedestrians filed past. He looked around at nothing in particular and disappeared around a corner. The loitering jogger was pushed from her thoughts by a sharp voice behind her.

"Who's your friend?" Alex sidled up and peered over Emma's shoulder at JT, who was walking to the car.

"No one," she replied dismissively, pretending to check her phone.

"He's a beast. Boyfriend?"

"Nope."

"Brother?" She was relentless.

"No. Only child."

"Well, he could be a bodyguard with that build." Her gaze didn't waver from the glass in front of them. She knew exactly what Alex was doing. Emma had been carefully schooled in the art of interrogation, in many forms. Alex was spitballing until she got a reaction. Emma wasn't sure why, but she had her suspicions. As soon as she volunteered an explanation, Alex would know she had scored a hit. Well, surprise Alex, this wasn't her first rodeo.

"Or an undercover cop . . . ." she continued.

"He could," Emma conceded, "or he could be an NFL player taking an old friend to lunch." She winked and walked out of the building, leaving Alex huffing in frustration and beating a hasty retreat to her office.

Emma climbed into the back of the Suburban around the corner from prying eyes and rested her head against the tinted glass. She had given a lot of thought to telling Nathan her whole truth. Two things had given her pause. She was reluctant to rock the boat this early. This was her first relationship, her first sexual experience, and her first time falling in love. The idea of adding more complications felt like aiming a fan at a house of cards. That was her chicken shit reason. The other reason was a bit more substantial. Nathan was clearly keeping secrets of his own. If her suspicions were correct, he, like Emma, was hiding another identity. And if that was, in fact, the case then they were currently on equal footing. Her lack of experience was an easy excuse to put the burden on Nathan to decide when they pulled aside the curtain. God, she hoped it was soon. She wanted to know every part of him, and, more shockingly, she wanted him to see every part of her.

CHAPTER TWENTY

Emma sat cross-legged on the chaise on her balcony, thankful the sun had gone behind a huge storm cloud, as she searched her mind and reviewed the notes she had written. Again. She had never had a memory of her abduction, so despite the potential damage to her psyche, she wanted to cling to every detail of the flashback. She was wearing one of Nathan's Harvard Business School T-shirts and her favorite cut-offs. Her hair was piled on top of her head in a messy bun. She doodled on the legal pad she held in her lap, wanting to begin the exercise, but also stalling. Thunder rumbled in the distance. She started to scribble down notes.

She had had enough therapists assure her that if she did, in fact, recover any memories, they might not be reliable. Nevertheless, this is what she remembered, so she recreated it on the page, starting with the small tattoo: a rectangle with an ornate cross flaring out at the four ends. She admired her handiwork.

"How many pairs of sunglasses do I need in LA?" Caroline was leaning against the open French doors, scrolling through her iPad.

"For three days? I don't know, seven?"

"You think? I was hoping to get by with four."

"I was kidding, you loon."

She sat at the foot of the chaise and shielded her screen with her hand as she showed Emma a variety of celebrity sunglass candids.

"I'm not. It's LA. It's a movie star interview. I'm considering changing sunglasses midway through."

"Car, you are entering a race you can't win."

"I know," she sighed defeated. "I can't pull off a Christine-style interview."

Christine Lamont was her mentor at CNN and more of a diva than any actress Caroline could imagine. She once notoriously cleared out an entire wing of the Bellagio to accommodate her needs during a Britney Spears one-on-one.

"Car," Emma pinched her forearm and she looked up, annoyed. "This is going to be the easiest pep talk in pep talk history."

"Okay, I'm ready." She set her tablet aside and gave Emma her full focus.

"Don't strive for a Christine Lamont-style interview. Strive for a Caroline Fitzhugh interview. You're sunglass shopping when you have the most beautiful eyes ever. You're preparing questions that Christine would ask. Ask him what Caroline wants to know. Remember when we would sit up and watch *A Walk in the Park* or *Broken Vow* and you would ask me if I thought he would like popcorn with Junior Mints mixed in? Or if he did anything crazy at night before bed, like when you checked for ghosts?"

"I still do that."

"Ask him! Clark Rhodes wants a change, and you are the biggest breath of fresh air out there. You can't win trying to be a cheap imitation of Christine, because Christine is a cheap imitation of herself as it is. But if you go out there as you, real and unedited you? You with no filter and inappropriate sense of humor? Clark Rhodes won't know what hit him."

"Damn."

"Good, right?"

"Seriously, that should go in some sort of book of pep talks."

Emma made a tiny bow from her yoga pose. "Thank you, thank you."

"I'm going to go pack." She snatched Emma's legal pad. Their friendship had absolutely no boundaries. "What's this?"

"I've been writing down everything I remember from the flashback."

"That's the tattoo?"

"Yeah."

"It's weird. It looks Middle Eastern or Eastern European." She squinted and amended, "Maybe Egyptian?" She pinched the thin skin between her thumb and index finger. "And it was here?"

"Yes, right hand."

"You know, there's a guy at work who hunts down shit like this. He sources weird symbols associated with terrorist groups and stuff. I could ask him to research it. See if it's a common symbol, or if it has meaning."

"Yeah, that would be great. I'll tell Dad you're doing that when I give him the notes. We can all put our heads together when you get back."

Caroline snapped a photo of the drawing with her phone.

"I'm gone for three days. I think the flight will last longer."

"Maybe you'll fall in love and stay."

"Ew, Em, he's like a hundred. I'm not falling in love with Clark Rhodes."

"I wasn't referring to Clark Rhodes, but it's interesting that you went there. Also, interesting how defensive you got."

"I'm going for coffee and not taking that bait." She rifled through her bag for some cash. "Maybe he has a son." She blinked innocently.

"He's thirty-six, not fifty, you spaz."

"Maybe I should bring him some adult diapers."

"I'll take a cappuccino if you're going," Emma said, refusing to acknowledge the last comment.

"No problem. I'll stop by Duane Reade and pick Clark up some Rogaine on my way."

Emma's only response was to throw her pencil at Caroline. She laughed as she retreated and shouted from the hall, "And prune juice!"

Emma chuckled, then sobered at the thought of seeing Nathan the next day, *their day*. Emma had given it a lot of thought and concluded she was being foolish. For one thing, whatever Nathan's secret, it surely paled in comparison to her own. For another, Nathan already held her heart. This tether that joined them was unbreakable. She wouldn't insult or threaten their bond with a lie. She had a plan. The time for secrets was over.

CHAPTER TWENTY-ONE

It was her birthday. Her real birthday. Emily Webster's birthday. July 7. It was also Nathan Bishop's birthday. Emma could remember their parents laughing about the coincidence—five years to the day apart—and she could remember the double cakes. Nathan's was chocolate, hers was pink, and they would all celebrate on the beach in Nantucket. Her father would start the singing and the rest of the group would join in. Nathan made it all about Emily, mostly because she was a spoiled little girl, but also because it was his natural tendency to fly under the radar. He never liked attention about his birthday, and not much had changed, apparently, because as she walked up to his office, there was no indication that this was anything other than a normal day. Her contact lenses were gone, and her violet eyes sparkled with anticipation. Wearing a jade silk slip dress and paillette splash pumps, she had carefully wrapped a small box containing a chocolate cupcake and a pink cupcake from Magnolia Bakery. In another box, she'd put his present, the present that would tell him everything.

She had been playing on the front lawn with one of Mariella's dishcloths stuck to her head with bobby pins and a fistful of violets in her hand when he'd walked down his drive, hauling a bulging backpack. She had chased after him.

"Nave, come marry me!"

"I can't today, Em-em, I'm heading back to school again."

Her eyes grew glassy. "But it's summer."

"Hey, hey, hey. I'm coming back in a few weeks for the long weekend."

I'll be back for our birthday. I'll bring you a present."

"Will you have time to marry me when you get back?" She fiddled with the violets in her hand.

"You bet, Em-em. I will come back, and I will marry you. Sound good?"

"Okay. When?"

He thought for a minute, then reached to his wrist and unhooked a black rubber sports watch. He held it open and Emily extended her arm. It was huge but there were holes punched all the way to the bezel, so he strapped it on.

"See the little window on the face? There's the date."

He did a quick calculation in his head.

"In twenty-three days, I will be back. I will bring you an awesome present for our birthday, and we can get married. Again."

"Okay."

She stared at the watch and waved to him without looking up.

"Bye, Em-em."

"Bye, Nave."

She was taken four days later. She had spent her ninth—and Nathan's fourteenth—birthday in captivity. The watch stayed on her wrist the entire time. As she wrapped it this morning, she felt a tremor of anxiety, but it was quickly replaced by the image of Nathan opening the box and realizing . . . .

She pushed open his office door with a beaming smile and was met with a stony stare that knocked the joy right off her face. Nathan looked at her, but it wasn't Nathan. It was a cold, empty man with barely contained rage flowing through him.

"What's wrong?" she asked, birthday surprises forgotten.

"Who are you?"

"What?"

"Who. The. Fuck. Are. You?"

He'd found out. She shouldn't have been surprised. This was a guy who uncovered secrets for a living. He clearly didn't have the whole truth, but he had part of it. And having a partial truth was a dangerous thing.

"Nathan, I can explain."

"I've spent the last three hours running through our conversations in my head. What I've told you, what I let slip, who you could have told . . ."

"Nathan, no, it's not like that."

"Really? What's it like then? Because Emma Porter didn't exist until fourteen years ago. Emma Porter's birth certificate in Georgia is a very good fake. Emma Porter's childhood home was purchased through a shell corporation."

"Nathan, please, just let me tell you the truth."

"The truth!" he bellowed. "Now you want to tell me the truth? I fucking trusted you. I never let my guard down like that. For anyone. Ever! Stupid. Fucking stupid."

"Nave."

"That whole fucking sob story. Was it all just a hook to draw me in?"

"Oh, God." She felt sick. "No."

He talked over her.

"Get out."

"Please, Nave."

He looked confused, but his anger was consuming him.

"Security is on the way. If you move quickly, you can escape getting thrown on your ass onto Sixth Avenue."

She set the packages on the edge of his desk, and pleading violet eyes met fiery greens.

"I'm going, but you need to open these. Please. It will explain everything, and I promise you it's not what you think. Remember that night at the bar? When you came in with that woman? Remember how bad it looked?" He wouldn't budge.

"Out. Now."

"Nave, I swear. Only good surprises."

She turned without a word and left the office. As she rode down in the elevator with a suited executive who never looked up from his phone, she sent up a silent prayer that Nathan would open the boxes and not send the bomb squad to destroy them. Deep down he had to know. Emma knew he had to know, so she relied on the faith she had put in him.

She emerged onto Sixth Avenue and stopped on the sidewalk at a loss. Pedestrians moved around her, altering the flow of foot traffic like minnows avoiding a rock in a steam. The Suburban was parked on a side street, JT leaning against the driver's door reading something on his phone. Nathan's Range Rover pulled up out front. Chat emerged from the driver's seat, came around the hood, and stopped abruptly when he saw her. Emma looked at him with a desperation that had him widening his eyes. Chat stood for a moment, assessing. Then he navigated the crowd, took Emma by her shoulders, and guided her back to the expansive recessed entrance of the building. With a serious face and soothing voice, he said, "Everything is going to be okay. You'll see." Then he turned to the glass front doors, pulled the closest one open, and gestured toward Emma as Nathan came charging through. Then Chat disappeared inside, a secret smile on his lips.

Fat rain clouds moved across the sky, blocking the July sun. Unnaturally still, nostrils flaring, breathing hard, Nathan looked like a bull about to charge. Emma glanced down and saw that he held the small wrapped package in his hand.

"Who are you?" he asked again, but this time his voice was quiet, desolate.

"Nathan, please. Open the gift."

He stared at the package as if he hadn't realized it was in his hand. Thunder rumbled and fat drops of rain hit the sidewalk. In the shelter of the alcove, he tore off the paper and shoved it into his jacket pocket. Emma watched him carefully lift the lid and look inside. He stared down at the black rubber sports watch. He didn't move, didn't speak. A full minute later, he slowly pulled it from the box and rubbed the bezel between his thumb and index finger. Finally, he looked up at her through glassy eyes.

"Emily?"

The one word was saturated with hope and grief and love.

She'd barely finished her nod of confirmation when he jumped on her like he wanted to swallow her whole. He kissed every inch of her face and pulled her body into his. A few hoots and whistles from passersby had Nathan grabbing her hand and pulling her through the rain to the back of the Range Rover. There, cocooned in the quiet backseat, he drank in her face and repeated his question.

"Emily?"

"Yes, Nave."

He silenced her with another blistering kiss. A kiss that seemed to exorcise fifteen years of demons, fifteen years of pain.

"I can't. I don't . . . ." He couldn't sort through the avalanche of questions to form one.

"I need to talk to you," she gasped. "I need to tell you."

"I need to marry you," he blurted.

That got her attention.

"What?"

"I promised you. It was the last thing I said to you. God, Emily." He rained kisses on her face and her neck.

"Nave?"

"Fuck, don't ever stop calling me that."

"Never."

He pulled back an inch and just stared at her, drinking her in, and she did the same. She wasn't seeing him anew, but she was seeing him through Emily Webster's eyes. In finding him, she had found herself. He ran his nose down the length of hers.

"You can't imagine what it's been like for me."

"What do you mean?"

"The loss, just the thought of this perfect little girl . . . ." He couldn't finish the thought. It was horrific. "Not knowing. It was brutal."

"I know."

"I used to imagine what you'd grown up to look like."

"Are you disappointed? I can't compare to a fantasy."

"You don't. You exceed it. In. Every. Way." He punctuated each word with a hot kiss.

"Nathan . . . ." She wanted to beg him to take her home, to give herself to him, but he wasn't finished.

"Every woman that I've dated, every woman that I've been with, every woman that I've ever made some miserable attempt . . ." he brushed a hand down his face, ". . . lost out to the memory of an eight-year-old girl and the woman she would have become."

"It's the same for me, Nave. That's why . . . that's part of the reason I can't . . . . When you left for boarding school before I was taken," Nathan stilled at her words and gripped her like a vice, anchoring her to him, "it was like something inside me wasn't there anymore. I would get up in the middle of the night and stare out the window into the dark at your empty bedroom across the yard and just cry. It was crazy."

"You want to hear crazy?" She nodded, relieved he felt this as much as she did. "That night at the Jane? When you burst into that conference room? I saw you, and I just knew."

"Knew?"

"Knew what had happened. Knew you needed me. Knew there was something about you. I don't even remember crossing the room to get to you."

"That's not crazy."

"I haven't gotten to the crazy part. After I caught you, after you passed out in my arms half choking me with my tie, the words on my lips, the thought in my head . . . it was something I had never thought, never meant in my life."

"I used to tell you I loved you all the time." She didn't pretend she didn't understand what he meant.

"I remember. You used to pat my cheeks with your tiny hands."

"Do you remember what you said back?"

He searched her eyes, looking for an answer, but nothing came. He shook his head once.

"You'd say, *and you are my sunshine*, and you'd pull my nose." Her eyes grew moist, but the sentimentality of the moment was quickly lost when she looked at Nathan. He had gone pale.

"What? Nathan?"

He puffed out a laugh and reached for his phone. He scrolled through his contacts and brought up the info. He showed her the nickname that he had flirtatiously withheld when they first exchanged contact information:

Sunshine.

His kiss bruised her lips, slicked her thighs, curled her toes.

"I need to tell you what happened to me; at least what I can remember. I can't lie to you anymore. I don't want anything between us." She was babbling, pent up, and nervous. She wanted to give herself to this man, and it was a feeling she had never experienced. Instead of her trademark lockdown, she was saying too much, spilling out every thought. It was like he had pulled the cork on her bottled-up emotions. Nathan just nodded while she prattled on. He understood with a completeness she could not fathom. "I need to explain. I need . . . ." Her voice failed her as she looked into grass green eyes filled with wonder and, yes, love.

"What do you need, Emily Webster?"

"I need you."

"You have me, Emily. You always have."

"It's the same for me, Nave."

"Let's go home."

Home.

He kissed her slowly, meaningfully, and she lost her breath and every thought in her head that ten seconds ago was dying to get out. She just stared at him and beamed. He ran his knuckles down her cheek.

"Happy birthday, Emily."

"Happy birthday, Nave."

CHAPTER TWENTY-TWO

Nathan led her into the dark apartment. With a quiet command of "dim lighting," the room brightened to a romantic glow. He never broke stride as he headed toward his bedroom.

Outside the bedroom door, he cupped her face. "I'm going to make love to you, and then I'm going to fuck you. Then we'll see how the rest of the night goes."

"Oh."

"Yeah. Oh."

His bedroom was dark and sparse. Decorated in nautical blue and gray, a huge bed was the centerpiece flanked by two end tables. The dresser was dotted with a few knick-knacks and photos she couldn't make out. The far wall was one seamless floor-to-ceiling glass wall, oddly cohesive with the traditional pre-war architecture of the building, and beyond that was a stone balcony overlooking the park. A block to the south, the Metropolitan Museum of Art glowed like a palace from another era.

She felt the heat from Nathan's body at her back as he stood behind her. He cupped her breast with one hand. With the other, he reached up to pull down the zipper of the slip dress. He did it with such agonizing slowness, she felt like she could hear each individual tooth come open until the pale green fabric fell gently to her feet. Her bra followed. She slid off her sandals and turned to face him in only a nude thong. Nathan stepped back and just stared. He looked at her like . . . like a man gazing upon beauty for the first time. His eyes traveled from her face to her breasts to the flat of her stomach, the curve of her hips, down her thighs to her painted pink toes. Emily stood still as a statue and let him look, reveled in it. On the journey back up her body, his gaze changed. His entire body shifted to that of a predator held in check, a lion waiting for the gazelle to wander juuuuuust a little further from the herd. Then he pounced. He snapped the delicate lace from her body and devoured her mouth in a searing kiss.

"You keep tearing them."

"I don't see that changing in the foreseeable future. I have a house account at La Perla. Buy a hundred pairs."

Emily had never been jealous in her life. Never had reason to be, but the idea of Nathan shopping for lacy unmentionables with leggy super-models gave her pause. Nathan sensed her unease.

"We're going to have a long fucking talk, but now is not the time. I think we both know at this point that perceptions are not reality."

Emily didn't reply with words. She did something she had never in her life done, but it felt as natural as breathing. She reached out and palmed his erection, her eyes only leaving his when the sheer size filling her palm pulled her gaze. Nathan chuckled.

"We'll get you good and ready. I want this to be the best night of your life."

"It already is."

With that green light, Nathan leaped into action. He swung her into his arms and dropped her unceremoniously on the bed. He pulled the tie from his collar and set it on the mattress with a wicked gleam in his eye.

His suit jacket was somewhere on the living room floor. Monogrammed platinum cufflinks hit the carpet with a plunk. As each button opened, she stared at the chest slowly being revealed. He had a light smattering of chest hair and an assortment of scars. She wanted to explore him more, but as his hand went to his belt, his lips latched on to her breast, and she lost every sane thought in her head. Every stroke of his tongue, every pull with his teeth left her throbbing, aching to be complete.

"I want you inside me. So much."

He kissed down her belly, then met her gaze with one that seemed to say, *not yet.* Then he winked. She yanked his hair in admonishment, but as his lips traveled down, her desire turned to need. Nathan licked her as if nothing had ever tasted so good, his precision only shaken by lust and urgency. He tongued her to a shattering orgasm then pushed two fingers into her and stretched her as she continued to quake.

"Emily, I've never had sex without a condom."

"I'm on birth control. I got the implant when I moved to New York. I want you bare."

If there were magic sex words, those four words were it. Nathan was above her in an instant. His cock poised at her entrance, his eyes on her.

"We'll go slow."

"Now. Please."

Nathan pushed inside and she lost her breath. Jesus, he was big. He stopped after a few inches, allowing her to accommodate him. He stared at the ceiling, seeming to gather himself.

"Just do it. I'm ready. God, Nathan, I need you."

That broke whatever restraint he was clinging to, and with one forceful thrust, he pushed fully into her. Her body gave way as he plunged to the hilt. Nathan stilled. He kissed away her tears as her body adjusted.

"You good?" He pinched her nipple and the combination of reassuring words and the arousing tweak caused her hips to tilt.

"So good."

"That's good."

"Let me show you how good." She squeezed her inner muscles. She may have had zero sexual experience, but she couldn't be best friends with Caroline Fitzhugh and not learn a thing or two about satisfying a man. Nathan groaned. "Gotta move, Sunshine." He started in long slow strokes. Every withdrawal left her feeling hollow, every thrust complete. She grabbed his ass to return him to her, her body building to a zenith.

"Jesus, Emily, I'm not gonna last. I need you with me. Come with me."

Her garbled shout was her only response as her body blew every circuit. Her inner walls contracted violently, and Nathan's groan echoed off the walls as he emptied himself inside her.

They were both still. Stunned. Nathan's forehead touching hers, their bodies joined. A bead of sweat ran down his temple, hit her cheek, and disappeared into her hair like they were one being. Nathan kissed her forehead, her jawline, her lips, then slowly pulled out of her. He looked briefly down between her legs, then kissed between her breasts. "Be right back." He climbed off the bed with remarkable grace and retreated into the master bath. She sat up smiling and satisfied, brushing the massive tangle of hair over her shoulder. She glanced down between her legs and stilled. Emily knew her hymen had already been broken, most likely from years of dressage and gymnastics as a child. It was one of the reasons the doctors couldn't conclusively say whether she had been sexually abused during her abduction. But in this moment, she *knew* she had never been violated. She knew Nathan had been the first man to know her body. The feeling overwhelmed her, and Emily collapsed into tears of relief and joy. Nathan emerged with a warm washcloth and immediately paled when he saw her. He rushed to the bed and pulled her into his lap. Emily was the type of girl who needed space. If she needed to work out a problem or process an emotion, she did it alone. But that was never how it was with Nathan. It was as if their souls were somehow joined—like he was part of her. Their pain, their lust, their happiness, they were shared. He stroked her back and let her cry. After minutes that felt like hours, she looked up at his concerned face.

"I really was a virgin." His face was a picture of pain and confusion. She beamed at him with so much love in her eyes, he calmed instantly. She touched his beautiful face, his rough stubble abrading her palm. "I guess it's time for that talk."

He stood without effort and carried her into the cavernous shower. He set her on her feet with military precision and held her face.

"Shower, hydrate, eat, talk. In that order."

"Yes, sir."

His gaze heated. "I've never really been into that, but Jesus, that gets me hot." The shower started on its own, a sensor triggering the water. Emily reached for the hand-milled soap and gave him a wicked smile.

They sat opposite one another on the floor of the dark paneled study. A wooden tray laden with fruit, cheese, smoked almonds, and truffles sat between them. Nathan, shirtless in pale blue drawstring pajama bottoms, opened the beer he had retrieved from the fridge and took a long pull from the bottle. He watched Emily with rapt attention. Despite the gravity of the conversation, he chuckled when he noticed her eyes rake over his eight-pack and the V leading to his waistband. He pinched a grape from the bunch and held it out to her. She used her palms on the mahogany wood floor to prop herself forward and plucked it from his fingers with her mouth. When she licked the juice from her lips, Nathan felt the beer bottle in his hand slip and tightened his hold to secure it before it hit the floor, along with his jaw.

"Jesus, Emily."

"What?"

"I think the sexiest thing about you is that you seduce me without even realizing you're doing it."

"I think some of Caroline's tutorials paid off."

Nathan chuffed. "What you do can't be taught."

"Caroline would beg to differ."

"Caroline knows, I take it."

"She's known all along. She lived in Georgia, where I grew up, and then was my roommate in college."

He looked a little wounded, so Emily clarified. "Dad and Mr. Fitz go way back. It wasn't about you, Nathan. I don't think he trusted your father."

"He was right not to trust him." He took a long pull of his beer. "I just . . . Fuck, it's so hard to say this when you were the one taken, I struggled with it."

Emily pushed to stand and went to him. She straddled him and settled in the nest of his crossed legs. She pushed her face into his chest and wrapped her arms around his waist. "I know."

"I tried to contact your dad, but he never had answers. Eventually, he stopped taking my calls."

"And you moved on," she finished for him.

"Hardly."

She pushed back and cocked an eyebrow. "What?"

He sighed and took a final swig of his Stella. "Come with me."

He led her into the closet where she had had the flashback. She hadn't even thought about the box until he pulled it from the rack. It was marked 'Webster' and he hauled it under one long arm as he led them back out into the unused guest room. He set the box on the bed and lifted the lid. Inside was a series of files, alphabetized and meticulously labeled. The first file she recognized immediately. It was an Eastern European crime syndicate heavily involved in arms dealing. Two of her kidnappers, the two who had been killed in prison, were both associated with the group. The file held photos and Interpol reports. She looked up at Nathan, realization dawning.

"You looked for me."

"Most of the stuff is on my computer. This is information I don't want to be hacked or leaked."

"Oh, Nathan." Tears streaked down her cheeks.

"I couldn't just sit around; it ate me up inside. I know my imagination was worse than reality . . . ."

"It was," she reassured him.

"You sort of became my hobby." He shrugged.

"That would be an interesting interview response," she quipped. "And what do you do in your free time, Mr. Bishop? I like to do jigsaw puzzles and Emily Webster." He set the box on the floor and pushed her back onto the bed.

"You have no idea how much I like to do Emily Webster."

"So, this hobby . . . ."

Nathan sighed. "Yeah, about that. It's not as cloak and dagger as you might be imagining. K-B has a small division that handles mostly on-the-books hostage and rescue ops."

"Mostly?"

"Any civilian can hire Bishop Security for an abduction/rescue situation. Just last month we negotiated the release of a group of college kids caught with drugs at the Thai border. I also have a contact, a liaison between various government agencies and my team. If he reaches out, the assignment is more sensitive."

"What sorts of assignments? Can you tell me?" Nathan saw through her attempt to distract him. Plus, he really couldn't tell her much.

"Talk to me, Emily."

Emily sighed, nuzzled below Nathan's ear, and took a deep inhale. Several therapists had offered breathing techniques to help her overcome sudden panic. Too bad none of them knew about the crook of Nathan's neck; it was restorative. It was time. Nathan leaned against the headboard and brought Emily into the nook at his side. She spoke with her head on his broad shoulder, her hand resting gently on his chest.

"I don't remember much." He didn't reply, just stroked his thumb over her bare shoulder. "The nanny was taking me to Half Shell for ice cream. She was the one who filled in when Mariella went to Guatemala to visit her family." The nanny's name was Rena Smalls. Nathan already knew that after the kidnapping, she had walked back to her 1995 Ford Focus and driven away. And disappeared. Emily told him about the van with the logo and the man with the sleeve of tattoos and the sound of the sliding door. She tried to keep her few memories in order. "So. The flashback." She tangled her hand in the sheet that covered them. His hold on her tightened.

"If you can, Emily."

"Yeah, I'm good." She sensed rather than saw his smile. He could tell she was still with him; she hadn't switched into robot-mode. "I saw the banker's box labeled Webster, so I stuck my hands up through the shelf grate to inch it forward."

"Snoop."

"I admit to it, but you have to admit that was irresistible."

"Agreed." He kissed her hair.

"So, my hands were through and you came up behind me." Just as the words came out, she realized Nathan would feel responsible. "Wait. Stop. Please don't blame yourself. You didn't do anything wrong." She was on her stomach now looking up into his pained eyes. Her hands gripped his shoulders, begging him to hear her.

"I know, it's just . . . I triggered it."

"Yes, you did, and you have no idea how grateful I am." That got his attention. "You're giving me strength, Nave. If my mind wasn't ready to remember, it would still be blocked. You're helping me. I am so sick of this shit; you have no idea. Before that happened, I don't think I even fully realized all the fear and dread I was pushing down every day, and for what? It's the *fear* of the memory that's consuming me, not the memory itself. I'm glad something triggered a flashback. I hope it happens again. I think I need to know what happened to me. It's like an ugly scar that's worse than the original wound. I guess I need to cut it open again so it can heal properly."

Nathan looked stricken. "Emily, some of these abductions . . . ."

"I know." She sighed; this would be hard for him to hear. "I've also seen my medical report. It's not that bad." He sat up with her and held her face in his hands.

"Oh, Emily."

"Cuts and scrapes mostly. Some welts on my bottom, some bruises on my thighs. And a bite mark." She tapped the top curve of her right shoulder. "Here. All healed without a trace."

Nathan nodded as he composed himself. "And the flashback?"

She told him about the cage she had remembered and the room and the man and what he had said. She told him she remembered his sports watch on her small wrist. He gave her a sad smile. When Emily told him about the tattoo, she moved to scoot off the bed to retrieve the sketch she had drawn, but Nathan was unwilling to let her go, like if their skin broke contact they would dissolve into dust. Emily clearly shared his reluctance because she scooted back into his lap without a second thought and described the small image: a rectangle, with a cross in the center and a small flower at each corner. Nathan was pensive.

"What kind of flower?"

"I don't know. It was just the blossom, like a carnation."

"So, no stem or leaves."

"Yes, I think so. I mean the whole tattoo was tiny, the size of a domino."

"And the cross?"

"It flared out at the ends, I think."

His forehead touched the top of her head.

"Nathan?"

He sighed. "Seems benign enough. I need to check with some people."

"Okay. The only thing I remember after that is being in the SUV with the FBI agents and my father." Nathan didn't respond.

"I want to remember, dammit."

"Don't try to force it. You know that."

Emily had been told numerous times by numerous therapists that straining to recover memories was the surest way to keep them at bay.

"I know that. How do you know that?"

"I had some exposure to PTSD in the Navy."

"Oh, I see." Her index finger skated idly over his forearm.

"How do you do that?"

"Do what?"

"Know when to leave it? Sometimes you push and needle and ask a dozen follow-up questions about something. Then, other times, you just drop it. It's like you know."

"I'm not sure. I guess I just feel it when you can't or aren't ready to say more."

He stared at her with the most loving, possessive gaze she had ever seen, and she remembered what his mother used to say about their eyes. She touched the corner of hers. "Like a violet." She touched the corner of his. "And a leaf." He pulled her back, so she was resting on his chest.

"Emily?"

"Yes?"

"Thank you for coming back to me."

"Thank you for waiting."

CHAPTER TWENTY-THREE

Emily was sitting at her desk at *The Sentry* going over her notes for the first installment of "The Bishop Chronicles," as she was now calling them. She had been mildly concerned before she had even started that her childhood affection for Nathan would somehow show in the story; now she was panicked that the story would scream *I am hopelessly in love with this man!*

Nathan Bishop was a lot of things to a lot of people. The surprising thing was that he didn't seem to mind being thought of like a careless partier, a shameless playboy, or a ruthless shark; what he did not want to be portrayed as was a hero. He discouraged any mention of his time in the military and out-and-out forbade her to recount any of the stories he had shared "off the record" about his service. If he was going to be a hero, he was going to be the unsung kind. It was funny, but Emily understood. He was not bothered by misperception; he just didn't want anyone to know the real him. His need for privacy was innate. He didn't care if a sex tape leaked, but he would hate it if the world knew his secret habit of keeping a small seashell in his pocket and rubbing it for luck. He didn't want the world to see the most private parts of him, the parts he showed to her, and that made her feel . . . cherished.

She had notes typed on her tablet, handwritten on a legal pad, and scrawled on Post-its, but slowly she was making sense of it all. She glanced up as her phone buzzed, dancing on her desk. She scrolled to the text.

Mr. Wonderful: *Pack a bag.*

Emily: *Is that an order, sir?*

Mr. Wonderful: *I like the "sir," but no, it's a request.*

Emily: *Any specifics?*

Mr. Wonderful: *Pack for a sunny surprise.*

Emily: *So just sunscreen then?*

Mr. Wonderful: *You just made me drop my phone.*

Emily: *So, I'm getting better at this flirting thing?*

Mr. Wonderful: *I've created a monster. Should I be worried?*

Emily: *Never.*

Mr. Wonderful: *Friday at 2. I'll send a car.*

Emily: *I have a job.*

Mr. Wonderful: *I thought I was your job.*

Emily: *You have a point.*

Mr. Wonderful: *See you then, Emily.*

Emily: *Looking forward to it . . .*

She noticed that since he'd discovered the truth, he only called her Emily, not Em, no endearment. It was like he couldn't say it enough. She certainly couldn't hear it enough.

On Friday, Emily stood in her lobby holding a Louis Vuitton week-end duffle and a small La Perla shopping bag. Her tease was wasted, as it turned out because only Andrew greeted her when the Range Rover pulled up to the curb. He was a bit more conversational than he had been in their past interactions. He asked about her day. When Emily mentioned he didn't say much, he confessed that was the face-tious source of his call sign, "Chat." Nathan had a work emergency. Andrew clarified, "He said it's nothing of concern and he would meet you at the airport." By airport, he meant Teterboro, where one of the Knightsgrove-Bishop Gulfstreams sat poised near the runway. Emily flew private all the time, but even for her, this was beyond. After depositing her things in the plush bedroom, she settled into a cream leather seat and sipped on the bottled water the attendant, a gangly man named Brian, offered up.

Emily had done a lot to overcome the claustrophobia that had gripped her intensely when she first came home, but extended time peri-ods alone in small spaces still induced panic. After twenty minutes, she started to shake, and she knew a panic attack was in the offing. Fortunately, the cabin hatch was still open, awaiting Nathan's arrival, and she quickly moved to the doorway. She sat on the top step and took even breaths, focusing on the sky. In the distance, a black Bugatti Chiron tore across the tarmac. She rolled her eyes. Seriously? Sometimes she forgot the Nathan Bishop of today had an image to uphold. He parked, and the doors popped out and up like the wings on Mercury's helmet. He emerged and jogged to her, taking the stairs two at a time.

"What are you doing out here?"

"Just getting some air." It was the truth.

"Emily?" He leaned into her face, kissing the small wrinkle between her eyebrows.

"Sometimes small spaces . . . it's not a big deal."

He sighed into her neck. "I'm sorry. I didn't think . . ."

"Stop. You can't anticipate every little quirk I'm going to have. And trust me, there are plenty."

He kissed her then. "And I look forward to discovering, and in the future, anticipating every single one." She smiled against his lips, and he spoke against hers, "Can you go back in?"

"Yes, I'm fine."

"I hate that word." He took her hand and pulled her up and together they ducked back inside the plane.

"Fine?"

"Yes," he grumbled.

"It seems innocuous enough," she shrugged.

"That's why I hate it. That, and nobody who uses it ever is."

She chuckled at the truth of the comment. "True. It should be a safe word."

Nathan had started his plunge into the leather seat but that jolted him back upright. "How the hell do you know about safe words?"

"I haven't been living under a rock, Nave. Plus, I've been researching you for the past several weeks. You'd be amazed what comes up when you Google 'Nathan Bishop and kink.'"

He kissed the end of her nose. "Not falling for it, Emily."

"Darn."

"Even if I admit to a mildly checkered past, I am the picture of discretion."

"I see." He didn't miss the chill in her voice.

"Hey. What?"

"You asked me that. That first night. You asked me if I had a safe word."

"Jesus. I forgot. I could kick my own ass for the way I behaved that night."

"I was ... I couldn't believe you were the same person I remembered."

"I'm not. I wasn't. I was preoccupied with you ever since the night you were drugged and burst into that meeting. I was angry with myself for letting a woman get to me. I thought if I spent the night with you . . ."

"You'd get me out of your system."

"I should have known then."

"Known?"

"That you weren't like the others. A night with you, even before I knew who you were, it would have mattered. It never mattered before."

"I don't like thinking about that stuff."

He pulled them both down into the seats as Brian finished the preflight check.

"About sex?"

"About you having sex with other women."

He looked at the ceiling, shaking his head.

"Emily, it has only ever been you. I'm not a saint, but no woman has ever . . . . Before you came back to me, I was . . . ." He scrubbed his face with his hand and then came nose to nose with her. "There has never been anyone but you, beautiful Emily. In here." He pointed to the left side of his chest. "Got it?"

She did nothing to stop the lone tear that trailed down her cheek and nodded against his forehead, "Got it."

"Nathan?"

"Hmm?"

"I love you." She could feel his grin against her cheek. He stayed that way for a solid minute and just rubbed his hand along her arm. He pulled back slowly and met her gaze. For the first time since her revelation, he seemed . . . not distant, but maybe wistful.

"Good. Now buckle up." He signaled to Brian for a beer and nestled Emily into his side. She paused at his lack of response to her declaration, but his body spoke volumes, so she snuggled in and off they went.

Even before the plane began its descent, Emily knew where they were going. Nantucket.

"Nave? I thought your family sold your place."

"We did. I bought a new house. I can't wait for you to see it. The rest of the island can wait though. This weekend we are just going to relax and unwind."

"Sounds perfect."

As they hopped into a battered Jeep with no doors, Emily thought of the Bugatti back in New York. With a secret smile, she thought, *this is the real Nathan.* It was peak season in Nantucket, and as they wound up Cliff Road, she shivered in anticipation. Both of their childhood homes were sold but Nathan, while low key as billionaires went, liked his creature comforts. She knew his home would be incredible but inconspicuous. When they pulled into the entrance to her old home, her jaw dropped.

"Nathan?"

"First thing I bought when I got access to my accounts at twenty-five." His smile was hopeful. "I asked your father to hang on to it until then, for me." Emily remembered her father selling the house on her twentieth birthday. Now she understood.

"I think you're trying to kill me." She stared at the roll bar of the Jeep, trying to stop yet another bout of tears.

"Nah, but I would like to make you smile for once instead of cry. You only had eight summers here with me, but they were perfect summers. I want you to have every summer here."

"You're setting the bar kind of high." *Every perfect summer* was a lot of expectation.

"No, I'm not. You don't have to do anything to make them perfect, Emily. You just have to be here."

She smiled then. He followed the line of her lips with his finger.

"Aha, success."

She took his hand. "Let's go look. Is it different?"

"A little. I made some changes. Knocked out a wall, updated the kitchen and bathrooms. Oh, and I bought the house on the other side and tore it down."

"You *what*?"

"You never saw it. It was a blight. It looked like a maximum-security prison, and it blocked the view."

She just shook her head as she walked ahead of him up the winding drive. "So, you spent five million dollars for a view."

"Eight," he corrected as he jogged to catch up, "and worth every damn dime."

The exterior of the house looked just the same—the gray shingles and black shutters, the flagpole in the center of the large patch of grass circled by the pebbled driveway, white window boxes overflowing with cascading white petunias and lobelia. Inside was another story. The ten-thousand-square-foot home was a classic Nantucket estate. A wide, open hallway bisected the house straight to large French doors at the back that led out to the pool and the beach, which was accessed by a steep set of wooden steps typical of the houses along the cliff. Inside, a wide staircase started about halfway back and led up to a landing with another set of doors that opened onto a small balcony. The stairs then turned back toward the front of the house to complete the ascent to the second floor. It was all very traditional, but for the fact that there were no walls.

The walls that had once separated the living and dining rooms from the center hall had been removed and replaced with sleek white columns. Behind the dining room, a massive space had been created from combining the original kitchen, staff quarters, butler's pantry, and breakfast room into a kitchen/living space that any chef would dream of and any family could camp in. Decorated in white and slate blue, the kitchen was sleek but homey. A long French provincial farm table held a vase of Nikko blue hydrangeas. The island was white honed marble with a graphite vein, and the cabinets were white cottage board. The kitchen opened to a bells-and-whistles outdoor cooking area under a covered patio. The space was punctuated with heavy wrought iron furniture covered in cushions upholstered in broad yellow and white stripes. The guest house to the right of the pool had a party room, a smaller kitchen, and five bedrooms.

But the real kicker was the view. Every room Emily stood in looked out over the vast Atlantic. It was a bit of a hike down the wooden stairs to the private beach but perched up here looking out at such beauty . . . transcendent.

"Beach or food?"

"Those are my only choices?"

Nathan grabbed her hand and hauled her toward the master bedroom. "What was I thinking?"

"I would like those other two, though," Emily laughed.

"We'll get to it. Perhaps all at the same time." Nathan carried her off. From behind the closed bedroom door, Emily let out a squeal.

The beach at night was heaven. Emily sat between Nathan's thighs. The waves slapped the shore, and the fire crackled as it died down. Nathan started to rub her shoulders.

"Mmm, that feels good."

"I'm an expert. If my business fails, I have a future as a masseuse. A very perverted masseuse." The thought made her stiffen. She didn't want to be jealous, but this was all so new. The thought of this little paradise being some sort of sex den for Nathan . . . . She tried to shake it off, but he accurately interpreted her tension.

"Emily, I've never brought a woman here."

199

"Okay."

"I mean it. My brothers have brought their wives here—oh, and my mom has come." He turned her to face him. "Only you, Emily."

"I'm sorry."

"Trust me, I get it. You may not have the same level of experience, but that doesn't mean I don't want to kill every guy who eye-fucks you when you walk into a room. I feel the same need to claim you."

"You're not going to pee on me, are you?"

He nearly spat his beer into her hair. "God, that mouth."

"Hit me over the head and drag me back to your cave? Kill a rival in a duel?"

"Trust me, Emily. I have every intention of marking my territory."

"Soon?" She wiggled closer into the space between his legs.

"Patience. I have a whole seduction planned for you."

"Oh, God, that sounds elaborate."

"I think so, but I'll let you be the judge."

"Now?"

"Right now, Emily."

He pulled her up and led her into the house.

Elaborate was not the right word, Emily decided. *Sinful,* she thought as he fed her a strawberry. *Illicit* popped into her head as he secured her hands to the bedposts and put his head between her thighs. *Wanton* crossed her mind as she straddled his narrow hips. *Dirty* was the descriptor when he put her on all fours and slammed into her. *Kinky* flitted in her brain as he dripped candle wax on a taut nipple. *Romantic,* she sighed as he moved above her, and *euphoric* as the pleasure crashed over them. And when they finally collapsed in a tangled mess in the knotted sheets, and she felt the echoes of their passion between her sore legs, she thought he had succeeded. She was *marked.*

CHAPTER TWENTY-FOUR

"I don't like this any more than you, but when you climb the stairs, you get the belt."

The leather lashed across her small bottom through the tattered nightgown. Her face was mashed up tight into a ball when the door flew open.

"What do you think you're doing? You idiot!"

"She went up the stairs."

"Who cares? Drop the belt, or I will put a bullet in your brain."

The belt hit the floor with a thud.

"She has to mind."

"She can't be marked, you fool!! You bit her! You want to keep her from going to the stairs? Watch."

The man who had come in grabbed her under her arms and picked her up. With a monogrammed handkerchief, he wiped her nose and eyes.

"There, there, Little One. You must stay away from the stairs, all right?"

She sniffled and nodded. He spoke with a soft voice.

"We have to keep this little one perfect. Because that's what you are; you are perfect."

He sighed, resigned.

"Little girls who go up the stairs get the box."

"Okay," she said, not quite understanding.

He walked a few steps with her in his arms and bent down. He tugged on a rope handle and a planked door in the floor pulled open, revealing a squared-off hole. Without a word or a glance, he dropped her in, and as the door closed above her, everything went black.

Emily shot up in bed, soaked in sweat, the scream lodged in her throat. Finally, it broke through as she covered her face with her hands and grabbed at her throat. Nathan was up in an instant. He switched on the small bedside lamp and squared her shoulders. He shook her gently.

"Emily, what is it? A nightmare?"

She clutched her throat with one hand and put her other flat on his chest, feeling his racing heart.

"Can't breathe. Can't breathe," she choked.

Nathan scooped her up and moved like a jungle cat through the house with Emily in his arms. He grabbed a bottled water he had left on the kitchen island and pushed open the French doors out to the patio. Then in long strides, he carried her down to the beach. The wind was fierce and nearly blew the air into her lungs. Nathan set her down and stepped back to let her breathe. She was on her hands and knees like a marathoner collapsed at the finish line. She was torn between the need for space and the need to touch him. One look at his concern, and the battle was over. She crawled the short distance to him as he fell to his knees. Her face nearly collided with his chest as she breathed him in. He was her air. Her hands went around his bare waist, and her cheek rested on his sternum. He knew what had happened, so he simply held her and waited.

When she moved them to sit, he scooped up a towel she hadn't seen him grab from the patio and spread it on the sand. Then he sat behind her, enveloping her with arms and legs. Her claustrophobia didn't re-emerge though. With the dark ocean in front of her and his warm body behind, Emily breathed out a sigh.

"I was there, in the house." She could feel Nathan stiffen, but he didn't speak. "A man was hitting me with a belt. I had walked up some stairs, gotten about halfway, I think, when he grabbed me and pulled me back down." Emily could hear the detachment in her own voice as she recounted the dream. Nathan stroked her arms rhythmically from shoulder to elbow and back. "Another man came in. The man who called me Little One and scolded the man for beating me. He said I shouldn't have marks." Nathan continued his hypnotic soothing as she told him the rest. She took a deep breath. When she told him about the hole in the floor, he felt her body shake, muttered a curse, and wrapped his arms more tightly around her, pulling her back into his body.

"Sky and sea, everything is wide open," he soothed.

She nuzzled into his neck.

"You doing okay?"

She nodded without moving from her spot.

"Can I ask some questions?"

She nodded again, feeling his smile.

"Could you see anything else?"

"Yes. In the dream, it was a basement. Part of it was carpeted, part was wood. The stairs went up. At the top of the stairs, there was a bare bulb in the ceiling." She described the Baltimore house where they found her to a T. "Oh, I was holding a stuffed animal—a bunny maybe? That's how the FBI made the connection. Something about a neighbor seeing grown men with stuffed animals. I remember clutching it when I was being whipped."

Nathan made a pained sound, almost a growl.

"I don't remember the pain. I just remember the sound."

"That's normal. Your body doesn't remember pain."

"Wait. Something about me is normal?" She leaned back and looked into his glowing eyes.

"Nothing about you is normal, Emily Webster. Nothing ever has been. I would never insult you by calling you normal." He leaned in to kiss her and tugged her bottom lip with his teeth.

"It goes a way toward explaining why I hate the word perfect."

"That's okay; I have a long list of adjectives I can use instead."

"Do you now?"

"I do."

"And what's at the top of your list?"

"*Mine.*"

"I love you, Nathan."

He sighed.

"Emily, I need you to listen to me." She turned on the towel to face him and pushed her shins into the space under his bent legs. "I don't say those words. Ever. I have my reasons, but please understand that I just . . . can't." He scrubbed his face with his palm and seemed to rethink. "My father," he hesitated, then plowed ahead, "he had this ritual on Sunday nights when I was a child. He would call me into his study and review my behavior of the past week. Then he would strike me with a switch. The number of hits depended upon my behavior."

"Oh, Nathan."

"The bothersome part for me was after the whipping, I had to stand at the door of his office and thank him and tell him I loved him."

Emily sat still and silent and rubbed his arm as he had done for her.

"It was like vomiting nails getting those words out. In my mind, I changed the definition. To me, they mean the exact opposite of what they mean to everyone else. It doesn't mean I don't feel what you feel— exactly. In fact, even if I weren't fucked up about it, I'm not sure 'love' is the word I would use for you. I have loved in my life. I love my mom and my brothers. I loved my dog." He stopped to run the backs of his knuckles down her face. "But you . . . it's like 'love' isn't a big enough word for what I feel. Like they need to invent some new word for it because what I feel for you makes love seem very small."

She touched her lips to his. He kissed her tears. They both turned to the ocean, only the white caps visible against an endless starry night.

"I sky you, Nathan."

He smiled and met her violet gaze.

"I sky you, Emily. And I may be shit at telling you, but I'm fucking great at showing you." And with that Nathan lowered her onto the beach towel peeled her camisole over her head and her boy shorts down her legs. She wrapped her legs around his hips and urged him toward her. He groaned into her neck.

"Someone's getting the hang of it."

"I'm getting the hang of you." He pushed inside her, stretching her, filling her.

"You always did."

CHAPTER TWENTY-FIVE

The jolt of the plane hitting the runway startled Emily awake. She had been dreaming of the weekend, of their walk on the beach, their failed attempt at breakfast that morning when Nathan's sudden need to eat *her* had resulted in burnt pancakes and the relentless beeping of the smoke detector. Emily was a restless sleeper, so the fact that she had passed out against Nathan's arm spoke volumes. He kissed her the rest of the way awake, and she smiled into his mouth.

"Thank you. For the trip. For everything really."

"First of many, Emily. I want us to go every chance we get."

"Sounds perfect."

Nathan reached into his pocket and withdrew his phone. He prepared to power it on, and she did the same.

"Ready for the real world?" He gave a tired smile.

"As I'll ever be."

It was as if an alarm had sounded at a firehouse. Dozens of email alerts, texts, and missed calls. Emily quickly scrolled through for a message from her father, worried that something had happened to him. Even

Caroline had tried to call from LA Then she saw it. Caroline had sent the link in her first text. She set the phone on her lap and stared at the screen with her hands hanging limply at her sides. She was slipping away mentally as she read the *New York Post* headline:

> *Emily Webster "The Vanished Baby" Found Alive in New York City*
>
> *The child abduction that broke the heart of a nation has a surprise happy ending this week as the breathtaking child of privilege, Emily Webster, was discovered rescued and living a quiet, anonymous life working for a news blog in upper Manhattan.*

Emily just stared at the screen. She could see the words, but it was like they had no meaning, like she was reading a foreign language. It took her a moment to notice the two strong hands on her thighs, and for the echo of Nathan's voice to grow clearer.

"Emily, look at me."

Her neutral gaze met his.

"I've been outed."

"So it would seem."

"Okay, I should call my father."

"Emily."

"He has a plan in place for this."

"Emily."

"It means going dark. Again. But we knew this was a possibility."

Nathan stopped her by putting both hands on her cheeks and squaring her face to his as he kneeled before her.

"Emily, come back to me."

"I will. You know I will find a way to contact you."

"No. Now. Come back to me right now."

She stared at him for a long moment, but slowly she reengaged. She kept her eyes locked with his and braced herself as a wave of anguish washed over her. She slid to her knees in front of him and buried her head in his lap.

"I hate myself like this."

"Are you kidding? I'm crazy about you like this. Anything is preferable to that emotional disappearing act."

"Caroline calls it 'robot mode.' I can't control it."

"I know."

"What now?" she asked on a deep inhale.

"Emily, I think this is my fault."

"What do you mean?"

"When my people told me you had some red flags in your background before I knew the whole truth, I wasn't as careful with that information as I should have been. I assumed you had falsified your identity to get to me, not to protect yourself. I was selfish and careless."

She listened to him scold himself as the guilt washed over him, and she felt the strangest sense of calm. She could hear Caroline's voice: *You're Emily Webster, you always have been.* Her father's voice: *He's a good man, truth be told I trust him too.* And for quite possibly the first time, her own voice. Loud and clear.

"Nathan, stop."

"God, I'm so sorry."

"No. Don't." She grinned.

"What's got you so cheery suddenly? I can't let you disappear again, Emily. I won't."

"I won't."

"Then what?"

"I've been outed. So, I'm coming out."

"What do you mean exactly?"

"I mean if someone wants to try to take me after all this time, bring it on. I have my father and JT. I have Caroline and all of her work resources." She got nose to nose with him. "I have you. That's really all I need."

"And I have an army, literally."

"Nathan, you are an army."

"I'm ready to fight if you are."

She needed to make something perfectly clear.

"I don't mean I'm ready to face this because you have an arsenal of weapons or a team of Navy SEALS, Nathan. I'm ready to face this because you have this." She took his hand and placed it on her chest over the swell of her breast. "You have my heart. And that makes me feel like I can handle anything."

"I'm going to take such good care of it, Emily. You have no idea." He took her hand and placed it on his chest mirroring her actions. "And I expect you to do the same."

She leaned down and placed a kiss where her hand had been. She stared up into his wide, brimming eyes. They didn't need words. They were making a commitment, a silent pledge. Nathan reached up to tuck a loose strand of hair behind her ear as the pilot popped his head out of the cockpit.

"Nathan, I just got a call from the terminal building. The paps are gathered in droves. Someone tipped them off."

"Fuck," Nathan muttered. "Let me call Chat."

"He's on the tarmac. In a rented sedan. The Range Rover is out front as a decoy. He knew your phone would be flooded so he sent me the info. We've cleared an exit for you out a service road. You'll be back home before the photographers realize you've taxied."

"Thanks, Will."

"You never need to thank me."

"I know, but thanks anyway."

The pilot just shook his head good-naturedly and disappeared back into the cabin.

"Well, you're officially famous. For fifteen minutes anyway."

She laughed.

"That's fifteen minutes too long."

"Ready to make your escape?"

"Are we going to your place?"

"Emily, if I had my way, you'd never leave my side. I just don't want to scare you."

"I'm not scared." Wow. That felt good to say, and mean, for once.

"Good. Let's go. When we get home, we need to talk a bit more."

Emily was still a little gaga over his use of the word "home" when she replied, "Hmm?"

He chuckled softly. "Time for you to know my secrets as well."

CHAPTER TWENTY-SIX

Nathan dropped their bags in his front hall and went straight to the bar. He poured a hefty glug of fifty-year-old Macallan, downing what Emily estimated to be several hundred dollars' worth of scotch in one swallow. She sat on the small loveseat; Nathan remained standing.

"I could downplay your influence on my path, Emily, but once you hear the story, I think you'll see the impact you had."

She remained silent, giving him the same focus he had afforded her.

"I was *haunted* by your abduction. But I will say that somewhere in my mind I felt that maybe you were safe. Mainly it was a feeling, but it was also your dad. He may not have even known he was doing it, but something about the wording of his emails, little things that an untrained reader wouldn't see, planted a seed of hope.

"The SEALs I worked with went out on a lot of rescue missions. Other missions became rescue missions by default. We once discovered a captured Marine nobody knew was being held. Twice in Eastern Europe, we discovered groups of women preparing to be trafficked." He walked up to where she sat then and fell to his knees with such a look of despair, she had to bite back tears. "I know it made no sense, but I looked at each woman, each face with such dread, praying it wouldn't be you. Praying you had died rather than ended up like that." He dropped his face into her lap and was quiet for a long moment. When his emotions were under control he stood and began to pace.

"When I resigned my commission and came to work at K-B, I tried to push all that stuff out of my head. A fresh start, a new life. About six months in, my friend Tox, who runs my security division, came to me. His friend had been abducted from a gas station in his hometown. She'd only been missing about ten hours, and because she was twenty, the police wouldn't do much. It was a total no-brainer. We grabbed the guys from the old team who were close, five guys, three of whom work for me and two others, Finn and JJ, who both went to work for the CIA."

"The Giant works for you?"

"Hmm?"

"There was a guy who interrupted one of our interview sessions, I nicknamed The Giant. Bald. Enormous."

He chuckled. "That's Tox. You know Chat. There's also Twitch, she's the little redhead who runs cybersecurity, and Ren, who's sort of a utility player."

"Ren? Like Ren and Stimpy?"

"No, but I'll tell him you said that. He'll love it. Ren is short for Renaissance Man. The guy is like the Swiss Army knife of humans. If you ever find yourself stranded in the middle of nowhere, Ren is the guy you want."

He spoke with such fondness it warmed her heart.

"Anyway, Tox's friend. It wasn't exactly a high drama, headline news situation. Twitch hacked her cell phone records and found a frequently called number that belonged to a small-time dealer. Tox's friend, Katie, was pretty clean-cut, and I think she got in over her head with the guy.

Anyway, when she decided he was bad news, he didn't take it too well and locked her up. Just for shits and grins, we broke down his door, zip-tied him and his buddies, and walked Katie out. Talk about bringing a gun to a knife fight, these guys couldn't even speak, they were so outmanned. Tox stayed behind to drive the point home that his friend was not to be touched or even looked at again."

"Wow, that's amazing. You guys could do that as a business . . . ." The sentence died on her lips as realization dawned.

"And that's how The Perseus Project was born."

"The Perseus Project?"

"Tox, Ren, Chat, and I came up with it. It's more specialized than Bishop Security, less conventional. For people who can't go through normal channels, like the family of someone in a cult, who claims to be there voluntarily, or someone imprisoned or abducted on foreign soil where diplomacy isn't an option. Even an infant. We work with people when the victims, for whatever reason, have no voice."

"That's quite an altruistic business."

"Not a business, exactly, but a service. People who can afford to pay, do. People who can't, we cover."

"You really are a superhero."

"Nah, no superpowers, although after all this time we are really fucking good at it. I'd say it's more of a calling."

"That time I came here, and you were all banged up?"

"That was something else. Remember when I mentioned Bishop Security handles some off-the-books government work? In this case, the NSA and Homeland are tracking the possible sale of a biotoxin that was discovered in China. It's a vague and complicated story that started with a group of construction workers discovering something from a Japanese World War II research facility. I was doing what should have been simple recon. There is so much rumor and speculation about the discovery that Cerberus, our contact within the government, asked me to talk to the men who found the item. See if we could learn any actual facts. It was an uneventful and unproductive trip until someone chased me down and ran me off the road. The construction workers were being watched, but the men who came after me weren't expecting me to be armed and when I returned fire, they drove off. When I got back, I was banged up, but mostly just pissed I hadn't gotten any usable intel."

Emily couldn't help but notice Nathan was telling that story like he was talking about a ski weekend in Aspen.

"You love it."

"I do. All that daredevil cover shit I do to keep prying eyes off my real business? It's only partly for show. I love that stuff."

"Adrenaline junkie."

"Nah, I love it, but I could live without it. I'm an Emily junkie. Totally and completely addicted."

He stole her breath. "Come get your fix then."

"God, I love your mouth."

"That's good because there are some things I want to try that involve my mouth."

"Is that so?"

"Uh-huh."

"Happy to oblige. We can start with your experiment and move on to mine."

"Yours?"

"Gorgeous Emily, I have a few tricks up my sleeve. I want to take control. You're inexperienced, but this isn't about that. Surrendering sexually is something so liberating. For someone like you who has carried such a huge emotional burden, the freedom will be . . . unimaginable."

He kissed her senseless and only a glimpse at a scar near his hairline reminded her of their talk.

"Did we finish our conversation? About your secret life?"

He slipped his hand under her shirt and cupped her breast. "For now."

Nathan closed the door to the bedroom with a gentle snick. Emily started to pull on the button of her jeans but stopped and let her hands drop. She fiddled with the hem of her shirt, shifting on her feet.

"Emily, stop." She looked at him, desperate for some guidance.

"This isn't some dungeon. I'm not Sir. You're not Pet. You're Emily. I'm Nathan. This is about turning off your brain, letting go of everything outside of this room, outside of this." He gestured back and forth between them. "Let me take charge."

She sighed out a relieved breath and nodded. Nathan reached behind him, grabbed his Henley by the neck and pulled it over his head. His scars only enhanced his rugged beauty. His chest wasn't bodybuilder bulky, just muscular and defined, the inspiration for a sculpture. Emily didn't think or worry. She simply walked over to him, sank to her knees and unlatched his belt. Nathan pulled it through the loops and dropped it to the floor while she popped the buttons on his fly. He was already so hard, the crown of his cock was escaping out the waistband of his boxer briefs. She leaned forward and kissed the tip, tasted the salty drop beaded there. His answering groan was all the encouragement she needed. She pulled the gray cotton down his legs and took him into her mouth.

Whoa.

He was so big and soft and hard. She pulled him in slowly, as far as she could take him. Nathan placed gentle hands on either side of her face and guided her movements. Honestly, in that moment, if someone had asked her those questions they ask head injury patients—who's the president, what year is it, what state are we in—she couldn't have answered a single one. There was only Emily, in that moment, giving the man she loved her complete surrender. The power of her submission was heady—the more she let go, the more she owned him. She was molten from the intensity of it. The intimacy of the exchange overwhelming. She pulled him deeper, the tremble in his voice and the firming of his grip egging her on.

"Emily, Christ, *Emily.*"

He came so hard she felt him hit the back of her throat. She was so wet she was soaking her jeans. Nathan bent forward and kissed the top of her head, hauled her up and dropped her on the bed. Her jeans hit the floor with a *thwap.* Nathan stared down at her like every prayer he'd ever had had finally been answered; and she guessed, in a way, that was true.

"This body . . . ."

She tensed, fighting the residue of shallow appreciation.

"Emily, I love this body." He kissed her belly. "I love it because it's your body. It could be fat or thin or scarred," he placed his hands on either side of her waist, "or full and round, and I would love it just the same. Maybe more. Now turn off that brain and let me explore this amazing body. Amazing because it's your body."

"It's your body," she offered.

The heat flared in his eyes. "Bloody hell, I need to fuck you." In one swift motion, he nudged her thighs apart with his knees, lifted her hips, and pushed inside in one powerful thrust. It was the roughest he'd been, and she loved it. His eyes searched her glazed, lusty face, and she spread her legs further, giving him the green light in the best way she knew how. Nathan pounded into her, and he didn't mistake her cries, as she hurdled toward a shattering climax, as anything other than what they were. Ecstasy.

Later that night, Emily and Nathan sat on the balcony eating a chilled orzo primavera Nathan's housekeeper had left for him. She pushed a lima bean aside with her fork and stabbed a strip of bell pepper.

"I want to meet with your father. Make sure we're all on the same page."

"Would lunch at my apartment tomorrow work? We can have privacy that way."

Nathan nodded his agreement and resumed his pensive chewing.

"Nathan? Do you know who outed me?"

"I have my suspicions, yes."

She waited, holding her fork with an asparagus tip pierced on the tines.

"That day, our birthday, I tore open the watch, and it all came crashing back to me. Alex was standing in the doorway of my office, and I said *she's Emily Webster*. There may have been some choice profanity peppered in." He chuckled. "I ignored every security protocol and tore out of the office. Left the door open, my computer unlocked . . . ."

"She seemed very territorial about you."

"I took advantage of her attraction. I never encouraged her, but I used her as my safety date in a lot of situations." He tilted his head toward her, reminding Emily of their first meeting in his office when he had 911-ed Alex. "I knew she had ideas. I shouldn't have encouraged her."

"You can't possibly blame yourself for her pettiness and manipulations."

"I don't, but I blame myself for my carelessness with your security. All the more reason to meet with your father. I will have a fucking army guarding you if that's what it takes."

"Oh, good. That's my dream," she deadpanned.

Nathan chuckled. "Just until we're sure you're safe, Emily. Then it's just you and me."

"Much better."

The week flew by. After breakfast at Nathan's favorite greasy spoon on Sixth Avenue on Friday, they planned to walk the few remaining blocks to Knightsgrove-Bishop for a meeting with his team. Then, JT would drive Emily to *The Sentry* office and she, Nathan, and her father would convene at her apartment in SoHo for lunch.

"I just need to . . . ." Emily poked her thumb over her shoulder to indicate JT. Nathan nodded in JT's direction.

"I made him, you know. That day at the street fair."

"I know. I expected nothing less. Be right back."

Nathan held open the door of the diner for her, and they stepped out into the July Manhattan heat. He slipped his arm around her waist and kissed her until her knees went weak. Then she wobbled over to JT and explained that she was in good hands, and he could pick her up at K-B in an hour. The Suburban pulled away and she stood on the sidewalk and just stared back at Nathan. They looked like two love-struck idiots. Nathan rubbed his eyes with the heels of his hands and grinned at her like a teenager about to get laid—well, like a twenty-eight, no, twenty-nine-year-old as of last week about to get laid. She lifted her hand and smiled a smile of complete happiness as she took a step toward him. Then she heard the screech of tires and the nauseatingly familiar slide of a heavy metal door as she was pulled backward. The last thing she saw before she felt the fabric slide over her face and the needle pierce her skin was Nathan running toward her, his beautiful eyes filled with determination and terror.

CHAPTER TWENTY-SEVEN

Twitch sat at a bank of computers typing on a laptop like the hounds of hell were in pursuit. Nathan paced. Ren sat eating macadamia nuts and reading a mangled copy of *The World According to Garp*. Tox threw the door open with his butt, his hands balancing a cardboard tray of coffees and a bag of fast food burgers.

"What've we got?" Tox took a healthy slurp of his drink.

Twitch pushed the rolling chair back from the monitors and, using a remote pointer, activated the large screen on the wall.

"She had a tracker implant until about seventeen minutes ago. They were still moving when I lost the signal. Sorry, North."

"Last location?"

"West Side Highway and 96th. Based on the speed of the van, best guess is Henry Hudson Parkway out of the city. Chat's over at the precinct trying to get a look at the traffic cam footage. *Legally*," Twitch amended after Nathan quirked a brow.

"Well, they weren't planning on going far in that junker of a van. Westchester? Connecticut?" Tox started in on another burger.

"Connecticut plates on the van were stolen, *but,* in what could be a related story, an observant driver in Connecticut noticed the plates on her minivan had been changed out in a mall parking lot and reported it to the local PD in Waterbury."

Nathan crossed to another screen displaying a map that marked the van's known route. He touched the screen marking Waterbury, Connecticut, then stepped back to survey the area with a population of nearly fifteen million people. Ren looked up from his novel.

"The van lost a strip of tire tread as it sped away. A soil sample could give some indication of where the van has been."

Nathan nodded. "They bagged it. I'll confirm they're running an analysis."

A security monitor drew Twitch's eye. "We have a visitor."

"That's Emily's dad. I'll bring him up. If we can't chase these assholes, maybe we can get ahead of them, figure out what the fuck is going on."

Ren put down his book and stood. "Good thought, North. Because this is not a kidnapping. This is a vendetta."

CHAPTER TWENTY-EIGHT

Emily slowly came to in a dimly lit room and immediately began a checklist of her surroundings and an assessment of her body. The tranquilizer was fogging her brain and nauseating her, but Emily knew this moment of unobserved assessment was crucial. Once anyone noticed she was conscious, she would be closely watched. She was lying on a hospital bed, no, more like a labor and delivery bed with side guardrails and stirrups retracted to the sides. The bed was made with scratchy sheets, and she was naked beneath what felt like a paper gown. Her arms were tethered by wide leather restraints like she imagined doctors used to contain violent criminals. Her legs were free, thank God. There was a large window open a crack; her captors had confidence in her bindings. The leather strap was on its tightest fitting but still, her small wrist could rotate. Clearly, these cuffs could be used to confine a man twice her size.

Physically, other than the lingering effects of the tranquilizer, she was unharmed. She was connected to an IV, either keeping her sedated or providing fluids. Emily assumed the latter as her head seemed to be clearing. Her upper arm was bandaged, as was the back of her shoulder, where they, no doubt, had removed the tracking chip she and her father had implanted for just such an occasion.

The darkening sky outside looked to be out of a fairy tale; the rolling hills and leafy trees painted an idyllic scene. Where the fuck was she?

The smell of the ocean was faint but clear. That narrowed it down but not by much. Then she saw it. Well, she heard it first. *Tap tap tap.* A woodpecker was knocking away on a hollow branch of a dead tree. And not just any woodpecker, a red-headed woodpecker. Their gardener in Connecticut, Rodrigo, knew everything there was to know about birds. That's what it felt like to a seven-year-old at any rate. Emily would sit in the yard while he trimmed hedges and pointed out species of interest. She was sure in his native Colombia he saw all kinds of colorful birds, but he seemed to enjoy the avian life of Greenwich. *Look, niña, on the fence. That little fellow only lives around this area. He wears a red cap and a black coat, but he doesn't travel.* Emily had discovered later that year, on a second-grade field trip to a nearby bird sanctuary, that red-headed woodpeckers were endangered in Connecticut due to deforestation and farming decline, but the sanctuary had been committed to restoring the population and as a result, the little birds were thriving in the local area. Her assessment fell more into the "best guess" than the "pinpoint accuracy" category, but she had to work with what she had.

She assembled the puzzle pieces. If she was in Connecticut, near the ocean, in a secluded building on a large parcel of land, there were limited possibilities. Waterfront property from Florida to Maine was in high demand. She was either in an extremely isolated private home or some sort of country inn or resort or . . . . Something was itching the back of her brain. Then she recalled. Her first assignment for Farrell was researching fraud at rehab centers. A Pennsylvania family had come forward claiming their son had been held for months against his will. After voluntarily committing himself for prescription drug addiction, the young man was confined to the facility, Pinehurst, for nearly a year until his health insurance, and the family's nest egg, ran out. Farrell's conspiracy brain went haywire as he imagined sending her in undercover as a patient, like Joe Pulitzer sending Nelly Bly to uncover abuse in nineteenth-century asylums. In the months since the story broke, the facility had closed and had been put up for sale. Emily chuckled in her drug daze, wondering if they listed it as an evil lair.

The small surveillance camera picked up her return to consciousness, and after several minutes the heavy door pushed open. A serious man in a white lab coat walked slowly in the door looking at a tablet. He seemed kind, with ruddy cheeks and a bald head. His wedding ring was burnished and bore the telltale scratches of years of wear. She noticed that the door didn't shut all the way; the latch stuck on the door jam and the guard had to give it a final shove to secure it. The man, she assumed a doctor, rubbed his eyes with his free hand. Without comment, he examined the two bandaged wounds and probed the mild swelling around her knee. He then removed a large syringe and a vial from a tray in the corner.

"Gentlemen, wait outside."

One of the three guards hesitated, but the men shuffled out. This time when the door stalled before clicking shut, nobody corrected it. The doctor seated himself on the rolling stool at her side. He spoke slowly, softly as he prepared the vaccine.

"Yellow fever." He flicked the barrel of the syringe. "I gather you're taking a trip very soon."

Not good.

"There is video and audio in here. Don't nod or acknowledge me in any way. The guards have fifteen minutes for lunch at noon." He tipped his wrist, showing Emily the face of his watch: 11:43. "They threatened my family, but this . . . it's too much." He squeezed his eyes shut and stood to move to her side. He checked the IV in her arm and deftly loosened the restraint one notch using one hand while adjusting the drip with the other. "There are five guards here now. You can try to run if your head clears. It's your only chance." He straightened and spoke clearly as he administered the injection.

"You will have some injection site pain and perhaps some drowsiness. Other than that, you're in excellent health."

"Where am I?"

"I can only answer medical questions. Besides, it's my understanding you will be leaving soon. No time to visit the marina." He never looked up as he changed the bag of IV fluids.

He used a different syringe to inject something into the IV line. "I'm administering a sedative." He gave an imperceptible shake of his head. "You just relax."

He moved to the door and spoke to the men as he held it open. "Lunch should be here." He spoke for her to hear. "One floor down in the main floor dining room."

I'm on the second floor.

"She'll be out for a couple of hours." He ushered the men to proceed down the hall in front of him, then followed them without a look back.

Emily slipped out of the restraints and a moment later was standing on wobbly legs at the unlatched door, naked but for the paper gown. Right. Time to go. She moved down the hall in the opposite direction of the main stairs. If the guards were watching the video feed intently, she had maybe sixty seconds. If they were distracted or half watching, maybe another thirty. She whisked by an abandoned nurses' station and clipped an old, forgotten hoodie from a coat rack by the door. Ten seconds later she was standing in the ground floor back stairwell, plotting her next move. Boots hit the ground in the hallway, and she knew she had been found out. She peeked out the door and scooted into an empty industrial kitchen. Outside, there were two cars parked in the large rear-drive: a Prius with a "Zippy Maids" logo on the passenger door and a landscaping pickup towing a mower—the doctor must have already made a quick exit. This was the psychology of pursuit; where was the last place anyone would look? She pushed out the kitchen exit and moved. Just beyond the landscaping truck was a black Escalade with tinted windows. Bad guy lair? Check. Bad guy car? Check.

The four maids were at the back of the Prius, and the landscapers tossed their cigarettes to help the ladies load their supplies. Emily skirted past them. If they saw her, they pretended not to—much better for their longevity not to notice such things—and, hidden by the front of the pickup, she lifted the tailgate of the Escalade a scant ten inches and slipped inside. She pulled a black duffle over her body, assuming these guys wouldn't need to break out the tactical gear for one tiny woman. She heard the landscaping truck pull past and she assumed the Prius followed quietly behind. She just needed one of them to make it off the property so the guards would use the Escalade to follow. If the guards stopped and searched the Prius and the pickup on the property, the Escalade would stay put while they covered the rest of the grounds on foot. She closed her eyes and calmed her breathing. The Prius rolled by, the tires crunching gravel the only sound. Then came the landscaping truck, roaring its need for a new muffler. Then came the boots. All four doors of the Escalade flew open and the car lurched forward before three of them had shut. They caught the truck at the gate. *These guys think they're smart. They think a woman terrified and fleeing wouldn't race to a bunch of tatted-up yard men; she'd run to the maids.* So, after a cursory glance at the truck, the Escalade sped forward, spewing gravel. The guy riding shotgun instructed the driver, "To the right. Turning onto Front." Front Street. She knew the street. They were near where Emily grew up and her Pinehurst Hospital guess was spot on. The driver honked the horn, probably assuming the maids either didn't know they had a passenger or that the passenger they did have was a problem they would gladly surrender. They slowed and pulled over.

Emily rolled to the rear of the SUV. This was the tricky part. She waited for the noise of the passenger doors opening to mask the sound and pressed the button to release the tailgate latch. She rolled to the ground landing on her hands and knees. Fortunately, the hoodie was a men's XL and covered her bare butt. She gave the tailgate a gentle push and it retracted and shut almost silently. She risked a glance. One of the guards was using a translation app on his phone to instruct the women from the maid service to pop the trunk. The three other guards stood at the SUV with their backs to Emily.

"Hey, what are you doing?"

Emily froze and peered slowly toward the sidewalk. A man walking a French bulldog was marching in their direction. Emily braced herself as the man walked past, his attention focused on the paramilitary men looming over the frightened women.

"You guys cops?"

One of the men, sensing this nosy neighbor wasn't going to go away, came up with a plausible response. A plausible, *stupid* response. "Immigration." Immediately there was a commotion. One of the maids started yelling at the guard in Spanish. Another simply hurried off. The two women in the backseat were also shouting. French bulldog man simply backed away and continued on his walk. *Thank you, concerned citizen.* Nothing like a good distraction when you need it.

They were at a T intersection marked by stop signs. Two twenty-something girls in a BMW convertible pulled up alongside. They didn't notice Emily and weren't a good bet for a rescue. Girls her age rarely picked up strangers. The car behind them was a catering van. Perfect. She didn't need a ride. She needed a shield. As the van slowed, she skirted around the rear and headed toward the beach with the broad side of the van obscuring her from the view of the men still trying to get the trunk of the Prius open. This wasn't New York, where a woman walking around nude but for a papery hospital gown and a threadbare hoodie would barely raise an eyebrow. This was Connecticut, where the sight evoked images of a horror movie psycho on a suburban murder spree. The marina had two things Emily needed: abandoned clothing and an escape route.

It took less than a minute for her to grab some cutoffs and a pair of flip flops from a beach towel. With the old hoodie from the hospital, she didn't look too out of place. Time for phase two. At the edge of the parking lot, three guys were loading coolers and gear into the back of a 4Runner with New York plates. The tallest of the three was wearing an NYU T-shirt. Bingo. She looked a little psycho and a little drugged-up, so she went with it.

"Oh my God, are you guys heading into the city?" The tall one dismissed her but once the other two got a good look, they paused to hear her out.

"I was dating my TA and he brought me to the beach for the day. I got out of the car right when he saw his wife pull up with their kids. He peeled out and left me in the fucking parking lot."

"You're shitting me."

"I need to get back to the city so I can, you know, put orange dye in his showerhead or key his car or whatever psycho revenge plot I can come up with." The tall guy got on board.

"Allow us to be of service. I'm Marcus. That's Dwight and Brent."

"I'm Holly. Thanks so much. Shit. He drove off with my purse, so I can't even chip in for gas."

"Don't worry about it. That guy's an asshole."

"Thanks."

They piled in the 4Runner, Emily in the back with the ginger, Dwight. Just as they reached the mouth of the parking lot, she spotted the Escalade slowly inching down the road. She bent all the way forward and pretended to extract a pebble from between her toes. When she sat up, a solid minute later, Dwight was staring curiously at the hospital gown peeking out from between the hoodie and the cutoffs. So, she distracted him the easiest way she knew how. She started brushing off her thighs. "That asshole sprayed gravel and dirt all over me when he peeled out." When he finally looked up, Dwight blushed red as a beet and asked, "So, Holly, what do you do for fun in the city?"

CHAPTER TWENTY-NINE

Dario Sava thought of the next thing on his to-do list and sighed. It was his least favorite room in the house, but different aspects of his business had different location requirements. His meetings with his lawyers, for instance, required a conference room. Merchandise transactions needed a warehouse. Dealing with disloyal employees necessitated a soundproof room.

Dario left the serenity of his terrace, walked across gleaming teak floors, and glanced out French doors with billowing sheer curtains. He glimpsed the pristine pool that sat unused and the orchards beyond. He paused briefly in the main room, regarding his prized Goya, *Milkmaid at Eveningtime*. The woman in the painting reminded him so much of his Tala. He sighed wistfully and proceeded to the back of the house. He navigated the maze of halls to the remote wing. If Tala were still alive, he would handle this business at another location, but that was not the case, and Dario found that increasingly, the violent and distasteful aspects of his profession bled into the beauty and rewards. So be it. The profits and the costs of doing business were inextricably linked.

At the far end of the hall, he pushed open a heavy fire door to find his men standing dutifully in the unfurnished cinderblock room, awaiting his arrival. The man strung up above a drain in the center of the space cried quietly. Dario approached him and the man looked up.

"El Callado."

"You told someone my business." Dario's Spanish was so quiet, only the accused could hear him.

"No. Never. He's just my cousin. He wants a job with you. We were playing cards. I didn't tell him any details. I would never betray you, senōr."

Dario sighed. The explanation did seem reasonable. This man, Juan-Pablo, had worked for him for nearly a year—a lifetime in this business. Nonetheless.

"Rest assured, I will not leave your children fatherless. Your wife without a husband."

"Thank you. Thank you, El Callado."

"I will kill them, too." And with that Dario slit the man's throat with a single stroke. He turned to his men. "Now see if this cousin of his still wants a job. There is an opening."

As Dario was issuing further instructions while the dying man squirmed out his last moments, an urgent knock on the door interrupted him. A capable, broad-shouldered soldier opened the door but the nervous plea in his eyes as he watched Juan-Pablo dangle made a clear point: *don't shoot the messenger.*

"The girl escaped."

Dario calmly cleaned his blade on Juan-Pablo's shirt and replaced the knife in its sheath. He did not speak.

"They are tracking her and will inform us when the matter is resolved."

"The man whose services I engaged. Tell him I'm coming to fetch her myself. Perhaps his men will be able to handle the task without additional logistics to consider."

"Shall I inform Rigo?"

"No. Rigo is occupied. That is all." The man, relieved by his dismissal, already had his phone in hand as he turned to the door. The other men in the group shuffled toward the exit. The olive-skinned hulk the men all called El Roca, "the boulder," was last in line.

"Miguel." Dario stopped him.

"Si, El Callado?"

Dario stepped away from the dangling corpse, presumably because the blood, now trickling to the floor, was splattering his shoes.

"Come with me."

"Yes, sir."

Miguel Ramirez, whose real name was Camilo Canto, kept his face visibly blank and followed Dario back into the main part of the house, praying silently that the reason he was following his boss into another wing of his estate wasn't that the kill room was already occupied.

CHAPTER THIRTY

Emily walked calmly but with purpose as she maneuvered through the crowded streets. If she weren't terrified, she would have laughed at the fact that no one gave her hospital gown/hoodie/cutoffs ensemble a second look. She needed a phone, but she had no money and she needed to be extremely cautious with tech. The first order of business was clothes. The guys had dropped her near NYU, and she had hurried away after declining Dwight's request for her number. Now in the Meatpacking District just east of her neighborhood, she rounded a corner and saw the answer to her prayers.

Gansevoort Yoga, Caroline's yoga studio. Her feet were bleeding onto the flip flops from the run to the marina, and she was wearing a paper gown and a stained Mets hoodie, so she stuck her nose in the air and waltzed by the receptionist like she didn't exist. The young woman at the desk didn't spare Emily a glance.

She located Caroline's locker and entered her combination—she used her birthday for everything from her ATM PIN to her Amazon password—and jackpot: shoes and socks and a Lululemon outfit still in the bag. Emily thanked the stars for her sweet, sweet, shopaholic friend. She used the cosmetics and shower supplies set out for members and changed into the leggings, sneakers, and lavender tank. Time to bolt. She glanced around the corner and scanned the reception area. It was empty except for a guy in a suit chatting with the receptionist.

She would have thought nothing of it, if not for two things: every few seconds he spared a glance toward the hallway, and when he straightened, there was an unmistakable bulge under his suit jacket. Emily was forced to acknowledge the fact that they hadn't simply removed her tracker; they had replaced it. She retreated into the locker room and gingerly peeled back the adhesive bandage on her shoulder, relieved to see the unmistakable grid of a tracker was embedded in the latex strip and not reinserted into the wound. She removed the bandage then stuck it on the bottom of the tote bag of a woman just finishing a shower. Then Emily stepped out into the hall. She had something to do while she waited.

There was a fire exit at the end of the hall with a probably non-functioning alarm and roof access. There was also a huge tip-out window typical of these old converted factories. She walked casually to the end of the hall and pushed the two-ton window open. The back alley looked clear, and there was a thick pipe running down the side of the building that was within reach. Perfect. She hurried back to the locker room, fished the rumpled gown out of the trash and tore a small piece from the sleeve. Returning to the window she leaned over to the pipe and caught the paper fabric on an exposed bolt. She left the window ajar and walked back to the locker room. Next, she sought out the kindest-looking woman in the room. Bingo. A bubbly redhead was smiling as an older woman swiped through pictures of her grandchild on her phone.

"Excuse me. I'm sorry to interrupt, but I'm a pediatrician and my phone just died. Can I borrow yours to quickly check in with my office?"

The redhead didn't blink. She smiled and handed off her phone, then returned to the other woman's grandchild slideshow. Emily needed to get in touch with Nathan without tipping anyone off. She called the K-B main number and requested her party. Three rings later, she answered with a crisp, "Alex Peters."

"Alex, it's Emily Webster."

"I'm sorry, who?"

"Emma Porter?"

"What can I do for you, Emily?"

"I need you to give a message to Nathan."

"Yeah, I'm going to have to decline."

"This is life or death, Alex. Please."

"Unfortunately, I have to go. I'm late for a meeting."

Emily played the only card she had.

"Look, I know it was you who outed me to the press, and I can prove it." She was bluffing, but it was a good bet. "The very least Nathan will do is ruin you professionally. Do this for me, and I will owe you." After a pregnant pause and an audible sigh, she spoke.

"What's the message?"

"Tell him Emily said to meet her at the location of the first rescue at midnight tonight."

"Fine."

"Repeat it."

"Meet you at midnight at the first rescue. Is that a new club or something?"

"Or something."

"Whatever."

"Do it now Alex. Please. It's important."

"I'll do it as soon as I hang up on you."

And with that, the line went dead.

Assuming Alex did what she was asked, Nathan would get the message and meet her at The Jane Hotel where he had saved her two years ago. Emily returned the phone and was revisiting her mental checklist when the woman with the tracker-attached tote bag rushed by and exited through the back—the back door was something of a chic exit celebrities used to avoid attention, and regular members had taken to using it to look like celebrities. Emily waited five minutes, then opened the door to the locker room and walked right out the front door. The group of women who passed her at the entrance no doubt assumed her sweaty brow and messy hair were the result of a strenuous Bikram class. Warrior pose, indeed.

"The trackers aren't broken. The one in her shoe is currently heading down I-95 toward Miami. The one in her purse is in an alley in midtown. The one implanted in her shoulder stopped sending. Last ping was on the Upper West Side. After that, dead."

His phone chirped and he checked the screen. Alex. He silenced the call and continued peering over Twitch's shoulder at the three pulsing dots on the monitor. The phone squawked again.

"Alex, I can't talk right now.

"Emily Webster called me."

"When?"

"Just now."

Nathan put the phone on speaker and signaled for the team to circle.

"Emily called you?"

"She didn't think Big Brother would be watching me."

"Smart girl," Tox said around a bite of turkey club.

Alex conveyed the message and signed off.

"Holy shit. She busted out."

"That's . . . impressive." Ren chuckled in disbelief.

"The first rescue?" Tox asked, running a big hand over scruff that was about to cross into beard territory.

"The Jane Hotel. Two years ago, I helped her when some asshole slipped something in her drink. That's what she means."

"Marry that girl," Twitch said without humor.

"That's the plan."

"Okay." Ren smacked his hands together. "Let's get the girl and save the day."

Twitch clicked away on the keyboard. "We have to assume they can track her to The Jane. Odds are, whoever wants her is using hired guns. If he's foreign he'd need locals, and if he's local, he won't want his own security getting pinched."

"That's an advantage," Nathan nodded, "no loyalty."

"Although a big enough paycheck buys a lot of loyalty."

"Not the die-for-your-cause kind."

"True."

"I'm calling Harris."

"You sure?"

"I want to send a message. Whoever this guy is, he's not going after a little girl anymore."

"Our back-up plan needs a back-up plan?"

"Move the pieces around the chessboard, Twitch. Let's look at every scenario."

"On it. The Bishop will protect the queen."

Nathan threw a balled-up piece of paper at the back of Twitch's head and they got to work.

Counterintuitively, the hotel was quiet on a Saturday night. Summer weekends in the city were subdued, as most of the elite took their parties to the Hamptons. Emily looked out-of-place in her now grimy workout ensemble, but it was a hotel after all. People showed up in all manner of dress. The bitchy queen behind the desk, wearing a name tag that read 'David' and a fake smile, gave her an unabashed sweep with his disapproving glance and arched a brow. On any other day, Emily could have had this guy with his tail between his legs, but she was out of gas. She cleared her throat. "I . . . um, I need to get to the conference rooms." It never even occurred to her that she would have trouble getting past a fucking doorman.

"I see. And what sort of *conference* were you planning on attending?"

It was then she felt a warm palm on the small of her back. "David, she's with me."

Nathan had booked the hotel's most elaborate suite. He didn't keep a room here, like at The Gotham and one or two other boutique hotels around the city, but they knew who he was and the discretion he demanded. Everybody did.

David had the good grace to look thoroughly chastened as he stood. "Of course, Mr. Bishop. Can I send anything up?" Nathan's gaze never wavered from the now obsequious receptionist, but his hand trembled against Emily's back. "Two cheeseburgers, fries, milkshakes. From Shake Shack. Is the bar stocked?"

"Yes, sir, fully."

"Good. That's all."

Nathan strolled down the hall with Emily in tow as if this were just another night, but his radar was up. The small, nearly undetectable, earpiece was the only indication that things weren't as they seemed. Nathan walked slowly but with purpose toward the elevator and swiped his card for penthouse access. The gleaming brass doors swished open, and they walked inside like any chic Manhattan couple heading to their luxury accommodations after a grueling day of shopping and pedicures—minus the dirty clothes, bleeding feet, and stitches. Nathan seemed to need a moment to compose himself; his jaw was locked, and his hands were trembling. He glanced at the security camera in the ceiling and clocked the floor numbers as they lit and extinguished. He probably hated the kill box of an elevator as much as she did. At the top floor, they moved quickly down the hall.

"Nathan."

"In a moment. Let's get you secure."

"I found their tracker. I removed it."

"You did?"

"At Caroline's yoga studio. I sent it off with another member. I imagine it's at a West Village townhouse by now."

He shot her a look of pure lust.

"*That* turns you on?"

"Add it to an ever-growing list."

At the far end of the hall, a service elevator sounded its arrival. Nathan didn't tense so she didn't either. The doors groaned apart and two suited men stepped out. Nathan extended his hand.

"Harris, good to see you, man. Thanks for this." The whiskey-eyed man's lips quirked.

"Hey, I'll babysit you in a penthouse any day, North. Beats the hell out of Chiang Mai."

Nathan grunted in agreement and extended his hand to the smaller, at six feet, Middle Eastern man.

"Assam, good to see you."

"Just once could you give me a call when you're trolling for trim at a club? Does it always have to be this shit?" Assam gave him a toothpaste commercial smile.

Nathan shifted awkwardly, and Emily stuck her head out from behind him. "He's done trolling for the night."

"Oh shit . . . shoot. Sorry." Assam extended his hand while Harris chuckled and added, "Fifteen languages and six dialects, and he still puts his foot in it. You must be Emily. I'm Harris Mann. And this smooth talker is Assam Brudi."

"Yes, Emily. Hi."

"Also, the reason my trolling days are over."

Assam gripped her hand with both of his. "I can see why."

CHAPTER THIRTY-ONE

Twitch and the guys leapt to their feet, greeting Emily and nodding their admiration.

"Hooyah! Emily. It's good to see you safe." Tox turned to Nathan. "Her dad's been looped in. He's headed down shortly."

Harris headed straight for the food. "Emily, coffee? Nosh?"

Nathan turned his back to the group greeting them and headed for the nearest guest room with Emily in tow. "Go get yourselves some dinner."

Tox eyed the side table, piled high with sandwiches and snacks. Twitch jerked her head towards the door. Harris grabbed two go-cups of coffee, handed one to Assam, and the four of them headed out.

Nathan had no sooner kicked the door shut with his foot than he took Emily's face gently between his rough palms and kissed her like she was the air he needed to breathe. He led her into the small but elegantly appointed hotel bathroom, started the shower, and proceeded to peel her out of the yoga clothes. Emily went to work on his belt. In record time, they were entwined under the steady flow of water. Emily kissed his neck, bit his shoulder, and ground against him with an urgency that expressed her fear and vulnerability more clearly than words ever could.

"The foreplay will have to wait. I need you inside me now." She beat him to the punch with her words.

"You read my mind."

With that, Nathan hoisted her up as she wrapped her legs around his waist and plunged into her. He was moving harder than he meant to, faster than he meant to, but the primal need to mate had taken over. Thrust and retreat, over and over, as he held her ass in both hands and attacked her breasts with his mouth. Emily tightened around him and came with an explosive cry. He joined her a stroke later, spilled into her in what felt like an endless stream. They stood silently for a moment, still connected, the water beating down.

"You okay?"

"Never better." She smiled against his lips.

Nathan set her on her jellied legs and reached for the shampoo. He skimmed his hands down her arms and sides, stopping at the bandage on her arm.

"They removed a small tracker implant in my shoulder. The cut on my arm must have been an injury they stitched. My dad? Have you talked to him?"

"He's on his way."

"Good."

They finished the shower and entered the bedroom in thick white hotel robes. Nathan pulled Emily onto the bed and held her against his chest.

"Talk to me."

"I'm fine. That was nothing. My trainer in Georgia once hogtied me in a tree and left me to escape it. Strapped in a hospital bed is child's play."

Nathan didn't speak. He just waited calmly. Emily nuzzled Nathan's breastbone. They both let out a long-pained sigh, and Nathan wrapped her more tightly in his arms. Emily broke the silence.

"It's harder when you love someone. They didn't just take me; they took me *from you*. Emotion steals focus, but it was impossible to put all that stuff in a box in my mind and just do what I was trained to do."

"Unpack that box, Em. You've spent too long stuffing down your feelings. Emotions can cloud your judgment, but they can also drive you, give you strength."

"I was scared. I just wanted to get to you."

"I was on my way. You beat me to the punch."

She looked up at him with a grin, "Your girlfriend is a ninja."

"That may be the hottest thing I've ever heard."

After another, slower round of lovemaking, he stood and pulled Emily with him. "Come on. I've got some sweats in the closet. After we debrief, I plan on keeping you safe and sound at home with nothing but food and showers and sex and sleep for the next week."

Emily's eyes widened. "That's exactly what I imagined when I was running away. Only you were in a superhero costume."

"Please tell me it was combat stuff."

"Nope—tights, cape, the whole deal."

"Well, I needed to calm my hard-on down. That did it."

"You won't wear a spandex Captain America onesie for me?"

"Emily, for you I would wear nothing but a fig leaf and swing from a vine."

"Mmm."

"And there goes my hard-on again. Come on. Get changed so we can get back to the good stuff."

CHAPTER THIRTY-TWO

Two weeks passed filled with dead ends and misinformation. Emily had described in detail every moment of the abduction—the men in the van, the facility, the guards, the doctor. She had also told them everything she could recall of her childhood kidnapping—the trip to the ice cream shop, the man with the mermaid tattoos who had taken her from the nanny, the house in Baltimore, the evil man with the hand tattoo and the smooth voice. The facility where Emily had recently been held had been vacated. The new landscaping crew that had been hired by the property management company knew nothing. The one maid they had managed to track down was just as helpful. The maids assumed the men were the new owners, and they wanted to keep the easy job, so they cleaned quickly and thoroughly and didn't ask questions. There were hundreds of scattered fingerprints; if any of them belonged to the perps, it would take months to sort them.

Nathan was attached to Emily like a burr. While that was great in the bedroom—and the kitchen and the dining room, and on the balcony and in the shower, and on the desk in Nathan's office, and once in Central Park—it was agitating in her daily life. While pulling away from him made her feel like a piece of iron leaving a magnetic field, she was a woman used to being alone. Nathan knew that he couldn't be by her side every moment of the day, and she was oddly thankful for the work crisis that divided his attention.

Emily had also gotten to know the people in Nathan's life. Alex had been transferred, thankfully. Her call to Nathan had spared her from a worse fate. Chat was her favorite, although the guy almost never spoke. Emily had immediately picked up on an intuition that bordered on psychic. She enjoyed wheedling him into reluctant conversations. If it was possible, Tox was even harder to talk to, not because he was reticent, but because he was always eating. His six-foot, five-inch, 280-pound frame needed constant refueling. And when he wasn't eating, he was drinking, or fucking. Emily wondered if he slept. The dark circles under his eyes and the haunted look hidden behind a carefree mask gave her the answer.

Twitch, on the other hand, was like a fairy. She seemed so comfortable in her own skin and genuinely happy. She hunted down the worst kinds of people and saw so much horror, yet she had an unquenchable optimism that came with knowing she was doing her part. As far as Emily could see, nothing ruffled her. Ren was the most puzzling of the group. He really did seem to know everything about everything. He'd start off an explanation with a qualifier like, "Well, cuneiform isn't my area of expertise but . . ." or "I'm not well versed in neuroscience but . . ." then proceed to deliver a professorial-level response to whatever question had been posed. Emily was vexed by the breadth of his knowledge, always trying to stump him with random trivia, from the B-side of rock albums to obscure world geography. Ren always seemed to have the answer. Emily loved her new life so far. She was getting to know people, a novel concept in her world, and she had the very good fortune to be surrounded by some very interesting friends.

Caroline's trip to LA had been extended and she was uncharacteristically vague as to the reason. Emily didn't look a gift horse in the mouth, though, and simply enjoyed her infrequent alone time in the apartment. Her state-of-the-art security had been deemed "adequate" by Nathan, but JT did note the lurking Bishop Security SUV that seemed to appear whenever Emily was in residence.

She continued to work on "The Bishop Chronicles," although she was fairly certain no self-respecting news publication would run a series of articles about a controversial businessman written by the woman who was in love with him. Nevertheless, she persevered. As was her wont, Emily used her focus on Nathan to prevent her own self-reflection. Farrell had waited a decent amount of time since her "outing," three weeks, no doubt waiting for the more aggressive hyenas to tire the lion out. When he called her into his office, he was solicitous and relaxed— relaxed like an Olympic swimmer on the starting block. Emily put him out of his misery immediately.

"My name is Emily Webster, and when I was eight, I was abducted."

Farrell stood, walked around his desk, and hugged her. He hugged her for the story she was about to give him. He hugged her for the ordeal she had survived. But most of all, he hugged her because deep down, Farrell had sensed a well of discontent in Emma Porter. A feeling he seemed to understand. Emily was not a hugger, but she hugged Farrell that day for a good long time.

They hammered out the details and agreed that her colleague Calliope Garland would conduct the interview. Emily didn't know Calliope well, because she didn't know anyone well, but what she knew she liked. The daughter of a Greek poet and novelist, hence her given name, and a Swiss banker, Calliope had moved to New York to, in her words, "find some normalcy." If that weren't an indication of the craziness of her life, Emily didn't know what was. They had their first meeting at a nail salon on Elizabeth Street. Emily thought it was an odd choice, but Calliope insisted that getting a pedicure, with the added twenty-minute massage, was exactly what they both needed. With her ebony hair and ice-blue eyes, Calliope was easy to spot, and for an hour they sat side by side in the big cushioned chairs and talked. When they emerged, both with sky blue toes, Emily was surprised to see Tox standing outside, holding the leash of the scariest looking Rottweiler she had ever seen.

"Ladies," Tox nodded as the dog strained the leash.

"Um, Tox?" Emily pointed to the eighty pounds of fur and teeth.

"This," Tox sighed heavily, "is Fraidy."

"Fraidy?" Calliope queried.

"Fraidy," Tox confirmed.

"Oh, and this is Tox. Tox, Calliope Garland."

"Pleasure." Tox tipped his Yankees cap.

"Can you tighten your hold on that beast?"

"Relax, Emily. Fraidy is short for Fraidy Cat. A buddy of mine got her for security at a warehouse he owns in Jersey. Kids were graffitiing the corrugated metal walls. He thought a Rottweiler would take care of the problem. Turns out she's so friendly the kids breaking in graffitied her too. My buddy came into work the next day and she was all pink and red, wagging her little stub like she thought she looked great."

Emily smiled and held out her hand. Fraidy's entire backside started shaking side to side. Calliope laughed and rubbed behind her ears.

"I need to find her a home. Frank, that's my buddy, he was going to take her to a shelter. I told him I'd take her, but I'm gone all the time."

"Aw, Tox, you're a softy."

"Only with dogs. Humans, not so much."

"I'll take her."

Emily and Tox looked over to see Calliope was still petting the dog.

"My place is big and empty. I live near a small park. My schedule is pretty consistent, and she clearly loves me."

"She loves everybody. Don't you want to think it over?" And with Tox's comment and tug on her leash, Fraidy did the first aggressive thing she had ever done; she turned to Tox and growled. "When should I drop her off?" Tox asked flatly.

"I'll take her now. I'm headed home. I think I can request an Uber that will take dogs." Calliope took the leash and was already fiddling with her phone and walking toward a two-way cross street to make it easier for the car to find her, with Fraidy trotting along beside her. And just like that, Fraidy had a home. Tox looked at Emily.

"That was easy."

"When you know, you know."

"What's her deal?"

"No idea. What's your deal?"

Tox didn't pretend to misunderstand. "I live nearby, and Fraidy needed a walk, so I told Nathan I'd see you back to your place."

"Sounds simple enough."

"It was until about ten minutes ago. Nathan texted to bring you, and my ass, but that's neither here nor there, to his office. There've been some developments.

CHAPTER THIRTY-THREE

Miguel followed Dario into the richly appointed study, the image of the dangling, bleeding man still fresh in his mind. Nevertheless, he was calm and impassive; he hadn't made it this far in the organization by letting shit rattle him. Miguel had never been in this room before, and as he looked around, he stifled a chuckle, imagining a scene from a mob movie. Dario was a small man, but his quiet confidence and the height of the custom desk chair picked up the slack as he seated himself behind the Edwardian walnut desk. He interlaced his fingers on the surface and looked at Miguel with an unreadable expression. Miguel stood equally impassive and waited.

"You show a lot of potential."

"Thank you, senõr."

"A lot of my muscle, their brains are in their biceps, you know?"

Miguel nodded.

"But you, you think."

Another nod.

Dario mirrored the nod, as though satisfied with what he saw, and withdrew a small case from beneath his desk. He opened it, the lid blocking the view of its contents from Miguel. Dario withdrew a pair of loose-fitting gauzy gloves from the box, and then what appeared to be a book. He held it up for Miguel to see. It was housed in an opaque covering, but Miguel could still make out the cover.

"*Ulysses.*"

"First edition," Dario confirmed. "I bought it ten years ago. Paid seventy-three thousand."

Miguel arched a brow.

"I can only imagine what it's worth now. Well, that's not true. I know exactly what it's worth." He chuckled. Dario replaced the book and withdrew another, a frail copy of *The Grapes of Wrath*. He replaced it and withdrew a leather journal. Dario handled it as if it were the Centenary Diamond or an unstable isotope; perhaps it was both.

"The *Journal of Yasunari Kawabata*. Are you familiar with his work?"

"No, senõr."

"Exceptional novelist. Won the Nobel Prize for literature."

Miguel nodded.

"I'm auctioning these off at the Torvald rare book auction in Manhattan. I'm assigning you the task of delivering them." Dario spun the case with uncharacteristic panache, showing the three books, each set in a recessed pocket of the case. Dario's lips parted in a smile, a gesture so rare Miguel thought it took effort to accomplish.

"You will fly out with the books next week and deliver them to my man at the auction house. Here are the details." Dario handed him an envelope. "My people at the other end will take it from there. Your job is to deliver the books." Dario was incredibly strategic in business. No one cog in the wheel ever knew what any other was doing. Miguel would take the case from Point A to Point B and that was that. Explaining to Miguel about the auction was an uncharacteristic and unnecessary sidestep. He felt a flash of irritation that perhaps Dario was doing a little handholding. As if there were anything remotely challenging about delivering a bunch of books to a bunch of stick-up-the-ass collectors. One thought quelled Miguel's pique; if Dario were auctioning off these books in a legitimate transaction, in a last-minute decision, he must need cash. That in itself was valuable information. Furthermore, accomplishing this errand without incident would improve his standing in Sava's organization. He of all people understood the patience involved in infiltrations such as this; he was playing a long game. Miguel stood impassive while Dario once again closed the case and returned it to his safe. His desk phone rang, and Dario gave Miguel a curt nod and dismissed him.

Miguel left the house and walked across the grounds to his quarters. He passed the building that held the lab and nodded to the guard outside. He pondered the idea of snatching the toxin from the lab and smuggling it back to his team, concealed in one of the books, but he dismissed the idea immediately. While he had a certain amount of autonomy and latitude in his fieldwork, that was crossing the line to rogue. Miguel continued walking without altering his pace, swinging his hands casually at his side, when another thought halted him. The last informant who'd tried to infiltrate Dario Sava's organization had been discovered. Sava had sent a spec ops team on a wild goose chase and the inside man on a fool's errand before skinning him alive. Miguel searched his brain to try to recall the specifics. Sava had sent the informant to Buenos Aires to retrieve a set of custom knives—the instruments of his own death. Miguel shuddered. He thought of the careful way Sava had handled the books, his knowledge of each one. He gave himself a mental *get your shit together*. He was doing a good job. He was given this task because he showed potential. Miguel continued to his quarters; confident his cover was still intact. But the seed of uncertainty had been planted.

CHAPTER THIRTY-FOUR

Inside Nathan's crowded office, Twitch was typing away on the keyboard. Emily was sitting next to her, fascinated by whatever Twitch was working on. Harris and Nathan had their heads together, and Chat and Ren were playing chess. Jack Webster was watching the match intently. Tox was about to bite into a gyro when a distinctive knock had him turning toward the door. Tox checked the peephole, did a double-take, and pulled the door open with a flourish.

"Well, look what the mutherfucking cat dragged in. Thought you were in Manila."

The two men embraced in a fierce hug.

Finn McIntyre was nearly as tall as Tox and built like a linebacker. With his sparkling navy blue eyes and Hollywood looks, he could have graced the Big Screen if it hadn't been for the burns and jagged scars marring the right side of his face. Finn could have retreated after his disfigurement, but instead, he did the opposite. He got in people's faces, dared them to comment, spoiled for a fight.

"Finished early. I was in Philly visiting my mom. Harris thought you guys could use a hand."

The others gathered around to greet him.

"Thanks, Finn. Appreciate the help." Harris clapped him on the back as the other two men broke apart.

"Hey, any excuse to get a John's Pizza." Half of Finn's face lit with a smile.

"Twitch, you know Finn."

"We've met." Twitch gave the icy reply without stopping her work.

"Hello to you too, Charlotte."

Emily noticed Twitch visibly stiffen at what Emily assumed was the use of her real name, but was prevented from analyzing the exchange further when Tox tugged her over.

"This is Emily Webster."

"Hey, great to meet you, Emily. Finn."

"What the frigging frack is going on with this bait shop?"

That got everyone's attention back on task.

"Bait shop?" Nathan looked over her shoulder.

"Earlier, I was pulling some threads on some dark web communication about the biotoxin and the IP address of this bait shop in South Carolina kept popping up. It's not the sender or the recipient, but somehow, this bait shop is intercepting messages."

"Who are these guys?" Tox scratched his stubbled jaw.

Twitch continued her rant. "That's what I'd like to know."

Finn offered his expertise. "Could be digital communication with a lo-fi component. Say you're doing some sketchy business, drug smuggling or trafficking. Most of the Alphabet agencies are onto you. ATF and CIA and Homeland know *who* and *what* these guys are, just not *where* they are. Anything you send electronically will be tracked down; it's humans that are hard to locate. There are two tricks around that. The first is to create a common email account with multiple users who communicate by writing emails and saving them as drafts without sending them at all. Other people log into the same account, check the draft folder and . . . bingo. Alphabet agencies are onto that trick, though, flagging suspicious accounts. The other way is to send an email with a coded message. Say it looks like a grocery list. The email goes to a coffee house in Delhi or a bakery in Istanbul or, in this case, a bait shop in South Carolina. A guy there takes the message and hoofs it to the next town to restart the digital chain on a new computer, or even makes a burner call to keep the message moving."

"Eliminating a digital trail," Tox nodded along.

"Worse. Leaving a digital trail that goes nowhere."

Twitch shook her head. "It's not that. At least I don't think so anymore. I think there's a signal piggybacking on the original transmission. The tracker signal, the routing, communications sources all trace back to this rinky-dink website, but then the electronic signal bifurcates."

"Dude. English," Tox huffed.

"I don't think the bait shop is the intended recipient of these emails. I think someone planted a tracking program at the source, and whoever is monitoring the bait shop is listening in . . . or reading in, in this case."

"Somebody's sending you on a wild goose chase, Charlotte."

"Stop calling me that, and no, they aren't messing with me. I'm past all the messing-with-me stuff. The original transmission bounces around the world. I've been to Bangladesh, Berlin, Belfast, and Beijing. The secondary signal is embedded."

"Quite the alliterative wild goose chase," Assam chuckled.

"We have that capability." Finn looked nonplussed. Twitch met his gaze then. Finn shrugged. "It's a pretty simple malware program. If you can attach it to the source device—that's the tricky part—the program attaches to the transmissions, then when the transmission is sent, the malware sends it to another destination, like an automatic, undetectable BCC."

"Like a suckerfish on a shark," Tox added between bites.

"Yes. Exactly."

"Then once they hit the bait shop, the suckerfish swims away."

"And the shark swims on." Twitch stared at the screen with something like admiration.

"Where does the shark go?" Tox asked.

"I'm not sure. It's taken me this long to track the suckerfish to South Carolina. But that's not the weird part."

Nathan and the rest of the men knew Twitch's command of understatement and waited.

"I'm not working on the biotoxin transmissions. Well, I was, but this transmission from a few weeks ago; it's about Emily's abduction. I can't tell where it ends up yet, but it originates from the same source as the emails regarding the sale of the toxin. It appears to be a message to the local contractors after Emily escaped." She looked up. "The sender writes he's coming to the U.S. to handle the situation personally."

"The person selling the bioagent and the person trying to abduct Emily are one and the same." Ren looked poleaxed.

"Busy guy." Tox walked over and handed Nathan the folder. "You know the two kidnappers taken out in prison after Emily's original abduction?"

"Yeah, but that's a dead end."

"I know. But remember how one was stabbed three times? Right eye, right ear, throat."

"Yeah, that's a signature but the other guy was stabbed in the gut."

"Right, but I think that was a fuck up. Maybe the hitter was interrupted, maybe he just got lazy, because the guy suspected of the second hit got taken out six months later. Guess how?"

"Right eye, right ear, throat."

"Ding, ding, ding."

"But that trail leads nowhere. We always assumed those two were taken out by the mastermind."

"Right, but," Tox shuffled through the papers Nathan held, "three months earlier outside of Hartford—that would have been just days after Emily had been taken as a child—a body was found floating in the Connecticut River, stabbed once in the eye, once in the ear, and once in the throat. A low-level dealer named Cyril Bond."

The sound of shattering glass had everyone turning toward a recessed bar where Jack Webster stood surrounded by a shattered tumbler, the smell of whiskey filling the air.

"Dad?"

"Cyril Bond . . . was an acquaintance of your mother's."

CHAPTER THIRTY-FIVE

Jack Webster stepped carefully over the broken glass and joined the group. "Nathan, you might remember Emily's mother, Vivienne. She left when Emily was a baby. She passed away shortly after that."

"Vaguely. Mom has some pictures of her."

"She tried to clean up. She stayed sober for the pregnancy, but after a year or so . . ." he trailed off, his eyes filled with pain, ". . . she relapsed. She met Cyril at a dive bar she used to frequent. Cyril Bond knew a fat bank account when he saw it. He got her hooked on anything and everything that would keep her coming back. Her descent was remarkable. She could have been a model, a movie star—but after a month with Cyril . . . ." He cleared his throat. "I didn't go after her, but I kept tabs on her. It happened so fast. She was dead six weeks after she moved in with him."

"Dad, we've talked about this. You couldn't control, he addiction. There was nothing you could have done."

Jack continued as if she hadn't spoken. "We tried."

"We?" Nathan queried.

261

"Your father and I. I recruited him one night to help because of his . . ." he gestured at the pack of testosterone gathered in the room, ". . . private security contacts. We brought some muscle and paid Cyril a visit."

"What happened?" Tox was a bag of popcorn away from looking like he was watching a movie.

"She refused to leave. Cyril wanted money. I offered to pay what he asked. Five thousand dollars." Jack gave a humorless chuckle. "He knew she had money, but Cyril didn't realize what a cash cow he had. Vivi said she would pay him twice that to let her stay. The one conscientious neighbor in that hellhole called the police. As you would say, we aborted the mission."

"Cyril would have known about Emily. If Vivienne was doped up, she would mention it."

"He knew about Emily because he came to the house." Jack went to the bar and poured himself another scotch. "He claimed he had video footage of Vivienne." He shot an apologetic glance to Emily. "I won't go into detail, but he wanted money again. When I refused, he offered to sell me guns. Emily barged in, as she was prone to do even at the age of three. I quickly sent her off, but he saw her clear as day."

Nathan gave a dry laugh. "Living next door to us, you had access to a veritable armory."

Harris agreed. "Rule number one in sales: know your buyer."

"Yes, well, when I pulled the Glock out of my desk and assured him I was adequately armed, he got the message. Jackass probably stole the silver on his way out."

Ren quirked a brow.

"He must have offered up some info when Savo's men were trolling. He may even have been the guy in the van. The tattoos Emily described match." He tossed a gruesome photo of the body onto the table.

"A criminal, but more importantly, an opportunist." Nathan nodded.

"A dead opportunist," Tox reminded him.

"Must've seized the wrong opportunity."

Tox retrieved a whiteboard from the corner of the room. "Okay, let's get this shit sorted." He drew a large rectangle at the top with a question mark inside. Directly below it, he drew another box and wrote inside "Tattoo Man," then, next to it, quickly copied a version of the tattoo Emily had drawn. Below that, boxes with the dead kidnappers, Cyril Bond, and the prison assassin. Then he sighed and scratched his face with the end of the marker. "Well, that certainly clears things up."

"That tattoo." Ren looked at the rudimentary drawing, then tapped something into his tablet. "Did it look like this?" He flipped the tablet around to reveal a stone relief elaborately carved with a cross atop a rosette.

Emily's eyes lit as she stood. "Yes! That's it, almost exactly."

The group waited for Ren's revelation.

"It's a *khachkar*. An Armenian religious icon, a symbol for salvation of the soul."

"So, our guy's Armenian," Nathan said.

"But the man I remembered from the house was in a Middle Eastern tunic," Emily clarified.

"Most Armenians fled Turkey during the Christian genocide, but he could have lived or worked in the Middle East," Ren offered.

"Which means he works for someone from that part of the world." Nathan pondered a moment, then scrolled through a file. "Jack, how long were you in Qatar?"

"Four months." Jack searched the ceiling. "It would have been sixteen years ago and was utterly uneventful."

"Nothing? No violence, no unrest?" Tox queried.

"I had barely settled in. I planned to get things ready and then bring Emily over for the two-year appointment. When I flew home to get her after three months, she was sick—chickenpox of all things. So, I left her with my parents and flew back alone. About two weeks after that, I came down with Emily's bug."

"Chickenpox is very dangerous in adults," Twitch commented absently.

"Yes. I had to be hospitalized after I fainted at a diplomatic event. After that, I returned home to recuperate and resigned the post. The doctors were worried about complications from the virus. Barbara Coffer, the current Secretary of Health and Human Services, took my place."

The group was still absorbing this information when Twitch turned troubled blue eyes to the group. "Add another box."

"What?" Nathan asked warily.

"On the whiteboard. A highly disreputable private investigator, Mac Ferguson, was found murdered in an alley in Midtown last week. Cause of death was injected cyanide. He was also stabbed post-mortem. Any guesses as to where?"

"Right eye, right ear, throat," Tox surmised.

"Give that man a cigar."

"Fifty bucks says Ferguson found you." Tox pointed his sandwich at Emily.

"That explains how they were able to coordinate so quickly after the news of Emily's identity was leaked." Nathan gave her hand a reassuring squeeze.

"They already knew," Finn agreed.

Emily barely had time to process the information when Chat entered calmly but urgently.

"We have a situation." Chat handed the tablet to Nathan. Nathan read the information and passed it to Ren, who set his novel aside and took the file.

"Damn. I was hoping this was all some sort of black-market lore."

Emily stayed where she was on the small couch, but this was all too much. "What's going on?"

Nathan gave Ren a quick nod and he began the explanation with the calm tone of a professor delivering a history lecture.

"During World War II, the Japanese had a facility in a remote part of Manchuria, officially known as the Epidemic Prevention and Water Purification Department."

Tox snorted as Ren continued.

"It was actually a massive bio and chemical warfare research laboratory known as Detachment 731, run by the notorious Surgeon General Shiro Ishii, the Dr. Mengele of Japan. They experimented on prisoners using any number of pathogens: anthrax, smallpox, cholera, botulism, venereal diseases. Prisoners were infected, studied. Women were impregnated then exposed. It was a level of inhumanity nearly beyond comprehension." Ren took a moment to shake off the images he had no doubt conjured. "When the Red Army was on the move and the war was all but lost, the government ordered Detachment 731 be destroyed. General Ishii had the remaining prisoners executed, as well as low-level workers with knowledge of the facility, burned down the building, and ordered his staff to scatter and never mention the true purpose of Detachment 731."

Emily had her eyes closed and both hands covering her mouth. Nathan sat beside her and gathered her up.

"Fast forward to a year ago. A group of construction workers in Manchuria unearthed human remains while they were digging a foundation. Along with the skeleton, there was some sort of unidentified package. The information is sketchy. It was dated 1945, and the Japanese writing indicated the contents were from the Epidemic Prevention and Water Purification Department. The workers reported it to the locals, but before anyone knew what they had, the men were duped into surrendering the package to a group of men impersonating government officials. Now bear in mind, the perpetrators of Detachment 731 went largely unpunished—some people even go so far as to say Ishii went to work for the U.S. after the war—and the vast majority of their victims were Chinese, so even today China has a vested interest in condemning the atrocities. Rather than face the wrath of higher-ups for losing such potentially damning evidence, the locals simply 'lost' the report." Ren put air quotes around "lost."

Nathan jumped in. "Which means, there is the distinct possibility that someone smuggled an engineered biotoxin or some sort of pathogen out of Detachment 731 that, if properly contained, could still be viable."

Ren took the volley. "And judging from the rumors of testing done for months since the discovery, we have to assume that whatever was in that package, stuffed in the jacket of a dead man, and buried in the middle of Manchuria, was something extremely valuable and extremely deadly."

"I talked to one of the original construction workers who discovered the remains." The group looked up at Nathan's announcement. "Cerberus sent me. After the chatter that a bioweapon was going up for sale, he wanted to know exactly what was in that package."

"Any good intel?"

"Not much. The one guy I tracked down was nervous to talk to me. Said the package felt solid. The writing was Japanese. He was the guy who found the body, mentioned there was a bullet hole in the skull of the remains. They never opened the package, and they were happy to hand it over to the first person who showed up wanting it. When I asked him how big it was, he said probably the only English word he knew, 'Xbox.'"

"So, yea big." Tox held his hands about eight inches apart.

"That it?" Chat added, seeming to sense there was more to the story.

"Small detail. After I left, two guys in a Humvee ran me off the road. Flipped my Jeep. When I fired at them, they took off."

"That worker's got someone watching his back. Explains why the bad guys didn't just kill him."

Nathan pointed at Tox in agreement.

"Maybe it didn't even go down the way he said. Maybe he knew someone who might want the package. It's not a big leap to think this construction worker might have a friend or relative with criminal ties. Doesn't really matter. All I got from the trip was a tidbit of information and a bad case of road rash."

Twitch took over, her cheery disposition lightening the despondent mood. "Here is the good news. Well, 'good' in a glass-half-full kind of way. Our contact at the Port Authority in Savannah noticed a couple of the dockworkers driving shiny new decked out pickups. That's a big red flag that some palms have been greased."

"Or they won the lottery," Tox theorized.

"Which they did not. They play the same numbers in the Georgia State Lottery every week and, to date, they have not won more than thirty bucks. A quick, *eh hem*, peek at their finances shows both men made five separate cash deposits of nine thousand dollars."

"Deposits of ten thousand dollars or more automatically get flagged by the IRS," Ren clarified.

"Meanwhile, and here's my big cliffhanger, so that bait shop in South Carolina? I think it's an outpost of some kind. The NSA or Homeland has been monitoring electronic communication and intercepted instructions from an IP originating in Paramaribo, Suriname, for a $90,000 wire transfer to be used as a cash payment."

"The bribe for the dock workers," Nathan surmised.

"So, we have a Middle Eastern kingpin with an Armenian right-hand man living in South America." Jack rubbed the heels of his hands against his eyes.

"Believe it or not, that will narrow it down considerably. Can't be too many of those." Twitch never looked up as she tapped away on her keyboard.

"Twitch, before you start digging, get in touch with Steady. I want him down at the Savannah docks keeping an eye on things."

"And whoever is moving this bioagent is also involved in this mess with Emily." Jack shook his head in confusion.

"And whoever is manning that bait shop knows it now too," Nathan confirmed.

"Maybe the good people at . . ." Twitch checked her screen, ". . . Royal Beach Fishing and Tackle have some intel."

Nathan looked up suddenly. "Royal Beach?" Twitch nodded in affirmation.

Tox stood and began pacing. "What the fuck is the connection between an eight-year-old girl and a bioterrorist?"

"Technically, this person is an arms dealer. He is the outfitter, not the executor," Ren corrected.

Tox returned a flat look. "I stand corrected. What the fuck is the connection between a fifteen-year-old abduction of an eight-year-old girl, an ongoing vendetta, and a fucking arms dealer?"

Chat chimed in for the first time, "That is the question."

"We need to go to Royal Beach." Nathan looked directly at Jack Webster while clinging tightly to Emily's hand.

"Charlie? Impossible." Jack paled. "Your uncle would never be mixed up in this mess. He's a former Secretary of Defense, for heaven's sake."

"He's not the shark, Mr. Webster," Twitch clarified. "He's the suckerfish."

"And he always has the most valuable thing any terrorist or arms dealer or alphabet agency needs," Nathan added.

"What's that?" Emily queried.

"Information."

CHAPTER THIRTY-SIX

Charlie Bishop was known around the small coastal town as The Tinker. Though he stood at only five feet, ten inches, his comportment, close-cropped gray hair, and lantern jaw made for an intimidating presence. He had appeared in Royal Beach, seemingly out of nowhere, more than a decade ago, lived in a modest but well-maintained cottage, and drove a wood-paneled Wagoneer that predated his arrival. He could fix just about anything, and the locals relied on his expertise for everything from boat engines to children's toys. He hadn't tried to conceal his identity, but he certainly didn't announce it. Turns out the small fishing hamlet neither knew nor cared who the former U.S. Secretary of Defense was, much less what he looked like. Only the nearly clairvoyant owner of the local diner, Maggie Malloy, recognized him, but to this day rarely mentioned it. Not even to Charlie himself. It was one of the many reasons why he'd married her.

Maggie Malloy-Bishop turned sixty this year and had the energy and demeanor of a woman half her age. Her three children, all boys, from a relatively brief and disastrous first marriage, were grown and off living productive lives. The grandson she had raised after her oldest boy had gotten his high school girlfriend pregnant, her little strong man, was off saving the world. Her other grandchildren, three girls that belonged to her middle son and his doctor wife, visited twice a year. Most of the time, she and Charlie had the place to themselves. Her hair had remained a glossy copper, and her pale gray eyes glimmered with a knowledge that belied education. When they had first met, Maggie had joked that with his love for gadgets, his surprising sewing skills, and his military background, Charlie was three of the four men described in the title of John le Carré's classic espionage novel. The only thing missing, or so she thought, was the spy. When the mysterious, dark-suited men began appearing at their door—and disappearing into the back room of the cottage—she reevaluated. She loved Charlie Bishop with her whole heart, and she didn't need or really want to know the secrets that room held. She knew in her soul he was a good man, and that was enough.

Charlie would have scoffed at Maggie's assessment. He wasn't a good man. He had sent young men into deadly circumstances, not that different from the ones he had been ordered into as a soldier. *Same shit, different war.* He had let evil men walk free in exchange for worse men or vital intelligence. His list of sins was long, but this last leg of his journey to Calvary was without moral ambiguity. He never acted without knowing the whole story. He, more than anyone, knew that people were not always what they seemed. When he was both satisfied he was doing what was right and had the means to do so, he interceded.

This mess with Emily and Jack Webster had plagued him for as long as he had lived in South Carolina. He knew more than most, and what was relevant he shared. When the man he suspected of abducting Emily disappeared from their lives for more than a decade, Charlie had thought the matter closed. Dario Sava had found a new career for himself, a much more volatile career, and a very peculiar choice for a man poised to step into a powerful political position. With a man inside and some discreet surveillance, Charlie had concluded Dario Sava was the arms dealer he sought. Then, out of the blue, there was another attempt to snatch Emily Webster just weeks ago. The timing could not have been more perplexing. Dario Sava was on the verge of pulling off an unprecedented exchange. Why on earth would he complicate such a delicate, intricately timed event with the abduction of a young woman? Was Emily Webster a distraction? A red herring? Or was this something else entirely? One thing was certain: now that Sava seemed to have reignited his interest in Emily, it was time to disclose as much information as he could to Emily and Jack Webster. It was that thought distracting him from the Homeland Security report on his screen when Maggie, quite uncharacteristically, knocked on the door.

"Charlie? There are some people here."

Her announcement conveyed no other information, but Charlie knew by the tone of her voice that this was not a typical visitor. Not a local needing a winch repaired on a trawler, and certainly not one of the laconic men who called themselves Mr. Jones or Mr. Brown. Yet still, when Charlie opened the door to his office, he couldn't contain his surprise. A phalanx of four men and a woman stood behind his nephew, his old friend, and the daughter his friend prized above all else. Nathan Bishop, Jack Webster, and Emily Webster. It seemed they had brought the proverbial mountain to Mohammed. There was no hesitation as Charlie rushed to embrace the group, his broad smile conveying his exuberance. The trio returned his affection in kind.

"God damn, it's good to see you." Charlie held them tight. "Saved me a trip to that rat trap up north."

That comment had Nathan's head shooting up. "You have information?"

Charlie's natural response was to assess the room. Jack commenced introductions.

"The big guy is Tox, that's Chat, Ren, and Finn, and the redhead is Twitch. And you remember Emily."

"Last time I saw you, you socked me in the nose with a sippy cup. Glad to see you're just as feisty."

"Good to see you, Charlie." Charlie didn't miss Nathan's possessive hold on Emily's waist. As if to convey the same attachment, he held out his hand for Maggie, who had been observing the interaction from the kitchen doorway. "This is my Maggie." There was no need to elaborate. After handshakes and hugs, Maggie said, "I'll whip something

FALSE FRONT

up. You must be hungry." Ren's eyes lit up. "I'll help. I'm pretty good in the kitchen."

Maggie smiled. "A man after my own heart. Amazing how this one," she cocked her head toward Charlie, "can build a motorcycle out of spare parts but can't crack an egg. I suspect some intentional incompetence." Charlie pinked and chuckled, quickly ushering the group into his inner sanctum.

Twitch eyeballed the electronics like a child on Christmas morning. The room seemed to be divided into two different centuries. On one side, a tech set-up rivaled Twitch's at Knightsgrove-Bishop. Monitors dotted the semicircular desk and a mainframe hummed quietly. A satellite phone was on the desk and a collection of disposable cell phones filled the open drawer below it. A digital lock marked the door of what was certainly a weapons closet, and a workbench held a variety of gadgets. The other side of the room looked like the office of the owner of a bait shop. A rutted desk held a landline and some homemade fishing flies. Paper files, with receipts and accounting records poking out, sat in a precarious stack. A bizarre-looking striped burrfish with bulging eyes and a rectangular body was mounted on the wall behind the desk. Mirroring the tech workbench was another. This one held a small motor, the work surface stained with grease and covered with a smattering of sawdust. Nathan, Charlie, Jack, and Emily settled in a small sitting area. Twitch sat at the computer desk out of habit. Chat, Finn, and Tox stood at various spots around the room.

Charlie slapped his thighs with both hands. "No sense beating about the bush. Let's talk about Dario Sava."

273

CHAPTER THIRTY-SEVEN

Twitch read as she researched. "Dario Sava is the oldest of eight children of Surinamese mining magnate Rodrigo Sava and his wife, Nasarra. He was raised in Paramaribo and educated in England. Withdrew from Oxford in his second year to undergo treatment for testicular cancer. Looks like he made a full recovery. MBA from Wharton. After that, he returned to London to work on the commodities exchange. Huh."

"What?" Nathan urged.

"He left the London job when the Emir of Qatar appointed him to a coveted Defense Ministry post." The group waited as Twitch worked her magic. "Now we're getting somewhere. Sava's mother was Nasarra al-Malik, a member of the Qatari royal family. She met Rodrigo Sava in Riyadh at a symposium on oil exploration. According to this bit in a London tabloid, her family initially forbade the courtship, but Qatar is fairly progressive as Muslim monarchies go, and at Nasarra's insistence, they reconsidered. The family lived in Suriname but remained close to the Qatari side. The Emir, Dario's great uncle, accurately pegged him early on as a brilliant strategist and born diplomat."

"Plus, it wouldn't hurt to have a government official with ties to another potentially oil-rich country," Finn theorized.

"Good point," Nathan echoed.

"I met him," Jack spoke softly. "At a diplomatic event, the opening of a collection of artifacts at the museum in Doha. He and his wife were there as representatives for the Emir. We exchanged a few words about the exhibit I believe, then moved on. I remember because that was the night I collapsed. It was the beginning of the end of my appointment at the Embassy."

Twitch continued to type. "The story gets weird after that. Sava's behavior became increasingly erratic. He had to be forcibly removed from a summit with OPEC after insisting that Qatar would become a nuclear power. Within a year he had been removed from his government post. He moved back to Suriname and has since become one of the most clever and elusive arms dealers in South America."

"What about his wife?" Emily asked.

"His wife, Tala, is the daughter of an American horse breeder from an old-money Baltimore family and a Jordanian diplomat who died of a heart attack when Tala was a child. Tala met Dario Sava when his Qatari uncle purchased a racehorse from Tala's family. They married quickly, and she went with him to the Middle East and then to Suriname when he burned his bridges in Qatar. No kids. They lived together in Paramaribo until she died . . ." Twitch searched the screen, ". . . ten years ago. Complications from lupus."

"So, he goes from being a high-level government official to a ruthless arms dealer in a year," Tox recapped.

"And not just any arms dealer," Nathan continued the story. "He's notorious for leading law enforcement on wild goose chases and conducting transactions right under their noses. He once offloaded a truck full of stolen Russian AKs at an open-air market in Damascus in broad daylight, while a SEAL platoon raided an abandoned house outside the city. Smug bastard."

"You're saying he has a bioweapon in some form, and he's going to try to smuggle it into the country using smoke and mirrors?" Emily asked.

"I don't know. Maybe. I mean, there's no better way to make the U.S. look incompetent than turning it into ground zero for a biological attack."

"You're sure they had no children?" Jack asked. Twitch double-checked and nodded. Jack rubbed his jaw, searching his memory. "When I met Tala, I think she was pregnant."

"Hold on a second." Twitch was scrolling through something on her screen. "Two weeks after you left your post in Qatar, Tala Savo was hospitalized. She had a D and C."

"What's that?" Tox asked.

"Dilation and Curettage," Ren offered. "It's performed after a miscarriage."

"Confirmed," Twitch added. "She suffered a miscarriage at seventeen weeks gestation." She looked up at the room through her glasses. "The cause is listed as complications from the Varicella Zoster virus. She had chickenpox." The same chickenpox that had waylaid Jack Webster.

You could have heard a pin drop.

Nathan scrubbed his face. "I think we know why Savo wanted Emily."

Ren added, "Between his cancer and her health issues, her chances of carrying a baby to term would have been slim. There's no way to know for sure chickenpox was a contributing factor."

"True, but with all the frustration and helplessness that comes with infertility, that was an obvious focus for his rage," Tox spoke with uncharacteristic sensitivity.

"An eye for an eye," Ren nodded.

"Between his testicular cancer and her autoimmune issues from lupus, that pregnancy was probably their only shot," Twitch added.

"Oh God, I feel awful." Jack Webster cupped his face in his hands.

"Dad, you couldn't have known. Should we blame me for giving them to you, or my friend Lizzie for giving them to me?"

"Not to mention that lots of people have fertility issues, and very few turn to international terrorism. You bear no responsibility for Dario Sava, Jack." Nathan stroked Emily's back as he reassured her father.

"Thank you, Nathan. It's just such a shame." Jack Webster looked around the room at the men who had probably seen more human suffering than anyone should and collected himself.

Charlie took over. "The CIA has had a man inside Dario Sava's organization for eighteen months. Spent a year doing shit jobs for suppliers and lieutenants. About a month ago, he was moved into security on the Sava compound. That's a crucial time for maintaining cover—everybody watches the new guy. Nevertheless, he did confirm a lab on the compound, but no actionable intel, and nothing to indicate the presence of a level three or four biohazard. My source is due to check-in," he glanced at his watch, "at the top of the hour. I'll have him update you as well, North."

Finn looked up from his phone. "I need to head back to Philly in the morning."

"How's your mom?" Ren asked.

"On the mend, but the other driver fled the scene, so on top of her medical care, there's a shit ton of paperwork dealing with the locals and insurance."

"Go," Nathan waved him off. "We'll call you if we need you. Thanks for the backup."

"Any time. You know that, North."

Nathan nodded in agreement.

"Okay, let's keep digging."

CHAPTER THIRTY-EIGHT

It was after midnight in Savannah, but the heat and humidity were unrelenting. The container ship, *Ariadne*, now relieved of cargo, sat empty and silent. Hercules Reynolds picked nervously at the yellow paint chipping from the metal railing skirting a platform near the dock. As a Marine sniper, he routinely had to sit still as a puddle for hours, sometimes days, but civilian life had sapped his discipline. His best friend, Billy Grimes, was talking on the phone, actually *fighting* on the phone, with his on-again girlfriend, Melinda. Herc shushed him. Again. Nothing about this felt right.

In the Marines, Herc was a by-the-book guy. He'd served his country with honor. As dangerous and uncertain and bureaucratic as the military was, there was a certain comfort for Herc in knowing he was doing exactly what he was supposed to be doing, when and where he was supposed to be doing it. That had all changed when he became a civilian.

"Dammit, Mel, I'm not with a woman. I'm with Herc, and we picked up an extra job. Track my phone, for gosh sake!"

Hercules quieted his friend again. Billy had landed the job on the docks after his Less Than Honorable Discharge and quickly learned that there were ways to supplement his income. Billy knew the guy in town who took delivery of the counterfeit purses and watches that came hidden in containers loaded with furniture. So, helping get the stuff offloaded was a fairly easy and lucrative process. This time, though, . . . this was something else.

Forty-five thousand dollars each was enough to have them both damning the consequences. Herc could pay off his bills and help his beloved Mhamó, the granny who raised him. Billy could afford the ring Melinda wanted and help with the wedding. Now that the thrill of the payday had settled, Herc had some serious reservations. Everything about this smelled.

It's a one-shot deal, Herc. We find the metal suitcase in the shipping container with this serial number and stow it. Then we meet this guy, hand off the case, and he pays us the rest. Could not be easier. Hell, I'm not a dope. I'm bringing my Sig.

Herc had his Sig too, but he also had something else, a rather unusual piece of equipment he was demoing for the owner of the shooting range where he had landed a job teaching part-time. Billy ended his call. Herc stopped picking the paint and stilled. Apparently, not all his military instinct had fled. He hadn't heard the sedan approach. In the dense fog with its headlights off, it was nearly invisible. The distinct sound of footsteps, however, was clear. The man emerged from the shadows dressed in a tailor-made suit and Italian leather loafers, looking not the least bit shady. Billy relaxed a bit, but Herc kept frosty.

"You have the case?" the man inquired.

"Yep." Billy dangled it from the handle.

"Open it. The combination is 72117." When Billy started to fiddle with the dial, Herc stilled his arm.

"Come around here. There's a table." Herc led them to the side of a warehouse where a wide plank was set on two sawhorses. He moved Billy to the side nearest the warehouse wall, seemingly giving the suited man a better vantage point to watch his surroundings. Billy popped the case revealing the contents.

"Very good."

"It's yours as soon as you pay up." Billy was sounding like a regular mobster. Billy wasn't a mobster, though. Billy was just a not-so-bright guy, so distracted by the thought of giving his pregnant girlfriend everything she wanted and deserved that he didn't even notice the gun as he reached for the envelope of cash. Just as the man fired the suppressed round into Billy's chest with a quiet *thwat*, a much louder sound rent the air. Herc had pressed the button on the fob in his hand, and the Paradigm SRP Talon remote-controlled sniper rifle sent the round. Herc had positioned his target in the right spot—quite the reverse of a normal sniper assignment—and the suited man's head exploded like a cantaloupe.

Herc stood there for a moment marveling at the luck of his aim—good or bad, he wasn't sure. He certainly hadn't intended this result; he simply thought a shot into the gravel from the remote-controlled weapon would make the suited man think they had backup. Herc scratched his stubbled jaw. Quite the snafu. In the military, at this point, his job was done. Someone else handled the logistics. Nevertheless, this was hardly the time to say *not my job*. Whatever was inside that case was very bad news. He didn't touch anything, though he desperately wanted to close Billy's lifeless eyes. He knew where he needed to go, and he knew what he needed to do. He pried the cash out of Billy's clenched fist, put the envelope in the case, clicked it shut, and walked with a forced calm to retrieve the weapon from its hiding place. Rifle secured, case in hand, Hercules Reynolds hurried off into the sultry night and disappeared, leaving Billy and Rigo Mendaz lying dead on the ground.

CHAPTER THIRTY-NINE

"Holy Mother of Christ, North, some shit just went down."

Jonah "Steady" Lockhart was normally unflappable. His olive complexion and tranquil nature allowed him to blend into almost any environment with ease. A former member of their SEAL team and Bishop Security operative, he had been monitoring the situation on the docks in Savannah. When Nathan heard his frantic voice, he knew to pay attention. Steady seemed to gather himself. His next words over the phone were a good deal more composed.

"One of the dockworkers is dead. The Armenian with the hand tattoo has donated his brain to the pavement. The other guy? Herc Reynolds? He had overwatch. Someone took out Rigo Mendaz and skedaddled. Reynolds retrieved the rifle and took it with him."

"Where's the package?"

"Reynolds has it. It's a silver suitcase. Inside is a metal cylinder. I'm following at a distance. It's the middle of the night, and the fucker's making stops around town like he's running Sunday afternoon errands. He went to the gun range, the all-night diner. He came out of a boarding house about forty minutes ago with a duffle. Now he's on the move."

"He went rogue? Found a buyer?"

"Here's the thing."

There was a pause over the line as Steady gathered his thoughts.

"What's the thing, Steady?"

"Hold on. One more exit and I'll know." Steady was silent for a moment, then muttered.

"Oh, shit."

"Steady, what the fuck is going on?"

"I think he's coming to you."

"What?"

"He's heading for Royal Beach."

"How could he know we're here?" Nathan whistled quick and short, rousing the group, and circled his finger in the air. Without speaking, Ren, Tox, Chat, Finn, and Twitch prepared their weapons. Nathan switched the phone to speaker.

"Beats the hell out of me, boss, but Reynolds just made the last turn. He's definitely headed your way. ETA twenty minutes."

Nathan's phone signaled another call. He checked the screen and replied to Steady, "I've got to take this. Text me in five with an update." Nathan switched the phone off speaker and walked into the empty kitchen to take the call.

After speaking to the man Cerberus had inside the Sava organization, Nathan placed another call, this one to his doorman, Leonard.

"Mr. Bishop."

"I hope I'm not calling too late?"

"Not at all. I'm knee-deep in *Midsomer Murders*. Makes me homesick."

"I won't be back when I had originally planned, so I'm hoping you can handle an errand for me."

"Of course, sir."

"I'll have the details delivered to you at the desk tomorrow. Take Mira out for a nice meal after. On me."

"She'd love that. Thank you."

Nathan glanced at the text from Steady as he ended the call and walked back into the main room. *How the hell had this kid figured out where they were?* Much like Dario Sava, Nathan prided himself on being one step ahead, but this unexpected turn of events had him wondering if he had somehow been outmaneuvered.

"Tox, Chat, come from behind the hedge. Twitch upstairs on overwatch. Ren and I will approach. Finn, stay in the house with Emily. We don't know what's in that case, but if he even makes a move to open it, take him out."

Murmured "copy thats" and nods. The group got into position as a mud-splattered late model Ford F250 turned into the gravel driveway.

Hercules Reynolds grabbed the silver suitcase and jumped out of the driver's seat onto the grass as two, that he saw, Sig Sauers rose to eye level in the darkness. He cast a quick glance around, caught the slight twitch of the hedges. He lifted his arms away from his body, the case dangling from his fingers, and too many questions in his head to even form one. A brief thought flashed through his head. He was nine and

Billy was goading him to jump off a forty-foot rock ledge into the quarry reservoir. Right before he'd jumped, he'd yelled to Billy, *you're gonna get me killed one day!* Looked like today was that day.

Just then, the front door burst open. Three dogs came tearing out the door, Maggie Molloy-Bishop hot on their heels. Waving her arms about her head, she yelled, "Hold your fire!" Charlie, a good deal calmer, poked his head out and pointed with his thumb at his wife. "What she said."

Nathan kept his gun out but pointed it to the ground. Maggie turned to Herc with her hands on her hips and used the only swear word that ever crossed her lips. "Hercules Hamish McManus Reynolds. What the hell is going on?"

Charlie ushered two of the dogs back to their kennels with a swift command. The third dog stayed at Herc's side. Charlie stepped onto the lawn next to his wife. "Goddamn, that name is a mouthful." The third dog was now circling Herc and wagging her tail as he bent to pet her.

"And get Crazy Daisy back to bed with the other two."

CHAPTER FORTY

A different soldier than the one who had delivered the news about Emily's escape stood at Dario's open office door. He lacked the air of relaxed confidence of the other man. He clasped his hands in front of him to hide the shaking.

"El Callado?"

Dario gestured to the man to enter. The man cleared his throat, but Dario cut him off before he could speak.

"Rigo is dead, yes?"

"Yes."

"I suspected as much."

"The case. It was taken."

"By . . .?"

"One of the dockworkers. He took it and ran."

"What an interesting turn of events."

"Rigo's driver said after the man took off, then a dark SUV pulled out of a warehouse and followed."

"The NSA following a trail of breadcrumbs, I suspect. Always following."

"Rigo put a tracker in the case."

"Excellent. Tell Rigo's driver to locate it and be sure to keep the tracker in range. When the dockworker stops, have him forward the location."

"Yes, sir. Anything else?"

"Just tell the men to keep an eye on things. This was a contingency I had planned for. I'm flying to the States to resolve another matter."

"You need to retrieve the case, no?"

"Shortly. For now, I have a hunch it's moving in the right direction. I need the government agencies chasing their tails a bit longer. This unexpected twist could be a remarkable turn of luck. Tell the men to keep watch. I'll instruct them if further action is needed."

The man turned and quickly fled. Dario pushed back from his desk, crossed to the elegant bar, removed the bottle of Louis XIII Cognac from its case, and poured himself a small measure. He lifted the snifter in a small toast to the framed photo of his wife that sat behind the bar on a shelf of mementos.

His moment of peace was interrupted by the clanging ring of the secure satellite phone on his desk. He returned to his work and answered it.

"El Callado, you won't believe it." The man on the line was Pedro, Rigo's driver. He was speaking quietly, and it was a bad connection. Dario didn't, as a rule, anticipate bad news, but apprehension coated his words.

"What now?"

"I followed the tracker on the case. I arrived just a moment ago. The dockworker is talking to a group of men. They drew their guns at first, but they seem to have resolved the issue."

"Don't get too close. I don't want you spotted."

"I have moved around the block, but senõr, the girl you are looking for, Emily Webster, she's there."

"You're sure."

"Positive, El Callado. It's dark, but I recognized her immediately. I was in the van . . . the last time," Pedro rushed through, not eager to remind Dario of the failure. "She's with the group of men in the house."

"Stay out of sight, Pedro. Update me every hour. Your good fortune will be rewarded."

"Of course. Thank you, senõr."

Dario disconnected the call feeling a tremendous sense of *rightness*. He quickly sent a text to his pilot to inform him of the new flight plan and raised his glass once again to the photo behind the bar.

"My God, sweet Tala, you really do look after me."

CHAPTER FORTY-ONE

Twitch, Emily, and the guys were draped on the overstuffed chintz living room furniture while Maggie whipped up Herc's favorite: a ham and cheddar sandwich with a pineapple slice, Ruffles potato chips, and homemade iced shortbread. Herc told them the story of the exchange at the dock, the remote-controlled rifle, Billy, and the unknown man. Elbows on his knees, head in his hands, he finished.

"I didn't mean to kill him. I just wanted to fire a warning shot. Make the guy think I had backup."

Nathan walked in from Charlie's office where they had put the case. Emily extended her hand to him. He took it with a soft kiss to her palm and perched on the arm of her chair. "Trust me, Hercules, one of you wasn't walking away from that meet. You did what you had to do."

"Did you open it?" This from Tox, who was eyeing the kitchen door along with Daisy, both waiting for the treats they smelled to emerge.

"He did. The guy. The case, I mean. He didn't open the cartridge inside. It looks like a spark plug with a latch near the top."

Ren looked at Twitch. "Volatile chemical transport cartridge."

"Sounds like it," Nathan agreed.

Twitch popped up from behind her laptop. "We got a confirm. It's Mendaz."

Emily looked up. "He's dead?"

Nathan kissed her forehead. "Dead and gone. Literally. My people will handle the cleanup." He turned to Herc. "There will be no evidence either you or Rigo Mendaz were at the dock tonight."

"What about Billy?"

"It's going to look like exactly what it was. Billy got shot doing something shady after hours at the warehouse. Suspect at large."

Hercules nodded in grim acceptance.

"Hercules." Emily's soft voice had him looking up. "That man, Rigo Mendaz. He abducted me when I was a child. Don't let his death weigh on your conscience."

"It doesn't." Hercules stared down at his feet. "Not anymore." He seemed to be speaking of more than just this incident.

Chat turned from where he was standing at the large circular bay window that framed the darkness and the roiling surf. "What number?"

Hercules looked into Chat's eyes, and seeing a kindred spirit, said without inflection, "Fifty-one."

There was a silent understanding among the group. Hercules had been a sniper and he'd gotten out at fifty kills, a boatload for any elite shooter. With one push of a button, he had crossed a moral and emotional line. Chat walked over, squatted next to Herc, and spoke softly. Chat nodded along. No one but Hercules could hear what Chat said, but Herc's whole posture changed. Emily scrambled off Nathan's lap and gave Chat a hug that took him by surprise, but he returned the gesture.

"You're something special. You know that, right?"

Chat smiled sadly at Emily. "It's a gift." He then turned back to the window and the night, leaving Emily feeling slightly puzzled.

Tox returned from the kitchen with half a sandwich in his hand and the other half in his mouth.

"What's your call sign?"

Herc turned a shade of cherry red that had the whole group waiting for his answer.

"Shorty."

"Why Shorty?" Emily asked. Herc was neither tall nor short at just shy of six feet.

At that moment, Maggie came out of the kitchen with a tray of goodies.

"Okay, Shortbread, I've got some snacks."

With that, Herc popped out of his chair, grabbed the plate of cookies off the tray, took four for himself, and sent the treats around the room. When Emily took a bite, she couldn't contain her groan.

"Oh my God, Maggie."

Herc shook his head. "That very sound got me my nickname. Maggie used to send them to me at the base."

Tox grabbed a handful. "That's not so bad. Ren," Tox snapped his fingers trying to recall, "that LT in Coronado . . . ."

Ren chuckled, "Rash." Emily made a face. "Pretty sure it was because he was impulsive, but there may be more to the story."

"I'm named for a cookie," Herc shook his head, "but when they call you Shorty and you're not short in height, people wonder."

Tox wiped the crumbs from his hands. "Have fun proving them wrong. Nail the chattiest chick at the bar. That'll clear things up real fast."

From seemingly out of nowhere, a shortbread cookie smacked him in the side of the head. The icing causing it to stick for a moment before dropping into his extended hand. Tox looked sharply to the source, but Twitch was engrossed in something on her monitor. He gave her a narrow-eyed glance as he took a bite.

"Tox!"

"Sorry, Emily. Now I just think of you as one of the guys."

Emily sat back against Nathan's chest, the offense forgotten.

Finn entered the room with a duffle slung over his shoulder. "You girls gonna be okay on your own?"

Tox stood and slapped him on the back. "Beat it, spook. We'll call you if we need you."

"Copy that. It's been a pleasure." And with that, he was out the door.

Charlie marched through the room into the kitchen, planted a Hollywood kiss on Maggie, then turned back to the group.

"Okay, your destination is the U.S. Naval Research Lab outpost in Norfolk. Lots of letters of the alphabet awaiting your arrival. I have cars ready nearby. Nathan, you take the case with Chat. Tox and I will take the lead car. Ren and Twitch, you follow. Wheels up from Charleston 0600."

Nathan walked Emily down the wide deck stairs, around the high grass and dunes, and to the long flat beach. She could barely make out the water, but the wind had kicked up and she could hear the rumble of the waves crashing and the slosh of their retreat.

"I don't want to leave you."

"I don't want you to leave, but it's okay. I've gotten pretty good at looking out for myself."

"I know that. I do. But you shouldn't have to."

"Dad and I are going to stay another day. Dad wants to catch up with Charlie, and I want to walk on the beach."

"Just walk?"

"Well, with you gone, walking is about the most exciting thing I can do on the beach."

Nathan dipped his head into the crook of her neck and kissed his way down to her clavicle. He palmed her breast beneath the cozy cardigan. "I'm not gone yet." Nathan pulled off his barn jacket and spread it on the sand. Emily hiked her skirt up and positioned herself on the coat. As he dropped his pants and boxer briefs to his ankles, Nathan disappeared under her flowy skirt. Emily shouted out his name, her cries swallowed by the surf. Nathan emerged with a devilish grin and brought Emily astride him. She impaled herself on his length and wrapped her legs around his waist as Nathan bent his knees to cradle her as they moved. They came together as Nathan roared. And there in the howling wind, beside the raging surf and under stars that blinked as clouds rushed by, Nathan held Emily until she fell asleep.

Emily awoke feeling out of sorts. She knew Nathan had carried her into bed, and she also knew he was gone. She chided herself for feeling so dependent that his absence made her physically ill. She had one day to herself, and she was going to enjoy every minute of it. She plotted a mental agenda as she shed her clothes from the night before and popped into the shower. Her need to steady herself on the tile wall as the water beat down had her wondering if this was some residual side effect from the drug she had been given; her equilibrium was off. When her head cleared, she dried off, slipped into cozy yoga pants and a sweater and followed the smell of bacon and cinnamon.

Maggie turned and smiled, looking like the star of a baking show with her bright apron and tray of warm sticky buns. Emily breathed deep and took a step forward to snatch a treat, then the room spun. She groped for the chair back nearby and finally steadied herself on the kitchen counter. Maggie set the tray down and calmly rested a hand on her back.

"Sweetie? You okay?"

"I think so. I've just been dizzy."

"When did it start?"

"This morning. Well, I guess I've noticed it for a day or two. I could be coming down with a bug. Or it's some type of residual effect of the drug I was given."

"Charlie always says when you see hoofprints—think horses, not zebras."

Emily didn't pretend to misunderstand.

"I'm not pregnant." She pointed to her arm. "I have an implant." Her eyes followed her finger to her right upper arm. More specifically, to the small healed cut on her upper arm. "Oh my God, they removed it. They must have thought it was a tracking implant." Emily looked at Maggie, who was beaming at her. "I think we need to visit Dr. Hardy. Great name for a doctor, isn't it?"

"Ohmygodohmygodohmygod." Emily covered her face with her hands.

"Emily." Maggie's voice was soft but stern. Emily looked up. "Herc came to me when his father, my son Angus, got his high school girlfriend pregnant. My neighbor Helen had a baby at forty-eight. She has a grandchild older than her youngest. My skunk of a first husband left me with three babies under the age of three." Maggie cupped Emily's face and thumbed away the tears. "Every baby is a miracle. You'll realize that soon enough."

Emily shook her head. "It's too soon."

Just then, Hercules stomped into the room in his boxers and a T-shirt wrinkled from sleep. "Smells awesome in here, Mhamó."

Maggie shook her head. "They also have terrible timing." Both women laughed.

CHAPTER FORTY-TWO

The sleek, black Bentley pulled silently to the curb. A pair of elegantly trousered legs and a gleaming, ebony cane emerged onto the pavement. The weathered hand that held the jade carved snake head at the handle followed. The man turned and extended his other hand to the delicate arm of the lady behind him. The petite woman, clad in a simple black sheath with a double strand of pearls at her neck, emerged and stood by his side. Next came a young Asian man, in a wrinkled button-down shirt and dark slacks, holding a laptop. The trio waited for the pair of hulking bodyguards to flank them, then they walked silently into the auction house. A professional-looking woman greeted them in the sparse but elegant lobby.

"Herr Dohrmann?"

The man nodded once and signaled for the guard to produce his credentials. When the employee had inspected them, she turned and directed them into a private elevator. The woman spoke more to fill the silence than to impart information.

"Obviously, the Gutenberg is the big draw. Although there are some collectors for the lot that interests you. The three I'm aware of are bidding remotely. You may end up with quite a steal."

The man gave his cane an imperceptible squeeze, and without taking his eyes from the mirrored doors, in thickly accented English, said simply, "I doubt that."

One hour later, Herr Dohrmann and his wife slowly walked to the curb and returned to the idling sedan. Their techie, phone at his ear, peeled off from the group and climbed into a nondescript SUV. One of the bodyguards placed the case in the rear footwell and got into the front passenger seat; the other guard was already behind the wheel. Only then did Herr Dohrman allow a small smile to tilt his lips. The driver's eyes met his in the rearview mirror.

"Congratulations, sir."

"Thank you. Let's deliver this, and if you wouldn't mind, we'd like to go to the Russian Tea Room."

"Of course."

"I'm taking my wife to lunch."

CHAPTER FORTY-THREE

Emily wrapped the cotton cardigan more tightly around her. Despite the warm weather, the breeze had picked up, and she felt an ominous chill. Dr. Hardy had kindly stopped by the cottage on his way to the office and confirmed Maggie's diagnosis. Although once Emily realized her birth control implant had been removed, it wasn't difficult to guess. She'd gone from virgin to sex maniac in a matter of days. Caroline's unabashed texts were filled with suggestions for bedroom antics. Nathan would snatch her phone and hold it out of reach as he read Caroline's pornographic ideas. *My god, half of this shit I've never heard of, and I've been around.* Emily had blanched at the remark, but Nathan was quick to ease her mind. *Emily, it was meaningless. A facade. I didn't have a different name like you did, but I was another person just the same.* Emily had given him a wicked smile and crawled into his lap. *Now, this reverse cowgirl sounds interesting . . . .*

It was odd for a woman who had been so solitary to perceive Nathan's absence with such intensity. Nevertheless, she felt a palpable ache, a phantom pain. Perhaps that feeling had been there all along, but like the memories of her captivity, she had packed it away, unresolved. And now she was carrying his child. Despite the unexpected news and the awful timing, Emily was filled with a foreign feeling that she correctly noted was . . . hope. She ran a gentle hand over her flat belly and imagined herself rounded and full. Lost in her thoughts, she hadn't noticed the burly man standing beside one of the marked beach exit trails through the dunes. The voice behind her had her spinning around as she skirted a beached jellyfish. Dario Sava stood with his hands in the pockets of a duster, a stylish fedora tilted just so.

"You were supposed to be mine, you know."

Emily studied him for a moment, struck by the utter lack of emotion in his wistful words. While attractive and quietly confident, the apathy in his dark eyes made her shudder. She examined her options. The man had no weapon that she could see, and she had taken down men bigger than his henchman.

"I would have taken good care of you. Tala would have spoiled you rotten. You would have wanted for nothing. Known no fear. Your life would have been so different."

"And yet, you were the cause of that fear. Is that something a father would do, Mr. Sava?"

If he was surprised by the use of his name, he didn't show it.

"Perhaps not. Nevertheless, your father took something from me, took *everything* from me, and order must be restored. I cannot go to Tala while this injustice lingers."

Emily noticed then his gaunt face and thin frame.

"The cancer has returned." It wasn't a question.

"With a vengeance, I'm afraid." Dario spoke with the disinterest of someone talking about the weather.

"You're one to speak of injustice."

"Ah, my dear, you understand little of the world. Moving from order to chaos is the natural way of things." Dario paused and looked out to the horizon. You make me mourn the loss of having you as a child. I could have taught you so much."

The hulk began to step toward her. Emily readied her stance.

"I must ask you not to resist. Pedro is merely our escort. You will come willingly, or I will detonate the small explosive in the case currently in the possession of your lover. You should pray the explosion kills him; the toxin that will be released brings a much more unpleasant end."

Emily thought for a moment. There was a chance he was bluffing. Tox and Ren had examined the case and found no explosive. But they hadn't opened the canister that contained the toxin.

"I see your mind working. I assure you I mean what I say. However, if the inevitable demise of Nathan Bishop and everyone in his vicinity isn't motivation enough, Pedro's brother is across the way with your father in his crosshairs as he reads on the porch. It's strange, really. You've lived a selfish existence thus far, focused solely on self-preservation. Your father has sacrificed everything for you. Have you ever danced with the notion of doing the same for him?"

No. She hadn't. It was a scenario she hadn't considered. Would she?

"Lead the way."

With that, Emily took her place between the guard and Dario as they walked off the beach and climbed into a black SUV. The man in the back seat beside her sat stone-faced and vigilant. Dario took the passenger seat and Pedro climbed behind the wheel. Again, Emily weighed her options.

"I apologize for the tranquilizer. We have a long drive ahead of us, and like you, I minimize risk."

Before Emily could resist or think about the effect of the drug on the new life inside her, she felt the prick in her arm, and knowing it was useless to struggle, sat back and watched the world go by. She couldn't even put her hand to the window as she watched Hercules Reynolds maneuver Charlie's three unwieldy dogs down the narrow sidewalk and stop to watch as the sleek SUV turned the corner and drove away.

CHAPTER FORTY-FOUR

"It's pancake syrup."

Charlie and Nathan stood there dazed and stared as the scientist, Navy Lieutenant Brooks, peeled off his protective gear. "Mrs. Butterworth's if I'm not mistaken. It has an additional additive that gives it a slightly different smell and taste than, say, Log Cabin or Aunt Jemima."

Tox leaned over to Ren. "Is he shitting us right now?"

"Well, it does taste different, but I see your point."

North got them back on track. "And as far as *other* additives?"

"Just plain old syrup. You could pour it on an Eggo."

"Damn, now I want waffles." Tox, of course.

"Fucking Sava and his fucking red herrings." Charlie Bishop allowed the rare burst of temper. "There's a biotoxin out there that we have no clue how to find."

"Not necessarily." Nathan's face was impassive, but his confidence betrayed his suspicion. "I think Dario Sava acquired something extremely valuable from Detachment 731, and I also think he's selling it, but I don't think it's a virus." Nathan had their full attention. "I think it's a formula. Or more specifically, a journal from one of the researchers, or even Ishii himself, containing methods of reengineering viruses, formulas, and results."

"My God," Ren reflected, "a bioterrorist guidebook."

"Exactly," Nathan confirmed. "The collective research from Detachment 731 has unfathomable potential for devastation."

"What made you conclude it's a journal?" Chat queried.

Nathan thanked Lieutenant Brooks, and the scientist retreated to his lab.

"As Charlie mentioned, the CIA has a man inside the Sava organization, Camilo Canto. You guys remember him? He was with the Teams for a couple of years. JJ?"

"Oh shit, yeah. El Jefe de Joder. The boss of fuck." Tox started to go on, but Ren's quelling look silenced him. Tox cleared his throat. "You were saying, North?"

"So, Sava's got all these balls in the air. He tries to abduct Emily. He's trying to smuggle some sort of bioweapon into the U.S., then out of the blue, he pulls Cam aside and tells him to deliver a set of books to a rare book auction in New York."

"But why would he even do that when he could just sell the book from the comfort of his home?"

Charlie knew the answer. "It's what happens when recklessness meets arrogance. Anyone can sell a weapon like that. Dario Sava auctioned off a collection of research on the most lethal biotoxins ever used right under our noses."

"About a week ago, I had a strange conversation with Anya Amirov, the wife of a very high-profile broker. I correctly assumed her husband would be at the front of the line for a biotoxin purchase. He has ties to both Chechen rebels and Syrian terror groups. I was working her for information on the auction, and she said her husband had complained about a meeting which must have been with Sava's people. She said he kept going on about how he wasn't a 'do-it-yourself-er.' I didn't put it together at the time, but Amirov must have been referencing the fact that the item discovered from Detachment 731 was research and not an actual toxin. So, when Cam called to update me and told me about his errand to the book auction, it clicked."

Charlie blew out an audible breath and looked at Nathan with something akin to pride.

Twitch looked up from her tablet. "Torvald Auction House held a rare book auction this morning. One of the items was the 1945 journal of Japanese writer Yasunari Kawabata."

"That's setting off some alarm bells."

"Not as much as this," Twitch added. "The journal's estimated value was between $90,000 and $150,000. It sold for $3.2 million."

"That's our book."

"How do we track it down?"

"We don't need to." The group waited for Nathan to elaborate. "It's sitting in my safe. My doorman Leonard Pipham has a very colorful background in England. My grandfather worked with him."

"He was in Parliament?"

"Oh, God no. Much less devious. He was a spy, back when they still used that term. A good one, too. Some of his exploits with the SAS are the stuff of legend."

Ren looked stunned. "Not the Mongoose?"

Twitch rolled her eyes. "Don't be ridiculous. The Mongoose is a Cold War myth invented by people who read too much Follett and Forsyth."

Nathan continued without denial or confirmation. "In any event, Leonard is perfect for certain odd jobs. Nobody suspects a seventy-five-year-old operative. Leonard bought the book. Teddy handled the electronic transfer."

"Teddy?" Twitch's voice was laced with irritation.

Teddy was Twitch's protégé of sorts. She had beaten him in some sort of legitimate hacking competition, and as payback, Teddy had done some rather nasty things, not the least of which was have ConEd cut off her electricity for lack of payment. Rather than her normal scorched earth approach, Twitch simply showed up at his door. When she discovered with amused shock that Teddy, hacker name the uninventive "Doom," lived with his aunt and uncle in a room that was basically under a staircase, she simply looked at him and said the only thing she could: *you're a wizard, Teddy*. From then on, Teddy had become like a little brother to her. He wasn't privy to her work at K-B, not yet anyway, but Twitch had an equally impressive set up in her Brooklyn brownstone, complete with a gaming system, and she and Teddy spent nearly all their free time there. Teddy had dangerous skills. Twitch shouldered the responsibility of keeping Teddy on the straight and narrow, or straight and broadband as the case may be.

"He was ready for a job, don't you think?"

"He should have told me."

"I was testing him. He tends to run his mouth. I wanted to see what he did."

"Looks like he passed."

"He did, but it's about to get tricky. He's following the money transfer, but Dario Sava is not some two-bit drug courier. Even with our virtual explosive dye pack, he's going to need your help."

Twitch nodded. "I'll have him meet me at the office. We headed to NYC?"

Nathan nodded as the group moved to pack up. "I'm going to accompany Charlie back to South Carolina and fetch Emily."

Charlie retrieved his phone from an interior coat pocket. "Four missed calls from Maggie. Something's not right." Charlie returned the call and had to listen twice to Maggie's frantic explanation before he finally got the gist. Nathan stared at him, straining to hear Maggie's words. Charlie ended the call.

"Emily's been taken. Maggie caught sight of her leaving the beach with two men. One tall, one short. Hercules clocked a black Escalade driving away. Tinted windows, SC plates, rental car sticker on the back tailgate."

Nathan went into battle mode without pause. "Twitch, get on it. Find out where they're going. We need the CIA's help with this. See if they know any holdings Sava has in the U.S. I need to contact Cerberus."

"Let me see what I can do." Charlie was already scrolling through contacts. Nathan stared for a moment as realization dawned. The computer set up in Charlie's cozy cottage, his intricate web of connections and channels of information. His three dogs. Always three.

"Cerberus." It wasn't a question. Charlie Bishop was Nathan's covert government contact. Charlie had, no doubt, chosen the code name—the mythological three-headed dog that guards the gates of hell—himself.

Charlie looked up and hit Nathan with a *took-you-long-enough* smile.

"Sofria Kirk should be able to help."

Twitch didn't look up from her ever-present laptop. "On it."

"In the meantime," Charlie continued, "let's head back to Royal. I work best from the home office, and you can get more detailed information from Mags. You also may want to bring Hercules along with you when you leave."

"Why's that?"

"He didn't elaborate on his military record. He never does, but he may be the best long-distance sniper the Marines have ever seen. If you need someone on overwatch, he's your guy."

Charlie followed the group out of the Naval Research Lab. His decision to withhold Maggie's other news about Emily not sitting quite right. A man had a right to know these things. Nevertheless, after quickly weighing his options, he determined that Nathan was already so emotionally impacted by yet another attempt to harm Emily, he'd never be able to hold it together if he knew Emily was pregnant. Still, Charlie had decided a long time ago he was through playing God. He lacked certain qualifications for the job.

Twitch, Ren, Chat, and Tox opted to drive back to New York. Twitch had heard back from CIA analyst Sofria Kirk almost immediately and needed to stop in Arlington to pick up the information Sofria hadn't wanted to transmit electronically. Tox wanted to pick up Finn, who was back at his mother's house in Philly. Chat gave a sharp nod of agreement, and Ren simply headed to the car.

Charlie and Nathan peeled off and climbed into the back of the other Suburban one of Charlie's contacts had kindly arranged. The Master at Arms naval officer at the wheel would return the car after dropping them at the private airfield where the K-B jet was fueled and ready. Nathan was already pulled tighter than a tripwire when Charlie turned to him.

"There's something else you need to know."

Nathan turned to him stone-faced.

"Maggie noticed Emily wasn't feeling quite right. Emily realized when her captors had removed her tracking implant, they also removed her birth control implant. They must have mistaken it for a backup."

Nathan continued to listen, but Charlie could see he wasn't connecting the dots.

"Nathan, son, Emily's pregnant."

Nathan's eyes were wide as saucers, and an enormous smile split his face. In an instant he composed himself. He took a deep breath, blew it out, and with a mastery of understatement deeply ingrained by his British mother, he calmly replied, "Well, we had better get her back then, hadn't we?"

"There," Twitch pointed through the rain-dotted windshield. "Pink umbrella out in front of the Starbucks. Pull over here and I'll walk over to her." Twitch hopped out and trotted across the street, shielding her head from the rain with her hands. Sofria was an analyst with a low-level clearance. As such, her identity wasn't closely guarded, but nevertheless, she had a barebones social media presence. Twitch had still managed to find a picture of her, but it didn't do her justice. Her exotic features—Indian, Twitch guessed—were framed by a sheet of jet-black hair. As Twitch approached, Sofria shifted her feet from side to side and scanned the area like a scalper looking for buyers. Twitch chuckled; she wouldn't last one day in the field.

"Sofria?" Twitch waved.

Sofria looked as though she was going to shush her but stopped herself with her lips pursed. She nodded once. Glanced around again.

"So. How do we do this?"

Twitch could barely contain her amusement.

"How long have you worked for the . . ."

At Sofria's panicked look, Twitch rephrased.

"How long have you been at your current job?"

"Six months."

"Okay, well, in situations like this, SOP is you retrieve the file from your bag, and very, *very* carefully place it in my hands."

Sofria listened intently, then caught on.

"There's no need to be a bitch about it. I've never done this before."

Twitch nodded in approval. The newbie analyst had a backbone.

"Sorry. I couldn't resist. It's just a file. You're just a worker bee. I'm just an IT grunt. Give it here, and you can be drinking a vanilla latte in no time."

"Oh, that does sound good." With that, Sofria retrieved the flash drive from her bag and gave it to Twitch.

"Awesome. Your first live drop was a success."

Twitch's use of the espionage term had Sofria glancing around again. Twitch pocketed the flash drive and waved.

"Thanks for this. See you around."

"Here," Sofria extended her hand. "Take my umbrella. I live right here, and the skies have opened."

"Thanks." Twitch gifted her with a genuine freckle-faced smile. "I'll try to get it back to you."

With that, Twitch, sheltered by the bright pink umbrella, trotted back to the car, and they were on their way to the roadside motel to get some sleep and prepare.

CHAPTER FORTY-FIVE

Finn McIntyre awoke to that familiar painful fog, not so unaware that he didn't sense the other presence in the bed.

"Get out."

The bottle blonde rolled and covered her mouth, suppressing a booze-laced yawn.

"So not a morning person," she drawled.

"Not a noon or night person either. I've got shit to do."

"So, I'm guessing breakfast is out?"

Finn didn't answer. He was looking at the text on his phone and furrowing his brow.

"Out."

"What did I ever do to get hooked up with an asshole like you?"

"I'm guessing there's a long list."

The woman peeled the skin-tight dress back over her thin frame, stuffed her thong into her bag, and hop-walked to the door slipping into her heels.

"You know, I had a nice time last night. I wasn't looking for anything more. For no reason at all, you turned the whole thing into a big pile of shit."

Finn hobbled to the shower. He had maybe thirty minutes before they came to pick him up. *Well,* he thought as he fumbled with the water pressure, *turning things into a big pile of shit? My specialty.*

✦

Nathan and Charlie were sitting in Charlie's Royal Beach office when the call came.

"Sofria really came through," Twitch spoke in one continuous stream. "I mean the kind of tenacity required to follow these threads is unbelievable. She's only worked for the CIA for six months and probably gathered more information about Sava's network than the entire team working before her arrival. I mean, wait till I give her the info that's coming in from the virtual explosive dye pack. They can dismantle the entire organization. And not just cut the head off the beast. I mean, take the entire thing apart piece by piece."

"Twitch!" Nathan rarely shouted, but circumstances were unusual.

"Sorry, Nathan. Okay, so the bad news is Dario Sava owns a lot of shit in the U.S. Because Tala was American and rich, they were able to purchase everything from vacation homes to office buildings with legitimate funds. There is good news, though."

Charlie waved in Hercules, who was standing in the doorway.

"Tala grew up on a horse farm outside of Baltimore. I mean, you should see this thing, Nathan; this is some *America's Castles* shit. Anyway, Tala was an only child and when she died, Sava inherited the farm. He keeps and maintains the property but only uses it once a year. At the exact same time."

"Why?"

"Tala's family cemetery is on the property. It's a historic site. Some of the graves date back to the eighteenth century. Sava visits on their wedding anniversary. Not the anniversary of her death which was last month, but their wedding which is . . . tomorrow."

That was it. Nathan knew it as soon as he heard it. Sava was a man who liked a certain artistry to his actions. Doing—he mentally skipped over whatever it was Dario Sava intended—this thing on their anniversary, at his wife's grave, was what, in Sava's dark mind, the situation demanded. Nathan stood with a warrior's focus and texted a quick message to his pilot. When he turned, he came face-to-face with Hercules, standing at ease, the lightweight case that held his Remington bolt-action sniper rifle slung across his back.

The two men couldn't be less alike, but Nathan liked the kid. He had a resolve that Nathan admired.

"I imagine you're looking for a job."

"Yes, sir."

"Good."

Nathan turned his attention back to the phone that Twitch had connected to the car's Bluetooth.

"Twitch, forward aerial and topographic maps. We're about two hours out. Where are you?"

"In a surprisingly crowded car. We just grabbed Finn in Philly and are headed back to Maryland." Twitch paused as she presumably checked something. "There's a diner in the small town near the estate. Molly's Kitchen on Route 3."

"Let's meet up there at 1800 hours."

Tox confirmed. "Copy that, North."

"This ends now."

"Hooyah."

Molly's Diner was more of a hipster coffee house than a roadside diner. The four behemoths standing in the doorway had every head looking up. Nevertheless, Twitch donned a bright smile and plowed ahead toward a large, unoccupied farm table in the back corner of the room. It was near the coffee-doctoring area which held a variety of milks and flavorings, but it was the only seating that would accommodate them. When the teenage waitress dropped off water, Twitch ordered two each of the five pizza specials listed on the chalkboard behind the counter. The waitress looked a bit puzzled.

"They're full-sized pizzas, you know. You want two for each person?"

Tox tipped his chair back onto two legs and grinned. "If we need more after those, we'll let you know." Then he winked. The waitress grew wide-eyed, then shook her head smiling as she hurried away.

"Down boy. She's twelve." Finn tipped Tox's chair back a bit more, forcing Tox to right himself.

"Just some good-natured ribbing."

The reminder of Finn's presence sobered Twitch, and she scolded them.

"Can we please focus on the task at hand?"

Finn smirked, "Focusing on a task has never been a problem."

Twitch gave him an icy glare but remained stoic. "Yes, Finnegan, job performance is not on your long list of flaws. Yet."

Finn started to respond, but the door hitting the wind chimes at the front had them looking up to see Nathan and Hercules striding purposefully across the room.

The new arrivals each took an empty seat, and the grave expression on Nathan's face silenced the banter.

"Sava is smart, but he's arrogant. He's pulled off too many exchanges to doubt his abilities. So, we have the element of surprise. Also, because Emily escaped last time, he doesn't know what he's dealing with."

"A private army," Tox nodded.

"No," Nathan clarified. "Me."

"I sent a drone to reconnoiter, and as we expected, the house is occupied. Looks like four heat signatures inside the house, four outside." Ren added.

"We're assuming Sava, Emily, and six guards?" Finn asked.

They paused while the waitress filled the table with pizzas as Twitch moved water glasses and her laptop to make room.

"Correct. There are no staff on-premises. Looks like even the caretaker has been sent away," Ren confirmed.

"He doesn't want to make the same mistake he made when she escaped the last time. No convenient rides out," Tox observed.

Nathan continued, "It's no longer an operational horse farm. There are no animals on the property, but all the outbuildings, barn, stable, guest house and storage shed are still there."

He looked as though he were trying to defuse a bomb that was ticking down on the table. Tox was quick to reassure him.

"Come on, North. A training exercise wouldn't be this easy."

Nathan rubbed his hand down his face. "I'll agree, it's ideal for an infil. Sava's making sure Emily can't escape, but he's not expecting someone to come in and get her."

Chat set his pizza slice down on his plate. "It seems to me your biggest problem is Emily."

Nathan looked up and waited for Chat to explain. "She's used to getting out of these situations on her own. Sava may have her guarded, but she's not just going to sit there like a damsel. We need to think of her as an asset on the inside, not a hostage."

Nathan nodded and smiled. "Yes. An asset. And this time she knows I'm coming."

CHAPTER FORTY-SIX

Emily had already released the zip ties around her wrists, methodically loosening them groove by groove until the plastic slipped off. She kept her hands behind her back and waited for an opportunity. One guard sat near her in the frilly bedroom. He squirmed a bit in the ladderback chair that was turned away from the small desk where his Glock rested and read something on his phone. They both heard the pebble hit the window, but only the guard looked up.

"Did you hear that?"

"Hear what?" Emily glanced his way from her seat against the head-board. "Can I have something to eat or at least read? I'm bored."

The guard picked up on Emily's attempt to distract him. A little reverse psychology had done the trick.

"Shut up."

He rose and crossed to the window. Emily only heard the quick break of the glass and the thud of the guard as he fell. Without pause, Emily shot to her feet, grabbed the Glock from the desk and waited. She knew Nathan and his men could neutralize the guards patrolling outside. That left the guard outside her door and Sava. He had still been downstairs when she was escorted to this hideous bedroom. She removed a pink case from the menagerie of pillows decorating the bed and waved it in front of the window. Hopefully signaling to the sniper that she was a friendly. When no shot came, she slipped in front of the glass and raised the window. The second-floor windows were not connected to the alarm system. Unfortunately, the shouts from the sentries outside accomplished the same objective, and the second guard threw open the bedroom door. Emily had never shot an actual person before. She had never killed a man. She had never been shot herself, but all three of those things happened in the next instant.

"Got him. He's heading to the cemetery," Twitch spoke into the comm unit to Nathan who was moving in the shadows across the grounds.

"How convenient."

"It's a smart move. Lots of cover, trees, and graves, and there's a shed where he could store an ATV. There's access to a service road there. He's not planning his funeral; he's planning his escape."

"Not this time."

The guard and Emily fired at the same time. Emily had aimed for center mass as she'd been taught but his shot caused her to flinch slightly and she hit the guard in the side of the neck. Same result. The guard's shot grazed Emily's torso. Blood was dripping down her side.

Ren appeared at the doorway, quickly assessed the situation, and crossed to Emily.

"Let's have a look."

"How do people in movies get shot, then run all around fighting bad guys? This freaking *hurts*."

Ren chuckled. "Imagine how an actual bullet wound would feel."

Emily glanced down at the injury. "Oh." She would describe it as a deep scratch. Then she remembered. "Ren, I'm pregnant." If he was surprised by the news, he didn't show it.

"Nothing to worry about, Emily. This barely qualifies as a *wound*, much less a gunshot wound."

She could hear Caroline's voice in her head: *Hey, it counts; a bullet from a gun caused bodily harm. You got shot.*

"You'll need a couple of stitches, I think. Let's get out of here, and I'll get you cleaned up."

"Is it over?"

Ren looked out the window into the night, then clicked his mic to signal something to the team and nodded once.

"Almost."

Dario Sava was out of breath when he reached the cemetery. Why was he even running? A bullet would be a more merciful end than what awaited him. The cancer was everywhere: his lungs, his liver, his brain. He nearly laughed. Perhaps that was the reason for the series of errors in judgment that had led him to this place. He moved across the graveyard, heading to his wife's headstone. He checked the time.

"Happy anniversary, darling. I'll be joining you soon."

"Yes. You will."

Dario spoke without turning. "Ah, Mr. Bishop. I hadn't factored you into the equation properly. Your reputation as a lothario is very effective."

"Thank you."

"I imagine you bought my book as well?"

"Yes."

He turned from his wife's grave to face his doom. A small object nestled in his hand.

"I didn't pursue justice for myself, you know. I did it for Tala." He paused, swallowed. "She was purity and light, and her only selfish wish was a child. If you could even call that selfish." He sighed in resignation. "Not the final act I had envisioned for myself, but perhaps not the one you had envisioned either. Because, you see, unlike my perfect wife, I am not an altruist."

With that, Sava revealed the small hand grenade and pulled the pin. He drew his hand back and aimed in Nathan's direction. Nathan took off at a run after voicing the command. "Send it."

The shot hit Dario square between the eyes, and he fell back against Tala Savo's headstone. The grenade rolled from his open palm into the soft grass. Nathan was barely out of the blast radius when he dove behind a small, now crumbling, gravestone. When the dust settled, Nathan was on his back looking up. Hercules, who had positioned himself in a tree in a small copse, was dangling from a branch by his arms and legs, rifle over his back.

"Shorty," Nathan chuckled into a coughing fit.

Hercules hopped down and squatted next to him. "You okay?"

Nathan rolled to his hands and knees and looked up at his sniper.

"You're hired."

Hercules helped Nathan to his feet, and they walked slowly back to the secluded area behind the barn where Twitch was running the show. Ren was slapping a bandage on Emily's side. Nathan forgot about his own battered body and rushed to her. Ren was quick to calm him.

"She just got nicked. She could maybe use a couple of stitches. It probably won't even scar." He grabbed Nathan's upper arm, met his gaze, and spoke with meaning. "Everything looks fine."

With that, Nathan dropped to his knees in front of her and placed a reverent kiss on her belly. Emily ran both hands through his hair. The rest of the team smiled and turned to gather their things, leaving them to their private moment.

CHAPTER FORTY-SEVEN

It was raining in Washington—no surprise for October—but Ren would be damned if he used the bright pink umbrella currently tucked under his arm. He was very evolved when it came to most things female, but his reluctance to use the fuchsia dome did have more to do with its girliness than, as he mentally justified it, with his natural aversion to standing out. He didn't really understand why Twitch had felt this obligation to return the darn thing. It was an umbrella. Weren't they disposable? Nevertheless, Twitch suggested he return it when Ren mentioned he was submitting an adjunct brief for an obscure land-use case being argued before the Supreme Court. After the Fifth Circuit Appeals Court had overturned the District Court's ruling on a Wildlife Sanctuary in the Louisiana Bayou, the Supremes had decided to hear the case, no doubt realizing its bearing on relaxed land-use restrictions on less invasive alternative energy sources.

Ren taught a course at Columbia called Environmentalism and the Economy. While his concern for the planet was profound, Ren knew first-hand that environmentalism was a cause ripe for manipulation by profiteers and people with less than altruistic motives. Like everything in his world—shadow and light.

Ren found the building and hit the buzzer for 2B ("or not to be" flashed through his mind and he chuckled) and waited. He looked up at the functioning security camera and waved the pink umbrella. After a long minute, the door chimed open. The building was very nice, no door-man, but clean and well-maintained, with plexiglass double doors at the entrance and a well-lit lobby with residents' mailboxes and a small sitting area. In other words, a dump by patrician Georgetown standards.

Outside 2B, he knocked softly and waited. *Sofria Kirk,* he mused, *what an incongruous name.* The given name so flowery and melodic, the surname so sharp and curt. She must have very interesting parents. Movement on the other side of the door alerted him to her presence. She was checking the peephole. Then the door opened a crack with the safety chain still in place.

"Sofria? Twitch sent me to deliver this." He waved the stupid umbrella. Again. "I can pass it through the crack if you like."

Sofria's mass of ebony hair was secured on her head in a bun that had morphed into a crooked ponytail. She seemed to gather herself while she blinked up at Ren, staring at him through dark-framed glasses that looked like something a dad in a 1950s TV show would wear. She closed the door, and while Ren knew she was unlatching the chain, he wondered if she had just retreated to her bedroom and left him out in the hall.

The door opened and there she stood. Ren had to remember to breathe. She wasn't super tall, just above average, but in the cutoff jeans and bare feet, her cocoa legs went on for days. God, she was breathtak-ing, not a traditional beauty—exotic, but not foreign. Everything about her, from her vintage Coney Island T-shirt to her toe ring screamed American. Why was that toe ring making him crazy? She was ner-vous and scrunched the scarlet toes of her right foot on top of her left, drawing his eye to the little band of silver. Her wide, whiskey-colored eyes darted around as if someone might be in the apartment or spying through the window. Then she held out her hand.

"Give it to me."

Ren complied. She hurried over to her office, which was once a dining nook, and set the umbrella on the desk. She unscrewed the handle and retrieved a flash drive from the hollowed-out center. Then she inserted it into her laptop and booted it up. All while Ren stood there with a *what the fuck is happening* look on his face. He inched closer to stare over her shoulder at the screen, where animated pigs were dancing in a kickline. Sofria clapped with glee.

"I'm sure it's none of my business . . . ."

"Twitch is helping me. I'm just an analyst, but I'd like to have some skill in fieldwork if the need ever arose."

Understanding dawned. "Ah, it's all very clear now. A few things to think about . . . ." Sofria gave him her full attention.

"You need to know *for a fact* I am who I say I am. If you don't know your contact, you need to make sure you're meeting the right person."

"So, like a code word?"

"Or an ID."

"I like a code word. Very Graham Greene. What else?"

"Well, and it's a small thing, your front door is wide open."

"Oh my God!" Sofria rushed to slam it shut. "I'll never be a spy."

"You know they don't use that term."

"I know. I know. 'Field agent.'" She air quoted it for some bizarre reason, and Ren had to chuckle.

"Probably not, but you should always be striving to improve."

Recognizing the familiar phrase, Sofria turned and really looked at him for the first time.

"Professor Jameson?"

Ren's eyes grew wide, but he didn't recognize the starry-eyed student staring up at him.

"Yes, but you can call me Ren. I work with Twitch. I don't remember you from my class."

"I took it last year. I wasn't officially enrolled, so I sat in the back."

"Which graduate program were you in? Or were you a Ph.D. candidate?"

Sofria looked a bit chagrined. "Undergrad."

Holy shit. Ren was ogling a teenager. Well, not literally, but close enough. Ren cleared his throat and backed towards the door. "Well, the CIA must have grabbed you up as you walked off the stage with your diploma."

"They actually grabbed me up after my sophomore year."

Holy double shit. She was an *actual teenager.* Trying to avoid making a Ren-shaped hole in the drywall, he nodded like a bobblehead. She didn't seem to pick up on his discomfort.

"I have a knack for seeing patterns in data."

Ren had a sneaking suspicion that was an understatement.

"I also practice radical honesty—involuntarily, I'm afraid. But I don't think that's why they recruited me."

"Probably also why you'll never be a field agent."

"Damn. I hadn't thought of that. Oh well, I'm still going to practice. *Striving to improve* as you say." She thrust her index finger in the air to punctuate her comment.

Who the fuck is this girl? Ren couldn't stop the small smile. She went from timid to chatterbox in the blink of an eye. She had returned to her laptop and was bending over it from a standing position, typing away. Ren felt his pants tighten. In his mind, a tiny version of him was waving two red semaphore flags and yelling, *get out!*

"Well, I've made the drop. So, see you around, I guess."

See you around, I guess?! Smooth, Ren.

"Wait." She walked right up to him and kissed him on the cheek while at the same time, with the subtlety of a freight train, dropping the pig-dancing flash drive into his outer coat pocket.

"Bye, Ren. Tell Twitch I said hello. And thanks for bringing my umbrella back."

She beamed at him, and Ren nearly blushed. Of course, if he had actually reddened, Sofria would have never seen it. He was down the stairs and out the door faster than the blood could rush to his face.

CHAPTER FORTY-EIGHT

Nathan led Emily down to the beach with the care one might extend to the gravely injured or elderly. She had lectured him twenty times in the six short weeks since they had returned to New York that pregnancy was not a debilitating condition, and she could work, exercise, and go about her normal life. Of course, that was before the two distinct beating hearts had been clearly visible in the internal ultrasound. Twins. She wasn't even showing, but Nathan still handled her like porcelain. Maybe he always would.

The house in Nantucket was full to bursting this weekend. His team was camped out in the guest house, except for Ren who was arriving later from D.C., and Twitch who declared Chat's snoring was unbearable and had claimed a room in the main house. *For a guy who says nothing, he is the noisiest mofo sleeping I've ever heard.*

Charlie and Maggie had come to New York to help Herc get settled, and the three of them had arrived on the island this morning. Emily's father Jack was there and Nathan's mother Serafina had arrived from London that morning. Emily was no fool. She knew what was coming. So, when Nathan took her hand and led her down to the beach, she was a little surprised by the flock of birds that had taken flight in her belly. Nathan was the picture of calm until he tripped on a piece of driftwood then quickly righted himself. Emily smiled; thank God she wasn't the only one feeling nervous. She realized belatedly that Nathan was leading her to the exact spot where the picture of them as children had been taken. The sun was again a ball of orange in the sky, and Nathan pulled her close as it sank to a half-circle on the horizon.

"This is long overdue. I think we were a bit of a foregone conclusion. Doesn't make me less nervous, though."

"There'll always be a bit of that goofy, insecure boy inside of you."

With that, Nathan strummed an air guitar and made a face. Emily laughed.

"You feel okay? How's the nausea?"

"Oh my God, if you don't hurry it along, I'll give birth on this beach."

"Emily, will you marry me?" he blurted. "Oh damn, I forgot to get down on one knee. Should I do it now? Oh shit, wait. I have a ring. It's right . . . ." Nathan patted his pockets, but his search was halted when Emily grabbed his face with both hands and kissed him, slow and sure.

"No, to the knee. Yes, to the ring. And yes, to the proposal. Yes, Nathan Bishop, I will marry you. Finally."

After an exhaustive search of his pockets, he located the small Harry Winston box in his pocket. Nathan cracked it open to reveal a four-carat, cushion-cut, pink diamond in a traditional platinum setting. He plucked it out of the velvet and slid in on her finger.

"You pick the violets; I'll scare up a hand towel for your veil."

And they did just that.

They were married on the beach four weeks later, the crisp October breeze cooling the air to a mild-for-Nantucket seventy degrees. Emily wore a simple white cap sleeve gown with a violet ribbon that ran along the empire waist and down the back of the skirt. Serafina had helped her choose it—well, if "helped her choose" meant "had the designer fly in at the last minute and create it to their specifications." With a Victorian lace hand towel pinned into her hair, she carried a nosegay of violets. Nathan waited with the minister as she walked barefoot down the runner with her father. It was a short walk—fifty were in attendance—but by the time Emily was halfway, Nathan was ready to meet her there and haul her under the bower. Tox's massive hand on his shoulder stayed him. When she finally arrived, after what Nathan estimated to be a good hour, she met his gaze with a serene and glassy smile. Caroline, dressed in a simple lavender sheath, took the small bouquet and gave Emily a wink. The guys had opted not to wear dress whites. Ren, Chat, and Tox stood behind Nathan in khaki pants, blue blazers, and matching pear green Ferragamo ties, a gift from Jack. Nathan was similarly clad, except he wore the cornflower blue tie. Emily clutched it as she steadied herself. Nathan held her elbows gently.

"Ready?"

"So ready."

He rested his hand on her barely rounded belly.

"How's the team?"

"Sleepy like mommy."

"Then let's get you married so we can get you to bed."

"Why do I think that won't get me any rest?"

The minister cleared his throat. Nathan grinned.

EPILOGUE

Six months later ...

Nathan sat in a recliner in the overly bright hospital room and gazed down at the bundle tucked into his arm like a football. John "Jack" Webster Bishop had weighed in at six pounds, five ounces and was sleeping like a rock. His little fists were both tucked up against his mouth, and his cheeks made an absent sucking motion. How anyone could sleep in this chaos was beyond him. In the propped-up bed, Emily sat with the lactation consultant and fiddled with the baby in her arms. Charles "Charlie" Emerson Bishop had been larger than his brother at birth—seven pounds, three ounces—but Jack was catching up quickly. Especially since Charlie seemed to have trouble grasping the whole nursing thing.

"He's not latching on," Emily complained.

"Give him a minute. He'll figure it out."

And when he does there'll be no stopping him. Nathan chuckled at the thought. His wife's breasts held quite an appeal.

"Ouch! Oh, wait, I think he's getting it."

Emily relaxed a bit and beamed at the little man who had discovered his food source.

"I'll leave you to it. You can text me if you have questions." The lactation consultant spoke in a stage whisper and quietly left the room. Nathan placed a gentle kiss on his son's head and turned to watch Emily, who seemed mesmerized by Charlie.

"Is it weird that you're turning me on right now?"

Emily rolled her eyes and ignored the comment.

"Isn't it amazing that they just know to do it?"

"He's obviously a genius."

"Well, goats and chipmunks and cats do it too, so genius may be a stretch." She smiled down at her little creation with so much serenity and joy, Nathan nearly choked.

"I love you."

Emily looked up, stunned.

"I finally connected the word to the feeling." He met her gaze. "This is love. You are love."

"I love you, too."

"Remember that when we take these chaps home tomorrow, and I'm yelling for help in the middle of the night."

"I will."

Tox's massive frame in the doorway was partially obscured by a giant stuffed gorilla. Finn stood behind him with an equally large giraffe.

"Happy babying." Tox gifted Emily with a grin.

"Oh, hell no." Nathan looked at Emily for backup. "Where would we even put those things?"

"In their cribs or highchairs," Finn replied. "I assume you have all that stuff."

"Not the babies, you idiot, those things."

Tox stepped in. "It was more to get a reaction out of you. We're taking them to the children's ward."

"That's really nice." Emily smiled, more relieved at not having to maneuver the stuffed animals into the car than the act of generosity. Tox walked up to Nathan and looked down at the sleeping baby.

"Nice work, man. That's a cute fucking kid."

"Oh my God." Emily's outrage startled Charlie into a tiny full-body quiver, and she calmed her voice. "Work? From where I'm sitting, I did the work."

"I just did the fun part," Nathan winked.

"A thousand pardons, milady. I just meant that he's a pretty cute baby. I mean normally they're all misshapen and red and they have this weird, wrinkly . . ."

"Quit while you're ahead, man." Finn stayed him with a hand on his shoulder.

"I understand there's yet another handsome and charming Charlie Bishop in the world." Charlie entered the room and set a vase of yellow roses on one of the few available surfaces, the windowsill. Maggie was on his heels with a basket of food. Charlie walked up to Emily's bedside, kissed her forehead, and looked down at the baby who was now passed out and satisfied.

"Which one is he? Because if he's asleep with food on his chin, he should be Charlie."

Emily laughed, then winced. "Yes, he's Charlie. Nathan has Jack." Well, he did have Jack until Maggie scooped him up with a maternal expertise that left Emily in awe.

"Oh, Emily. Please bring them down for a visit. I've missed having babies around."

"Actually, Charlie, I wanted to talk to you about something." Nathan rose, and Charlie followed him out in the hall. Finn eyed them, but Tox had found the fried chicken. Maggie was perched on the bed, talking to Emily and hypnotized by the baby in her arms.

Out in the hall, Charlie didn't mince words.

"Have you given it some thought?"

"Didn't need to give it much. Spinning off Bishop Security is the right move. Port Royal is off the beaten path, but it has a good private airstrip and larger commercial airports not too far. Emily loves the idea. She wasn't keen on raising the twins in the city."

"It's a big sacrifice, Nathan."

"It's no sacrifice. I never wanted to be the CEO of K-B. It was thrust upon me by my father. This, Bishop Security and The Perseus Project, this is what I was meant to do."

"My brother was not a good man. Maybe the morality gene skips a generation in our family."

"That's troubling coming from the man I've come to think of as my moral compass."

Charlie put a hand on his shoulder. "I'm a very proud uncle."

"Great-uncle," Nathan amended.

"I am great, aren't I?"

Seraphina Bishop, looking as elegant and beautiful at seventy as she had at thirty, swept past the men in a cloud of Chanel, Harrods bags, and excitement.

"I love you, darling, but I'm here to see my grandchildren. Hello, Charlie."

And she was gone.

The men got back to business.

"There's a building I have in mind. It's the damnedest thing. It was built as a grammar school in the 1950s. The basement was meant to be a bomb shelter, for a hundred and fifty students. It's one of the few buildings I've seen that actually has a basement, and this thing is the bat cave. Two stories, nondescript, nice perimeter. Other than the fact it's been sitting empty for twenty years, it's perfect."

"A renovation's a renovation."

"Sounds like your mind's made up."

"Lately, it all seems so clear."

Charlie glanced over Nathan's shoulder through the open door where Emily held up baby clothes, while Seraphina and Maggie each cuddled an infant.

"Son, a good woman will do that."

Nathan gestured to the front door with a flourish. Emily stood on the pale blue planks of the wide wrap-around front porch and checked her phone.

"Emily, the boys couldn't be in better hands."

"I know. I'm sorry. Oh, Nathan, wow."

He threw open the front door and . . . it promptly fell off its hinges.

"Damn. The contractor mentioned he hadn't hung it yet. Oh well."

Her gaze pulled her into the front hall. Located on a small lane that boasted modest homes on large lots, Emily was already captivated by the strollers and bikes she had spotted dotting the lawns. *This* was where they would raise their children. It was several blocks inland from Charlie and Maggie. Emily didn't want to be too close to either the ocean or the public beach. She was working through a new set of issues with Neil Tyson as she battled her understandable but irrational fears for her sons. Nathan had simply accepted her wish list and made it happen. *You are my home,* he had said.

The renovated Victorian had been neglected. The neighborhood kids had started rumors of hauntings and strange noises, but Nathan had been haunted for too long, and elbow grease and affection had exorcized any ghosts. Now the house boasted a country French kitchen, cheery rooms with pale yellow walls and vintage molding. The wood fireplace in the cozy den was stacked with logs and kindling. Upstairs, the large room off the master bedroom would serve as the nursery. But Emily wasn't looking at any of that. She walked straight back and looked out the restored French doors to the yard. The patio ended at a lush lawn dotted with violets. There were swings and a little cabin fort and . . . a lolling mastiff lying in a sunny patch of grass.

"Nathan?"

"That's Reggie. Say hello, Reggie."

In response, Reggie flopped his thick tail once.

"Charlie has a soft spot for these military dogs. Many of them can't be adopted into the general population, but Charlie works with the training center officers, and when he can, he finds homes for them. You met his beasts."

"Was he injured?" Emily approached him warily.

"Nope. Charlie said he was discharged. The trainer told him Reggie wasn't cut out for it. He said if he'd ever seen a dog that should be in a yard with kids and a tennis ball, Reggie was it."

"So, he was living a false identity in the military?"

"Fitting, I think."

Emily plopped down next to the dog and scratched behind his ears.

"And he's gentle?"

With that, Reggie made a lazy groan and rolled onto his back for a belly rub.

"Emily?"

"Yes?"

"Do you like the house?"

Emily smiled at the love of her life. "Let's go get the boys."

Nathan crossed the lawn in three long strides and held out his hand.

"Not yet."

Emily slipped her hand in his, captivated by the purpose and lust and love in his green eyes. She returned the look in equal measure, and they quietly slipped into their home.

The End

Made in the USA
Columbia, SC
07 May 2020